TWISTED WINGS

TINA SAXON

Twisted Wings

Copyright © 2019 by Tina Saxon

ISBN Digital: 978-0-9987762-8-6
ISBN Print: 978-0-9987762-9-3

Cover design by: Hang Le
Editing and Proofreading by:
My Brother's Editor

PROLOGUE

Max

The chair creaks as I sit down. I stare at Addison, her eyes pinned on the lake. I hate that I disappointed her, but I don't regret my decision.

My heart hammers against my chest watching my best friend's wife as tears roll down her face caused by me. I knew she searched for her every day. The loss muted the shine in her eyes whenever I was around her. Her best friend had vanished without saying anything. I had hoped Sydney would come back on her own.

But she didn't, and it's been a year.

Addison finally looks over at me. Her swollen eyes, red with anger. "How long have you known?"

Fifteen minutes ago she walked into my team's command room and found a picture of Sydney posing next to the Hollywood sign on our board.

I tense, opening and closing my hands, knowing the words I'm about to say might not be forgivable. "The whole time," I mutter, turning my gaze down to my hands. She draws in a ragged breath.

"You knew, Max..." She chokes on her tears and I clear the lump in my throat. "You knew what her leaving did to me." The chair teeters as she pushes off it and walks to the edge of the water, wrapping her arms tight around her waist. "Why didn't you tell me?" she whispers. I follow her, pulling in a deep sigh as I stand behind her.

"She told me not to," I say, folding my arms around her chest. She covers her eyes and cries. I'm at a loss at what to say to make this better. It wasn't my place to fix their relationship. I selfishly watched Sydney from afar, but she was living her life. It was her choice to stay away. "She called me the day after the funeral, asking me if I could fly her to California. I tried to get answers. Told her not to go. But she said it was something she had to do." And I would do anything for Sydney. I've yet to understand why though. Addison turns around in my arms.

She takes a couple deep breaths and squares her shoulders. "It's time," she states. "It's time to bring her home."

"I don't know if she'll come."

"I need you to try."

I close my eyes for a beat and nod. A year is enough time to squash my feelings, *right*?

———

Sydney

The nightmare burning holes in my heart awakens me. Shooting up in bed, I gasp for air as the suffocating feeling presses down on my heart with a heavy fist. The waterfall of tears soaks my face.

Why am I dreaming about this now? After all this time?

The ache subsides, and I'm able to calm my erratic breathing. The walls around me open back up and I take in a deep inhale, releasing it out slowly. Reaching over to my nightstand for my phone, I press the button to illuminate the time. The ache returns when the date jumps out at me.

One year today.

It's like my body has declared war on the part of my brain that has suppressed all the memories. It's a reminder that I can't hide them forever. The feelings linger deep inside me, tearing my insides up to get out.

My head sinks down into the pillow when I lay back on my side and I hold my phone close to my chest. The air is still and frigid. April in Los Angeles still requires heat at night, but I like the cold. A sliver of light peeps through the curtains from the full moon, lighting up Moxi's striped tail. Staring at the wild devil cat lying on the other pillow, I wonder if she even cares that I just almost died from suffocation. She holds her head up, meets my stare and meows before laying back down. *Did she just tell me I was exaggerating?* That could be my subconscious talking. Either way, she couldn't give a shit.

Rolling onto my back, I stare up at the blank ceiling. I can't believe it's been a year since I lost everything. Everyone. The memories that constantly threaten to surface, start leaking out, except this time I don't stop them.

Damon and I were like night and day. Totally opposite, but the transition was easy. Everything about our relationship was easy. When he asked me to marry him, my answer came without hesitation. I loved him. But for the wrong reasons.

Something was missing.

I squeeze my eyes shut; the guilt spreading inside of me. Guilt is a heavy beast. It can bury you in a shallow grave with just enough air that you're left to die a slow death if you let it. *I let it.*

Had I been satisfied with what he was offering, which was the world, he wouldn't have left upset before going out that night. But I was greedy. I wanted the universe. Instead, it buried me alive with the consequences of my doubts shadowing me. I deserved to be in hell. Everything was my fault.

I was alone.
I was lost.
I was dead.
That's why I became someone new.

CHAPTER ONE

SYDNEY

"Hey, sweet cheeks, I'm outta here," Graham yells through the bathroom door. I finish twisting the towel around my head and stand up, the humidity from my hot shower encasing me.

"Alright, love. See you later tonight."

I turn the music up loud enough to shake the walls. The upbeat thumping helps drown out the nervous energy. One would think over a year would make things easier. It hasn't. Rather, it's built a skyscraper out of my lies. Each day has built another floor, hiding me inside of it. People assume they know me.

They don't have a clue.

I warm up my voice as I put my false eyelashes on. Nothing but the best for one of the most important nights of my life. Jude Stonewall is coming to the show and I can't screw it up. Butterflies flutter in my stomach, knowing I'll be on stage in front of one of the top music producers in Los Angeles. This is the moment I've dreamt of since I was a little girl.

At what cost though?

Rushing around my room from dresser to closet, letting the music move me, I grab everything I need to get dressed. I glance at the clock. Graham's voice echoes in my mind, *tonight is not the night to be running late.*

One last glimpse in the full-length mirror and I freeze. I'm still not used to seeing the woman staring back. She looks nothing like the woman from a year ago. She's glamorous, sexy, a star. She's my shield. I turn away. When I stare too long, I think about *the old me* and I don't have time for that. My future hangs on tonight.

I blow out a breath. *It's showtime, Sky.*

"Who's the guy?"

I yelp and jump at the deep masculine voice coming from the teal velvet chair in the corner of the living room. My eyes widen when they meet steel- blue eyes. *Max Shaw.* One of my dead fiancé's best friends. I hold my hand over my heart. The beats so hard I'm having a tough time catching my breath. How did he get in? I glance at the front door to make sure I *still* have one. My lips pucker, annoyed that he finds that funny. He breaks into *my* home and then laughs at me for being alarmed. Jerk!

"You've lost your touch in hiding your jealousy," I sneer, but instantly regret my words when his laugh falls off his face, hitting a nerve.

"Bitch doesn't look good on you, Tink." He pushes his massive frame off the chair and it's not until then I see Moxi was in his lap. I glare at her. *Traitor.* Figures the cat who hates everyone, likes *him.* Max stalks toward me.

I take a couple steps back and shrug, acting aloof. "I guess life has made me a little tougher." My arms cross over my chest and I stand taller, which still doesn't compare to the six-foot Hulk size man towering over me. The hard shell I've put up around my heart begs to shatter. Begs to be let loose to feel again. But I can't. The only feelings that will pour out will kill me, and Max being here is already tapping on that fragile shell. His eyes move down my body and back up in a scrutinizing stare.

"Who the hell are you trying to be?"

Anger simmers under my skin. "Asshole doesn't look good on you," I say sarcastically. "Oh wait, you've always been an asshole."

"At least I'm not pretending to be something I'm not." He pulls on my long blonde hair extensions like a five-year-old. "You've got more makeup on than a drag-queen." Despite the accuracy, it stings coming from him. *Why do I care?*

"Why are you here, Max? If you're looking to make me feel bad, mission accomplished." I storm out of the room. I hear his heavy sigh, and then loud footsteps follow.

"Sydney, stop. I'm sorry."

I pinch my eyes closed and freeze. It's the first time I've heard my real name in almost a year. The foreignness of it surprises me. I spin around, ready for a fight. His eyes soften as he continues to get closer.

Tap, tap, tap.

I fight the tears welling up in my eyes. Asshole Max was easier to deal with. "Max, go home," I plead, my voice shakes.

"No." Warm, strong arms wrap around me and I relent, digging my face into his taut chest.

Tap, tap, tap.

"She misses you," he murmurs into my hair.

Crack.

My heart explodes, raw feelings that I buried long ago, pour out. I grip his shirt to hold on as my sobs rip through me. I miss her too. She's been my best friend since we were ten. I'm not surprised that he's here because of her. When I left, my plans were never to make my home here or to stop talking to her. I just needed a break. There was so much that happened all at once; guilt, resentment, and jealousy were destroying me. But it was easier to hide than deal with it. The loss, the heartache, the pain. *Everything.* I became a shell of my old self, building a new one in its place that included a guarded heart.

Max's arms squeeze me tight. When his hand gets caught up in my hair, it reminds me I have somewhere to be. I push back, swallowing my feelings. "Goddamn it, Max, I can't do this right now," I hiccup through my tears and swipe them off my cheek. I groan, not wanting to redo my makeup. I've become a pro hampering down my feelings and I can't let him being here pulling it out of me, destroy my night. He watches me stomp around, fixing myself. *Or try.* I murmur a few unpleasant words when I can't fix my puffy eyes. It'll work for now.

"Are you kidding me?" I mutter to myself, looking down at my phone. There isn't an Uber driver anywhere close. It's freaking Los Angeles, they're usually within a minute radius away. I can't wait fifteen minutes. "This is all your fault." Somehow Max being here has shifted my world already.

Max holds his palms in the air. "I can do a lot of things. But making Uber drivers disappear isn't in my bag of tricks."

I take in a long breath, letting it out slowly. Getting mad at Max won't fix the problem. "Do you have a car?"

He pulls keys out of his pocket, holds them in the air and shakes them. I snatch my purse off the counter and start for the front door. Sensing he's not moving, I twist in place, trying not to explode.

"Why aren't you coming?" I whine, sinking my hands to my sides. "Max, tonight is an enormous opportunity for me. Please give me a ride." My voice loses its steam. "We can have a heart to heart after the show, just *not* now. I need to go."

His eyes study me for a few moments. "Okay. But we're talking later."

"Can't wait," I quip, rolling my eyes.

CHAPTER TWO

SYDNEY

I t's what they want.

The list of songs in my hand isn't different. They're my normal songs, but they're leaving a sour taste in my mouth. It's Max. Being here is making me self-conscious. Demanding he leave was pointless. I'm delusional if I think he would listen to me. I've already spotted him speaking to security. *Twice.*

"Earth to Sky." I glance up at the sound of his irritated voice. Graham, with his snappy fingers, furrows his brows when our eyes meet. "What's up, babe? You've been acting strange since you got here. Now you're studying that list like it's the first time you've ever seen it."

The list crumples against my leg when I drop my hand. I need to pull my shit together. Graham has been my only true friend this past year, held me together when my life was ripping apart at the seams and helped sew me back together. Even though the seam was jagged, it was attached. A year ago, I didn't think I'd ever be able to trust someone enough to form a friendship. I couldn't give anymore. The burn at the end was too painful. People throwing me away so easy sent me down a spiral vortex, ending at the bottom of a black hole. I used to wear my heart on the outside, now I guard it with my life.

Graham weaseled his way in, using my voice. It terrified me I was letting him in because of my dependency on men until my therapist reminded me it was the intimacy I craved from men... and Graham definitely didn't fill that craving. Determined to repay him, I'll make sure tonight is great.

"Nothing's wrong, G. I'm just nervous about tonight." His body relaxes, lips curl up when I give him a reassuring nod. It's not a total lie. I close the gap between us and reach for his hand. "We got this. You just make sure Jude's not preoccupied when I'm performing."

"That I can do," he says, flashing a mischievous grin. I shake my head at him. He's always had a secret crush on Jude.

I point at him. "You better not do anything to run him out of here before I even start."

"I don't know what you're talking about." He feigns innocence as he wraps his arm through mine and walks up with me on the stage. "You have soundcheck in five."

"Behave," I reply, giving him the side-eye.

"Got it. Now, go shine like you were meant to." He leans down and kisses me on the cheek.

He hops off the stage and when I peek out at what I expect to be an empty bar, a set of steel-blue eyes freeze me in my spot. Their coldness sends a shiver up my back. Max stares at me, his jaw tics and it's obvious he isn't happy about something. Shaking my head, I snap out of the trance he put me in and stomp down the stairs in his direction.

"You can't stay here if you keep staring at me like you want to kill me all night," I snap, hitting him on the chest. I'm used to his broodiness. But this is different. He glances behind me and then back to me. Peering over my shoulder to catch who his attention went to, I only notice Graham going over tonight's line-up. You have got to be kidding me. I don't have time for this. I whip back around. "I'm not even goin' there with you, Max. My life here isn't any of your business."

Back in New York, I was used to his jealous glances. I saw them. Except it was his choice that we were nothing but a one-night stand. He made that crystal clear when Damon, *his best friend*, wanted to ask me out and got his approval. I'm not one to chase the disinterested. And Damon… was interested.

His jaw relaxes and his eyes cast down. He plays with the label on his beer. "Sorry. I just…" He pauses and shakes whatever his thoughts are out of his head. "… I'm glad you're doing something you love." I swallow the sour taste. The melody that comes out of my mouth is anything but love, but it's become a necessary evil to live. "If you want me to leave, I will."

Why is it now that he's offering me an out, I want him to stay? I blow out my cheeks. "Stay. Just don't give me the evil eye all night."

"Sky, you're on," the stage manager calls from behind me. Max winks at me and raises his glass.

I walk toward the stage and hear him murmur, "Go break a leg, or whatever they say."

"How about just good luck?" I call out over my shoulder.

"I've heard you sing, you don't require any luck."

SCANNING THE CROWD FROM BACKSTAGE, I search for familiar faces or a glimpse of the infamous Jude. When I first started singing at Dusty Rose, it was on amateur night. Graham talked Dusty, the owner, into letting me have a weekend night. There are only three of us that play on Fridays and it's become the busiest night for the bar. Especially since all three of us sing different genres, it attracts different crowds, but it blends well. Shanna Stellars sings country and Jarod Chavez does a cross between pop and funk. I'm the buffer between the two singing only pop. Before tonight, I did it with no regrets. It's not that I don't love pop music, I just imagined myself singing songs with more depth.

The reflections of my sequin skirt dance across the floor when the spotlight catches it. I cast my eyes down and wonder why I let Graham have the final decisions on what I wear. I'm overdressed. Throw me in some cutoff jean shorts and boots, and I'll shine more than my sparkly skirt.

"It's a packed house," Jarod says, throwing his arm around me. I note what he's wearing and sigh with a twinge of envy. He's wearing jeans paired with combat boots and a simple black t-shirt. The girls go wild over him, which isn't surprising because he's gorgeous in a bad boy kind of way. He has a slender frame, naturally tanned skin and a drop-dead smile that can make women's panties melt. "I heard Jude Stonewall's coming tonight."

"That's the rumor," I reply, innocently. A producer showing up is rarely announced. I'm uncertain how the word got out, but I won't mention my source. "I guess we'll have to bring our A-game."

"Pshhh." We don't turn, knowing who's behind us. "I always bring my best," Shanna snidely says, standing to our side. My mouth drops open when I notice her. Jarod barks out a laugh and I elbow him in the ribs.

"Really, Shanna?" I force out, gawking at her outfit. If it weren't for her dark chocolate hair, I'd think I was looking in a mirror. She's wearing the same thing I am. Short black sequin skirt with a white lace top over a black tank. The only difference, she's wearing the boots. Heat blazes up my cheeks.

"Oh, looky there. We're twins," she snickers, flashing her perfect white teeth. This is not a coincidence. She goes on first and considering she's never tried to sabotage me before, she must've also heard that Jude will be here. Though, she's not very smart showing me before the show starts. It's still annoying as hell to find something else at the last minute.

Graham, already out working the crowd, won't be able to

approve another outfit without people seeing me in this one. I grab Jarod's wrist and glance at his watch. Less than an hour to figure out a new outfit. I glare at Shanna. "You're goin' to need a lot more than stealin' my wardrobe to get noticed. It's a good thing you can't steal my voice." I force a sweet grin back at her before walking away. "I hated this outfit anyway," I snap. Getting under her skin right before she goes on shouldn't feel this good, but the way her face twists like she just ate a lemon, makes it better.

"There's my southern sweetness," Jarod croons. I roll my eyes. Anger brings out my southern drawl and Jarod loves it.

The thin dressing room walls shake from slamming the door. On a mission, I swipe each hanger looking through the options one by one. After finding an outfit that is more me, and one Graham would approve of, I quickly change. I'm slipping on my last shoe when Graham comes storming in. I figured as soon as he saw Shanna, he'd be on a rampage. His red, contorted face confirms my thoughts.

"Calm down," I say, spreading my arms out wide. "I like this better anyway." He has strong opinions about me showing off my legs so I picked something that did. His eyes move up and down my body and he twirls his finger in the air. I chuckle but spin in place for him. "Do I have the Graham approval?" I tease. I'm wearing short metallic silver shorts displaying my tan legs, a tight black tank and I finished the look with four-inch black peep-toe heels.

"Yes." He sighs, waving his hands around. "But that bitch is on my list. I'll make it my life mission that she never makes it anywhere near a recording studio."

THE AIR CRACKLES WITH ENERGY, my skin soaking all of it in like a sponge. There is nothing more exhilarating than being in front of hundreds of wired people, waiting on you to captivate them with your voice. Pull them in and give them an experience where they let go of all their daily grind for a night of fun. My body hums with adrenaline as the audience chants my name.

The lights go down. That's my cue. The microphone almost slips through my sweaty hand as I take my place on stage, surprising me. I take a few deep breaths trying to calm the nerves running amok. I rarely get nervous. But there are two new sets of eyes watching me. Judging me. It's my past and future colliding.

Lights illuminate the stage. "Hey y'all. Thanks for coming out to watch us tonight," I beam. The whistles and catcalls make me grin. I'm not naïve, I know why Graham has me looking like I've stepped out of a Barbie dressing room. Sex sells. The mask I put on, the sexy Sky, has helped me. It's a camouflage for my scarred and damaged heart. I shine on the surface to hide the darkness on the inside.

The things we do to survive.

The lyrics that come out of my mouth are nothing but words. To most people, music provokes thoughts and feelings. Not me. Not anymore. The words I sing are emotionless. All night I've tried to avoid Max's eyes. Yet, I've sensed them on me, like they're burning a hole right through the mask I wear. With a ten second break between songs, I'm thankful the lights go down so I can wipe the sweat dripping down my chest, between my boobs, and take a quick drink of water. They need to turn the air up.

"Is it me, or is it extra hot in here?" I ask the guys, fanning myself.

"Not any worse than normal," Tug, my drummer, responds. He pulls his sweat soaked shirt away from his slender tattooed body. I laugh because he's right, that is normal for him.

Taking my place in the front, we start our next song. We have three more songs in our set, so I hype up the crowd to finish strong. A grin spreads across Graham's face in the front row, and I know he's proud of me tonight. It's not until my eyes catch Max's that I know searching for him was a mistake.

I wanted him to see I'm doing better.

I wanted him to see I'm living.

I wanted to see if he was proud of me too.

What I didn't expect was my mind to replay the last time he saw me sing. The intense need to sing a song I swore I'd never sing again burns deep inside of me. Maybe it's proving to myself that I have moved on. Maybe it's proving it to him.

"I'm doing something different tonight," I say before starting my last song. My voice is on autopilot, my eyes pinned on Max. He quirks his head to the side. Even though I've stopped jumping and dancing, my heart picks up, beating erratically. It already knows it'll be a turbulent ride, but my mind is determined.

The band waits for me to start, I'm sure confused. I squeeze the mic being held up by the stand and close my eyes. The lyrics come out tender and slow, silencing the crowd. I'm holding still, afraid if I move, I'll fall to my knees. The fakeness is stripped from my voice, leaving behind naked honesty, and I'm taken back to the day I lost everything.

My heart is broken. The emotions I thought I would have are non-existent. Can someone feel nothing? I scan the church, filled with Damon's friends and family. A sea of black wallows across the room, the soft sound of cries floats above.

Why can't I cry? I love this man. I told him I would be his wife. And now he's… gone.

The extra large gold-framed picture on the stage stares at me, waiting for my words. The pressure of his eyes bearing down on me brings guilt. I wring the Kleenex in my hands. The one I had brought with me just in case the tears came. I glance at the picture again and softly grin.

Clearing my throat, I step up to the mic. "I'm sorry. I'm struggling with what to say." I stare down at the ring on my finger. I've only been wearing it for three weeks. "Um… Damon was an amazing man." I squeeze my eyes shut. Oh, that was endearing.

A small hand sneaks through mine and I look down to caramel eyes gleaming up at me. Lulu. My best friend's adopted six-year-old daughter who stole all our hearts the second we met her. I take a deep breath in and exhale it out slowly. I manage a small smile and she returns it.

"Damon loved you, sweet girl," I whisper down to her. She nods her head.

"I loved him too."

The sounds of sniffles and cries remind me of where we are. I glance at Addison in the front row and she's wiping tears from her cheek. Her lips curve up and she sends me a supportive nod. When Lulu begins to sing, the air goes silent and still. Our eyes meet and her pitch rises. I hum the melody.

The song is perfect.

The song is Damon.

Our voices blend in harmony as we sing "Lost Boy" by Ruth B. My voice cracks when we sing about him being home now. My heart breaks open and my emotions surge through me in a fractured instant. I swallow my cries, determined to get through the song. But it's no use. My heart's not broken now, I am.

Goodbye, Lost Boy.

EMOTIONS RICOCHET inside my body as I sing the song that broke me over a year ago. I feel the vise around my heart, squeezing it, the pain making it hard to breathe. I gasp for air, hanging onto the mic. Music is no longer my lifeline. Stars float in my vision right before blackness pulls me under.

CHAPTER THREE

SYDNEY

"**P**ut her down." Graham's voice echoes in my head.

A ball of worry twists in my stomach. I can't open my eyes and face what happened. Strong arms cradle me, carrying me backstage. Max smells the same as always. Spicy and clean with a mixture of woodsy scents. I lean my head into his chest and his arms tighten.

"Security! Where the hell is security?" Graham's voice raises a few octaves. I can imagine how red his face is. "Sky, don't worry, I won't let him hurt you."

"Who the fuck is this guy?" Max murmurs, rejecting all of Graham's threats.

"My manager," I whisper.

The crowd cheers in the background when I overhear the MC say my name. Those cheers have kept me going in the past, but I can't go back out there. I'm mortified I passed out. Max kicks open the door and places me on a couch. It's not until my head touches a pillow, I open my eyes and notice we're in my dressing room.

Graham runs to my side, struggling to get in between me and Max. "Would you move, you big oaf." He shoulders his way in. "Sky, are you all right?" I cover my face with my arms, tears stain my cheeks. *No, I'm not all right.* I'm a wreck. "Do I need to get a doctor? What hurts? Are you sick?"

"Dude, get the hell out of her face and give her a chance to catch her breath."

I open my mouth to tell Max it's okay, but Graham stands up and gets in his face. He's about the same height as Max, but the similarities stop there. He weighs as much as one of Max's legs. I sit up, debating if I should get in between them. Max regards him with humor in his eyes and crosses his arms.

"*Dude*? Who are you? If you're expecting money for helping…" He pauses and pulls out his wallet. "Here, this should be enough. Thanks. *You can go now.*" He shoves a twenty-dollar bill in Max's hand, whips around and kneels beside me. I pull my lips in to hide my chuckle that he just tried to pay off a millionaire. "Sky, we need to have you examined by a doctor."

I glance up at Max and his intense stare makes me fidget. Folding my hands in between my legs, I glance away. Graham sighs and turns, casting his eyes up to Max. "Why are you still here?"

Max doesn't take his gaze off me. "Why does he keep calling you Sky?"

Because I didn't want to be Sydney. It was exhausting being the person who lost everything. Being someone else was a way to start over. Graham knows my real name, but he's under contract never to use it again. When he convinced me the *sky was the limit* with my singing career, Sky was born.

"It's just a name." I keep my eyes down, messing with the edge of my shorts.

"I'm guessing you two know each other?" Graham says, pushing off the couch to stand. I nod. He lets out a long sigh. "I'll see if I can find Jude."

"I'm sorry, G."

"Don't be. You were already at the end of your set. Everyone stumbles. You just get back up and move on." He leans down, kisses me on the forehead and leaves the room.

The first couple months of living with Graham, I would wake to a sticky note on my bathroom mirror with a motivational saying on it. He's never asked questions nor expected anything from me. Unlike the man staring at me, sucking the air out of the room.

"Can you just go back and tell her I'm okay?"

"Is that what you want me to do?"

I nod so I don't have to lie. It would hurt too much to say it out loud. The place where Addison resides is already digging its way out of my heart.

"You can't keep hiding. She knows you're in California now."

I jerk my head up, my eyebrows creased. "Hiding? You didn't tell her?" When he shakes his head, I hop up. *Whoa.* Too soon. Getting lightheaded, I sit back down. This entire time I assumed she was too busy with her new life to reach out to me. The pity party of one thrown frequently where I was always the drunk girl attending was unnecessary.

"I don't understand. Why *now*?"

Max straightens, running his hand behind his neck. "She sort of found out I've been keeping track of you."

I do a double take. "You've been keeping track of me? What does that even mean?"

"I'm not sorry, let's get that straight," he states unapologetically yet shoves his hands in his pockets looking embarrassed. "I had Stone find you every couple months to make sure you were okay." My lips twitch, lifting to a small smile and I relax my shoulders. He shrugs. "I needed to know."

"Why didn't you tell Addie?"

"I figured you'd work your stuff out and come back when you were ready."

I let out a sarcastic laugh. "I'm great at working my stuff out, huh?" Max sits down next to me and I lean my head against him.

"Tink, you were amazing up there."

"She sure was," Graham boasts, walking into the room. "Better than amazing! Jude wants to sign you. He wants you in the studio A-SAP."

My eyes widen and I bolt off the couch into Graham's arms. "Really?"

"Really! Sweet cheeks, you did it!"

"I was a mess out there. I can't believe he still wants me."

"He liked the mess. He wants *that* part of you." I stare up at him, not sure I can give him the real me. It's raw and painful and it ended with me blacking out. Not the desired outcome I want every time I sing. I step back.

"I don't know, Graham."

His arms fly out. "What do you mean, *you don't know*? Sky, you sang with grit and passion. I've never heard you sing like that. It was phenomenal."

"Would you quit calling her Sky?" Max interrupts, standing.

Graham puts his hands on his narrow hips. "*You called her Tink.* What's the difference?"

Max chuckles. "That's like a pet name, it's not her *real* name."

I don't know if the shock of everything that's happened tonight caught up to me, but that comment just pushed me over the edge. I slap Max across the face. "I am *not* your pet, nor will I ever be." I catch a glimpse of Max's stunned expression as I stomp past him into the bathroom, slamming the door shut. My back slides down the door, memories flash from the night Max changed me forever.

ANGER PUSHES *me into the dark room, only lit up by the moon outside the window. "I can't believe you did that," I spit out, slamming the door behind me. I could have died from hypothermia from how cold that pool was. It's freaking almost winter. Max pushes off the bed, his large muscular body only covered with athletic shorts. He looks larger than life with the soft glow behind him. I swallow as he approaches me, the air turning still. "I'm still freezing because of—"*

I gasp as he slams me against the door and welds his mouth to mine. My body submits before my brain can catch up to what's happening. The raw emotions from hearing Addison's story tonight rages inside me and I practically crawl up his body. My fingers scrape against his back as his tongue assaults my mouth. He growls, grabbing my hands and pins them above my head.

He breaks the kiss but keeps his lips close. The heat of his breath tickles my lips, the heave of his chest rubs against my breasts. "Don't stop," I say, desperation grabbing hold. I need to feel something besides pain. My best friend's torture clasps around my heart, and it freaking hurts. Max shakes his head, squeezing his eyes shut. "Please, Max."

"You don't know what you're asking, Tink." His voice deep and raspy. I nod. Yes, I do. He smirks over his thunderous expression. "I'm not like other guys who will give you what you want. Treat you with white gloves like you're a princess. I take. What. Ever. The. Fuck. I want." The sharp staccato of his words, strikes a different chord inside my body, turning me on more than I expected.

"Then take, Max." The words fall out of my mouth, surprising even me.

With a low rumbling chuckle, he shakes his head again, holding on to whatever restraint is holding him back. He mutters a curse under his breath, pinning me with his stare. His tongue darts out to lick his lower lip. I try to release one of my hands still pinned above my head so I can touch him. He shakes his head.

"No."

I lift a brow. No, what?

"If you say stop, we're done. And you better mean it when you say it, because there's no going back."

Anticipation ignites sparks as I nod, yet not sure what I'm agreeing to.

"I need to hear you say okay."

"Okay."

"Don't fucking say I didn't warn you." In an instant, he releases my hands, but pulls up my shirt, knotting it right before it's pulled off all the

way, binding my hands above my head again. He takes a step back and his eyes flicker down to my chest. With one hand still holding the knot in place, his other squeezes one of my breasts. Hard. Pulling my white lace bra down, my full boobs pop out.

"Your boobs are perfect." My back arches off the door as he leans down and flicks his tongue over a nipple. While he assaults that one with his mouth, his hand takes the other one. The mixture of heat and pain from his bites and sucking has me pleading. I grind my hips against his hardness, begging for more. His hand slinks around my body, unclasping my bra.

His laugh catches me off guard. "Fuck, you have me off my game." He eyes my bra and then my tied hands and I figure out his conundrum. "Don't move," he commands, walking to the desk. It's so dark, I can't see what he picks up. It's not until my bra is free that I figure out that he just cut my bra off me. I stare at the destroyed bra on the ground, wide-eyed, while he reaches to put his knife back on the table.

"You could've—"

His finger on my lips stops me. "Don't talk. The only thing I want to hear out of your mouth is harder, and my name. Got it?" I pull my lips in and nod, willing to do anything for him right now. "You still want this?" He runs his fingers up my bare thigh, over the fabric of my pajama shorts, straight to my center, pushing his fingers against my swollen clit. I nod again, closing my eyes as heat streaks up my body. "Good."

He spins us around and walks me backward until the back of my legs hit the bed. He kneels down and drags down my shorts and panties at the same time. I step out of them and he throws them aside. His breath is hot against my stomach and my body shivers. He hums and runs his tongue over my sensitive clit, making me jerk. "I like this," he says, kissing my bare pubic area. I glide my tied hands through his thick golden hair and he looks up at me, shaking his head. I put my hands back, afraid I did something wrong. He stands, all six feet of him tower over my five-two body.

"Turn around," he orders. "Lay on the bed, ass up in the air and hold on to the headboard." I do as I'm told. The cool air hits my wet center as I *wait.* When the bed dips down, I glance back, and he situates his large naked body behind me. He rubs his hand across my ass, his thumb grazing over my entrance.

SLAP! I yelp from the pain of him slapping my ass. "That's for making me dunk you in the freezing water." I open my mouth to argue but snap it shut when he pushes two fingers inside me. The mixture of pain and pleasure has me so confused. While he fingers me, his other hand rubs my ass. He pulls them out and slaps me again on the other cheek. "That's for making me watch you shiver all fucking night long." He shoves his fingers in again, bringing me close to the edge, expertly working them in and out. I'm stunned that he's making me want another slap.

I stick my ass out farther in the air, pushing against his fingers, craving more. More of everything. What the hell is wrong with me? My body trembles, the heat tickling down my core. I whimper when he removes his fingers. But anticipation for another slap builds. My willing submission surprises the hell out of me. It's almost a relief when he slaps me again. The sting not as bad as the first time, but still there.

"That's for making me want what isn't mine."

This time, he buries his face into my vagina, licking and sucking like a madman. His tongue runs over my ass and down my entire center. My face burns with embarrassment. No guy has ever touched me there, let alone licked me. Thank god he can't see me. I moan when his mouth attaches to my clit and pulls me over the edge until I'm screaming out the most intense orgasm I've ever had.

"You're fucking perfect," he says, wiping his mouth off with the comforter. I see him from the corner of my eye, lean over to the nightstand and grab a condom. He lays his heavy cock against my ass and even though I can't see it, I feel it. It's very large.

"Fuuuck." A low growl erupts when he slides into me. "Your tight pussy takes all of me." Yeah, I'm surprised too. Fingers weave through my hair, and he yanks my head up. He drags his lips down my neck with light kisses, the only delicate thing he's done all night. When he bites my shoulder, I buck back into him, moaning from the pain and the delicious *fullness.* "The school teacher has a wicked side," he growls. *He thrusts hard again. My whimpers turn into unintelligible sounds as he plunges wildly. Loud sounds. I'm screaming his name, not holding anything back as pleasure explodes through my body once again.*

He roars through his release, collapsing next to me after he pulls out. Our bodies are slick with sweat and I've never been so thoroughly screwed. My knees give out and I fall to the cool sheets. He unties my hands, but I can't muster up the energy to move them at the moment. When he hops out of bed, I roll over so the cool air can cover my front.

After cleaning up, he falls back on the bed next to me. I turn into his side, laying my head on his chest, still trying to catch my breath. As I lie there, naked, listening to the drumming of his heart, I know I have to leave. Except, I want to stay. But like Max said, this has nothing to do with what I want. He has made no move to show me he wants me to stay. He's not even touching me right now. If he asks me to leave, I'll be humiliated. I might not be new to the sex scene, but I've never been with a man like Max. This is why I need to go. I roll off him and search the floor for my clothes.

Ask me to stay, I silently plead.

The silence stings but confirms my thoughts. I pull up my panties and shorts. I sense his gaze on me and I want to yell at him. For what, I'm not sure. I'm the one who stormed his room. I'm the one who said okay. I inwardly laugh when I attempt to put my bra on. That was my favorite bra, dammit. After I have my shirt on, I dare a peek back at him. Eyes trained on me, hand behind his head in a relaxed position and the sheet just past the well defined V, I swallow back the desire coming full tilt. He's gorgeous. And dangerous. Our eyes lock for a beat.

Ask me to stay.

The request doesn't come. So, I stand taller, walk over and kiss him until we're both breathless. It's the only time he's given me control. That's when it's time to go. I whirl around and walk to the door. "Thanks," I whisper over my shoulder.

He chuckles once. "Any time, Tink."

Once I'm past the door, my body deflates. I'm thankful he didn't ask me to stay. I need space to figure out what the hell just happened.

And why I liked it.

THE SOUND of a door shutting jolts me back to the present. My breaths are labored, my body overheating. *Jesus,* my libido hasn't stirred to life since Damon left me. I tap my head against the door, demanding it stops thinking of Max like this. I remember that the next morning, Max acted like nothing happened, so I followed his lead. I had always hoped he'd call me, but my phone never rang. I wasn't what he wanted.

Rolling my head to the side, I listen for anything on the other side of the door. Silence. I pull my emotional wreck of a body off the cold tile floor. I'm tempted to lie on it to cool off.

I'm met with intense eyes as soon as I walk through the door. Max sits on the couch, leaning forward with his elbows on his knees.

"I was hoping you had left."

"After what you just said?" he asks, standing up. "We need to clear that shit up. Right now. Do you even know what that means?"

"Yes," I huff. *Well, sort of.* "Sorry. I should've never said it."

"Is that what you think? That I have *pets*?"

I nervously wave my hand around. "Look, Max, I'm not judging your sexual preferences. It is what—"

His booming laugh interrupts me. "I'm not denying that I like to have full control in the bedroom." I swallow, the heat that hasn't had time to completely cool sizzles again. He takes a couple steps toward me and my heart beats quicker. "But I would never expect a woman to hand over control of her life to me. *That* isn't my thing."

Am I your thing?

My eyes widen, surprising myself by my thoughts. No. No. No.

I'm not his *thing*. He made that clear. I hurry past him and stuff my makeup into my bag. "I need to get out of here. Thanks Max, for coming to my rescue. *Again*." I squeeze my eyes shut for a second. How do we keep getting here? I'm like a damsel in distress for Max to save.

I rush out of the dressing room, thankful the sound of heavy steps isn't following me. The only thing I hear him say is, "Anytime, Tink."

CHAPTER FOUR

SYDNEY

"I need to go home."

"Now?" Graham whines, slamming his hands on his desk, standing up. "Sky, you get a break and you want to leave *now*?" He clears his throat as he reaches his upper register. He's freaking out.

"Not forever. Only a week," I reassure him.

He plops down into his black leather chair and eyeballs me with defeat. I'm not the only one that got a break. I'm his golden ticket, waving it as I walk out.

I couldn't sleep last night. Addison, unaware of my location, has me knotted up with guilt. Here, I was assuming she didn't have time for me, but the truth was I didn't make time for her. With too many unresolved emotions, I have to work through them if the music industry wants all of me. *The real me.*

"Are you going back to Addison?" he asks quietly. He might not have ever asked questions, but he knows our past and how close we were. *Were.* Tears gather in the corner of my eyes admitting to myself that we're not close anymore. For god's sake, she has a child that I've never seen before.

I glance behind him, at the lush scenery out his window. "I

am." He sighs loudly and I jerk my head his direction. "Graham, I want a singing career. I'm coming back."

"Promise?"

"Yes." My lips quirk up to a smile.

"You bringing that brooding sexy beast back with you?" His eyes light up and I laugh out loud.

"*Probably* not." He sticks out his bottom lip, pouting. "You know he doesn't hit for your team, right?"

"Oh girl, they *all* hit for my team, they just don't know it yet."

I smack my head, shaking it. "Max runs a security firm in Connecticut, he's only here for Addison."

"Are you sure about that?"

A bitter laugh slips out. "Max saves people for a living. He's doing his job. Nothing more." If it was anything else, he would've been here long ago, since he's known where I've been from the beginning.

"That's about as believable as him hitting for my team."

My STOMACH DROPS as we catapult into the air. The wheels folding up into the plane vibrate at my feet. I don't mind flying, but I hate taking off and landing.

"You all right over there?"

When we level out, I blow out a breath and open my eyes. "I'm good. Just not my favorite part." Max studies me. I wish he'd stop staring at me, not saying anything. "What, Max?"

He shrugs. "Nothing."

I huff and glare at him. "That's what a woman says when it's *something*."

"Well, since I'm sure I'm a man…" He puts up a finger with a sarcastic grin, pulls his shorts out and looks down his pants. *He did not just do that.* "Yep, I'm a man, so it doesn't apply to me."

The jab *I'm surprised you could see it* is at the tip of my tongue.

But I know better. One, it's *not* small. Two, he'll whip it out and prove it if I say it. He flashes a knowing smile and winks. Heat creeps up my face so I hop out of my seat and head for the bathroom. *Narcissistic ass.*

Thankfully he's on his laptop and working when I return. Digging through my bag, I pull out the most recent LA Now magazine, plop down in my seat and flip through the pages. The magazine comes out weekly with happenings around town. Graham demands I read it to keep up to date with the music industry. I stop flipping when I notice an article about my yoga studio. If you're looking to be in the spotlight, it's the place to be. Paparazzi camps outside, waiting for their chance to attack. I'm not famous so they never bother me. I never thought in a million years I'd be doing a downward dog next to Jennifer Garner though. It's almost impossible to act *normal* around celebrities. Graham reminds me they eat, sleep, and shit just like I do. *I bet their shit is rainbow colored though.*

I glance up and Max is still working. His black T-shirt stretches taut against his chest and arms. He tents his fingers against his lips, deep in thought over whatever is on the screen. Tats spread over his entire right arm down to his wrist. The artwork is beautiful. I wonder about the meaning behind each piece.

Max clears his throat and my eyes meet his. His eyebrow quirks up. "I was admiring your tats." He relaxes back against the seat and pops his foot on his knee. "Do they all have meaning?"

"Most of them."

I wait to hear if he'll share what they mean to him, but typical Max doesn't share. "I want one." His mouth twitches into a half smile and he nods. "Not a big one though." I point to my wrist. "A small one here."

"I know a great artist in New York City or I can find one in LA."

This is my week. I'm feeding my broken soul, mending it. Everything about it scares me, but I'm ready to confront all those fears. "I want to get it done this week," I murmur. "Does she hate me for leaving?" The words fall out of my mouth.

"You already know the answer to that."

"I'm scared to face her."

He nods. "She is a little scary." I giggle at his attempt to lighten my mood. "Sydney, you're going home. There's a lot you and Addison need to talk about. Don't be afraid."

"Thanks, Max."

His eyes soften. "Relax and *let it go.*" His voice is lighthearted, and he raises his brows. He didn't ask me a question, so I'm not sure what he's waiting for. My eyes flutter around the plane for a beat. His head shakes and he exhales sharply. I feel like a kid who just gave her parents a bad report card. I've disappointed him. "Tink, your wings are twisted tight," he mutters.

I narrow my eyes in confusion. "What?"

He stands up and walks over to me. "Something you need to figure out," he says before disappearing behind my seat. I turn my attention to the vast blue sky out the small window.

"*Twisted wings,*" I snicker to myself, thinking of the fall I took. The way my life has been this year, clipped wings are more appropriate. Not sure I'll ever be the person I used to be.

FOLDING my shaking hands into my lap, I only transfer the nervousness to my jittery foot. A large warm hand covers both of mine. Max rubs his thumb over them and the quiet gesture calms me. Bright lights and the sound of car horns welcome me home. I've missed the bustle of New York City. I lean my head against Max's muscular arm.

"Thank you for being my rock."

"I didn't think I was that hard," he jokes. "But you know I'll always be here for you."

Max is one of the most confusing guys I know. Ever since we

slept together, he's hot and cold, usually on the cold side. But his words are sincere, tender and ones that would come from a supportive lover. He's been there for me through some tough times. Our one-night stand was nothing but a by-product from an emotionally charged night.

The end.

We're just friends. I won't embarrass myself, *again.* I am not his type.

I pull in a deep breath and exhale when we park in front of Addison's building. "Is she expecting me?"

"No."

"What?" I jerk up, my eyes widen as I panic. "What if she's not home?"

"She is. Aiden knows, so he made sure Addison would be here. I didn't want to mention it to her and then you back out." I nod in agreement. That was a good plan. I'm not up there yet.

A few minutes thereafter, with a couple nudges along the way, we're standing in front of the penthouse. My nerves are firing off sparks inside of me, shocking my heart. Max stands silently next to me while I stare at the door.

"You should knock," he finally says.

I should have done a lot of things.

I squeeze my eyes shut, inhale and knock. We hear noises on the other side. My body's flight or fight response kicks in and I take a step back. Max's hand stops me.

"Uh-uh. Too late." I glare up at him and he smirks. He's enjoying this too much.

The door squeaks open and our eyes meet. Hers widen to the size of saucers and she jumps forward, wrapping her arms around me into a hug. "Sydney!" She pulls back and looks at me again. "Oh, my god! You're here." She looks over at Max and mouths, "Thank you."

She looks back and I sheepishly say, "Hey."

"Come in." She opens the door wider and Max and I walk past

her into the spacious penthouse. The last time I was here, it had boxes piled everywhere. Aiden walks up to me and gives me a warm hug.

"Good to see you," he murmurs into my hair.

Memories of why I left bubble up inside me, bringing me to tears. I should've stayed and dealt with everything instead of running away.

"You look good," Addie says, her eyes roaming over my entire body. "Different though. I've never seen your hair so long."

I smile and pull on my hair. "It's not real. They want me to resemble a Barbie."

"They?" she asks.

"Oh. Sorry…" I hesitate, reminding myself that she has no idea what I've been doing the last year. "My manager. When I'm on stage, he thinks I should look like what every girl wants to look like." I roll my eyes at how absurd that sounds. What happened to being original?

Addie narrows her eyes at me and crosses her arms. "On stage? Have you been performing?" Her words come out slow, a hint of irritation laces them.

"I have," I whisper, biting my inner cheek. I should've slowly eased into what I've been doing.

Her lips twist and she swallows. "You mean to tell me I've searched high and low for you, written letters every goddamn day because of the guilt I felt for not being there for you and you've been what" —she flails her arms out— "out chasing your dreams to become a singer!"

"Addison," Max warns.

"You stay out of this!" she yells at Max and then shifts her fury to me. "I can't believe you, Sydney. We all grieved for Damon. We were all here for each other, but you ran away!"

I can't say anything as I choke on my emotions. She's right. I left, but I can't get the words out to explain. The disappointment in her voice tears at my heart.

"Addison, you need to back the fuck off. Right now!" Max roars. His voice echoes throughout the penthouse. He steps in between us, blocking my view of Addison.

"Whoa, brother." Aiden steps forward, putting a hand on Max's chest. Max shoves it off, taking a step closer to Aiden. His eyes shoot daggers.

I put my hand on Max's arm. "It's okay, Max." I don't need him to end up with a wall between him and his best friend too.

He turns to me, his face carved in stone. "You had your reasons. Don't let her make you feel bad." Nothing he says will help. I feel guilty and ashamed of everything.

Max storms out, slamming the door behind him. "We'll be down at the bar," Aiden grumbles, following him out.

Once he's out of the room, Addie and I stare at each other. Tears flow between us.

"I'm sorry," I whimper.

She rubs the tears off her cheek. "Why did you leave, Syd?"

The words I need to say stick in my throat. "The night of the funeral…" I pause, the lump making it hard to breathe. "I lost our baby, too."

CHAPTER FIVE

MAX

"Johnny Walker, neat," I bark at the bartender before he has time to ask me what I want.

Aiden sits beside me. "Fink, just give us the whole bottle."

I shake my head, furious at him for getting in my face, furious at myself for getting so enraged. I know when Addison hears everything, she'll regret her words. I just couldn't take any more of the pain in Sydney's eyes.

Two glasses are placed in front of us with the bottle. He pours each of us a drink and walks off, leaving the bottle. We both take a much-needed swallow.

"I don't think you've ever been that pissed at me," Aiden says.

I turn my head to face him and grumble, "Sorry."

"Maybe we should have told Addison before Sydney got there. She wouldn't have been so blindsided," he says right before taking another drink. I told him everything before I left to go find Syd and gave specific instructions that it wasn't our story to tell. If Sydney wanted her to know, she'd have to tell her, herself.

I sigh and run my hands over my face. "You already know how I feel about that."

"She's hurt. You know how it affected her when Sydney left. She's letting her emotions get the best of her." He tries to justify Addison's outburst.

"I get it." I hold up my drink in a mock salute and he follows suit. The heat flows down my throat to the knots in my stomach. I thought watching Sydney and Damon together was the most trying time of my life. These past couple days have beat that tenfold. She's not mine. I can't have her, but my mind won't let her go. It was easy to push those thoughts aside when she wasn't around.

"You know it's been over a year," he says as if reading my mind. "Nobody would fault—"

"Don't fucking say it. No."

"I can still see it, Max. I can still see how you look at her and she's the only person who would cause you to get up in Addison's face. Shit, in my face."

"We don't need to have this conversation." I glare at him, silently demanding he stops. He shakes his head, pouring two more drinks. "How are the kids?"

"You can deflect all you want. You'll have to deal with that up there eventually." He points up. I thought I was past the regret and torment of letting her go. But the second I laid eyes on her, the levee broke, but it brought back guilt with it.

I snicker, ignoring his comment and say, "She has a new name."

"What?"

"Yeah, she goes by *Sky*. Her manager is an interesting character, but she kills it on stage."

"Is she going back?"

"She's only here a week." Another reason there's no need to deal with *that up there*.

I continue to tell him about my time in Los Angeles and the recording deal she got. I smile like a fool talking about her. As much as she's been through, I'm excited for her. She just needs to find herself again.

"Did you already run her security?" He smirks.

"Hell yeah. Hired one." I shrug one shoulder as he laughs out loud. "I needed to make sure she was safe."

"Mm-hmm." I flip him and his insinuating tone off.

"How's the new guy?" I eye him wondering why he's asking about Kase.

"He's doing great. The guys seem to like him a lot. I think he'll be a great addition." He nods slowly with a stern expression and then takes a drink. "Do you know something I don't know about him?"

"Nah. Addison seemed to like him, too." His voice is clipped. "I overheard her tell Katie he was–in her words–*scorchin' hot*." I chuckle as his jaw tics. "It's not fucking funny. I don't need my wife drooling over one of your guys."

"Honeymoon's over already, huh?"

He jerks his head in my direction. "We are *perfect*. Just leave your *scorchin' hot* SEAL at home next time you check on Addie and the kids."

I slap him on the back, laughing. That is definitely not going to happen now. Seeing Aiden squirm is awesome and rare. I also know that he and Addison are rock solid, so I'm not concerned.

"Uncle Max!"

I spin in the bar seat and stand just in time to catch Lulu flying toward me. Her little arms wrap around my neck. If Addison and Aiden hadn't adopted Lulu, I would have. I don't know what the hell I would've done with a five-year-old, but I would move mountains to make this little girl happy. And she knows it.

"Hey, Lulu."

"I missed you. Where've you been?"

"California, doing some work." I know she'll be over the moon when she sees Sydney. "How's school going?"

A small male fake cough grabs our attention. I look over at their nanny and she's standing with another kid about the same age as Lulu. She spins her little body in my arms and glares down at him.

"Snitches get stitches," she sneers at the little boy. I do a double take, looking at Lulu. Whoa. Where did this devil child come from and where did my sweet Lulu go?

"Alexandra Roberts," Aiden says sternly. The kid rolls his eyes like he's used to Lulu's threats. "We'll talk about this later, but you need to apologize."

Lulu's apology is half-assed. I bite my lip so I don't laugh. Aiden nods his head and walks over to take a sleeping Jett out of the nanny's arms. Lulu looks back at me.

I whisper, "*Snitches get stitches?*"

She shrugs. "He shouldn't tattle on people. If I tattled on half the things he's done, he would be in so much trouble." I'm *not* fond of this kid and his heathen ways already. I watch him and the nanny head to the elevator.

"Does he live in the building?" She dramatically nods her head. "So, what did you get in trouble for?"

A sly smile spreads across her cheeks. "Our teacher is mean. She said that she was sick and tired of kids not listening to her." She giggles to herself. "So I told her she should go take a nap. Since she was tired. She didn't like that, so I got put on red today."

Not gonna lie. I feel like giving her a high five for her wittiness, but I have a feeling Addison would kill me, so I shoot for the responsible uncle talk. "Well, unfortunately, we can't always have teachers we love, but you still have to be good for them." She nods, looking down. Addison tells me I need to be more firm with her when she does things wrong. Screw that. I'm the *best* uncle in the world, the last thing I want is to make her feel bad. "Hey, I have a surprise for you."

I grab her attention and her eyes brighten. "You brought me something from California?"

I nod.

Yes, because I kick ass.

CHAPTER SIX

SYDNEY

"**W**hy didn't you call me?" she cries into my arms.

"I did," I whisper, choking on my words.

That night was the hardest night of my life. Not only was I burying my fiancé with the burden of guilt that he died because of me, but I went home alone. There was only one person I wanted around me. My person. My sister. *My best friend.* I'd never been so lost in my life.

That was just the beginning.

"Addie, please pick up."

Something's wrong.

Her voicemail answers. I hang up and regret sending Katie home earlier. I just didn't want company.

I wince at the pain, the phone slips from my hand, crashing to the floor. My stomach twists in ways it shouldn't. The heartbreak has overwhelmed me the last couple days, so I haven't eaten. I must be hungry. I focus on swinging one leg at a time over the side of the bed. My feet contact the cool wood and I push off right before another sharp pain bites through me. Falling to my knees, my screams echo off the bedroom walls. Please God, make it stop.

The pain is so unbearable, my stomach twists. I turn and crawl on all fours to the trashcan, reaching it just in time to vomit. I haven't eaten, so I dry heave most the time.

The pain settles a few minutes later and I lean against the wall, exhausted. Something's wrong. I've never known of someone dying of heartbreak. Stretching my feet out, I moan at the slight wetness in my panties. That's awesome. Nothing like peeing yourself when you vomit. I draw in a couple deep breaths, taking note that the pain has diminished. I cautiously stand, using the wall to stabilize myself.

Bright red lines my panties when I pull them down. I gasp in disbelief, tears pool in my eyes. This cannot be happening. The pain stabs through my abdomen again and I double over. I have to get to my phone. I breathe through the pain and crawl out of the bathroom. Eyeing the phone on the floor, I slide over to it and call the only person who will drop everything to help.

"Max. Help."

ADDIE GASPS. "I remember when you called. I thought Katie had gone home with you." She clutches her chest, her eyes swell with apology. "I'm so sorry, Syd. Aiden was having a rough time that night. I *wanted* to answer. I told myself that I would call you back as soon as he fell asleep." Her head drops between her shoulders and her voice breaks when she adds, "And I forgot."

I should tell her it's okay, but I can't. The hurt still stings. My therapist tried to help me understand, forgive. But I couldn't.

I lost everything that night. Laying in bed the day after a long night at the hospital, my emotional state was volatile. Ugly crying over my loss overcame me one minute and the next my body would shake from rage and jealousy that Addison had everything. A husband, a healthy unborn child… she didn't even need me anymore. I became inconsequential to her. After all she'd been through and I was there by her side no matter what, this is what I received in return. Deep down, I knew I was being irrational, but I couldn't dig myself out of that hole.

I was being buried alive, and I had to leave.

"I would have been there for you," she cries, clutching my hand and squeezing it. "I was torn at *that* moment. You have to know how horrible I feel. Syd, *I love you*. It's killing me you went through this by yourself."

"I should have stayed. Max tried to change my mind, but I couldn't get past the suffering."

"Why California?"

I snicker. "My aunt Crystal lives there."

"You despised your aunt Crystal."

I still do.

"I thought she'd like to see her niece." I shrug. "There was never a plan for staying in California. I needed time to heal, and I didn't know where else to go. Max demanded that he meet my aunt when we arrived at her house. I guess it's good he did because when my aunt opened the door, she pretended she didn't know me. Claimed she didn't have a niece."

"She's still a bitch, huh?"

"You could say that. She asked Max if *he* wanted to come in though."

My mom and her sister are two peas in a pod. Grew up with silver spoons in their mouths and stones in their hearts. How my dad stayed married to her all those years, I'll never know. I was a mistake. Whenever I was an inconvenience in *her* life, she would remind my dad I was *his* problem. The therapist told me that is why I clung to Addison's friendship with a vise grip and why I took it so hard when she picked Aiden over me.

"After we left there, I had Max take me to a hotel."

Another person pushing me away only deepened the hole.

My self-worth was at an all-time low.

. . .

"I'M STAYING," he barks, dropping his keys and phone on the small kitchenette table.

"Max, I'll be okay. I just need some time alone." Sympathy weighs heavy in his eyes. He's stuck here with me because nobody else wants me. But I don't need him. I want to be alone. It seems to be what I'm destined for.

Having no more energy to fight, I drag my feet to the bedroom, strip off my shirt and pants, and crawl into the cold sheets. Wetness from my tears coats the pillow. I lost a child, and it's all my fault. No matter what the doctors claim, I'm the one who didn't take care of my body. I killed our child.

Minutes turn into hours. Hours of self-blame, self-loathing. Max checks on me frequently, but I ignore him. Maybe he'll tire of me too and leave.

But he doesn't.

"Tink, you need to eat something."

The sound of him setting something down beside my bed causes me to open my eyes. He unwraps a sandwich and puts it on a plate, along with some chips. "I didn't know what you preferred, so I guessed ham and Swiss cheese, and Doritos... because who doesn't like Doritos?"

My lip twitches. "I like Doritos. But I'm not hungry."

"I don't remember asking if you were hungry."

He sits on the bed beside me. I pull the covers to my neck remembering that I'm only in my bra and panties. He stands and snatches a shirt from the chair. Walking back over, he stares at me. "You putting this on or am I?"

I yank the shirt he's waving around. "I can dress myself, thanks." Like a gentleman, he twists around for me to slip it on. When I sit up, I wince from the ache in my lower stomach. Fresh tears graze my cheeks and I wish I could stop feeling. I pray for numbness.

Max sits down next to me again, wrapping his arms around my body and holds me tight while I cry.

• • •

"*Max!*" *I scream, squeezing my eyes shut, as sunlight floods into the room. Not even the thick white comforter I throw over my head can keep out the intruding brightness. The numbness that I longed for, finally hit. This is the first time in three days I've seen the sun and it sucks.*

"*I made you a doctor's appointment,*" *he says firmly. I've stopped bleeding and cramping so I don't know why he's making me go to the doctor. It's done.*

My baby is gone.

"*I don't need a doctor,*" *I grumble from under the covers.*

"*You need to talk to someone. You don't want to talk to me, so I found you a doctor.*"

That is the last thing I need right now. Sleep, that's what I need. Closing my eyes, my listless body turns heavy, pulling me under. I yelp again when my protective comforter shell rips off me. The cold air bites my body, sending chills all over it.

"*Really, Max?*" *I sneer, wrapping the sheet around me.*

"*Sydney, this isn't up for discussion. You're going.*" *His eyes bore into me and I know I don't have a choice. I throw my feet over the side of the bed and stomp to the chair holding my yoga pants. Stuffing each leg in, I yank them up and stare back.*

"*Let's go,*" *I say between gritted teeth, holding my arms out wondering why he's not moving. This was his idea.*

His eyes widen as he gets a good view of me. "*You... don't want to take a shower first?*"

I glance down my body. The same wrinkled shirt and black pants I showed up in days ago hang off me. Rubbing my eyeballs with my palms, I groan. "*No, Max. I don't. I don't want to talk to anyone either, for the record. I don't want to leave here. I don't want to do anything except go back to sleep.*"

"*Well, that was productive.*" *My voice drips with sarcasm as we exit the medical building. The doctor asked questions, I didn't answer them. She won't understand the loss I'm experiencing, no matter what I say. I* pull sunglasses down from the top of my head, walking down a street I don't remember walking before. Conveniently, the doctor was close to our hotel. I sigh. What exhausting thing did he plan now? "Where are we going?"

Max looks down at me, his eyebrows pinched with concern. "We're going back to the hotel."

I study the street, glancing around at the different buildings trying to locate anything that looks familiar. Did we come this way? Great! I'm losing my mind too. Add it to the list of stuff I've lost.

As soon as we step into the hotel room, I head for the shower—not because the doctor told me to—but because I got a whiff of my funky body sitting on her couch. I catch a glimpse of my reflection that I was trying hard to avoid. I do a double take because the person looking back is a stranger. Her cheeks are hollow and the dark circles under her eyes look like smeared makeup. Her hair is stringy and greasy. She's screaming inside of herself. She's lost, but I can't help her.

"I'm sorry," I whisper to her, moving away from the haunted reflection and slide into the hot shower.

"Feel better?" Max asks when I wander into the living room. I stare at him, dumbfounded. If he expects a hot shower will cure everything, he's an idiot. He throws his palms up. "Just asking. Don't kill me for being concerned."

I don't care if I hurt his feelings. I don't care that he's concerned.

I just don't care anymore.

While I'm preparing a cup of tea, he informs me he's going to take a shower. I watch him stroll out of the room and the only thing I can think is, leave. As soon as I hear the shower turn on, I rush around the room, grabbing my backpack and slip my shoes on and debate sneaking into the bedroom to grab my clothes.

No. I need to leave now.

I glance around the room one last time and I notice a small pad with hotel letterhead on the table next to the couch. Peering back toward the bedroom, my stomach twists. He's done so much for me, the least I can do is leave a note.

I scribble words on the paper.

PLEASE DON'T SEARCH *for me.*
    Thank you.
    Tink.

"HE KNEW WHERE YOU WERE." Addison squeezes my hand, pulling me from my story. It seems like it happened a lifetime ago.

I grin softly. "I know. Well, I know now. He mentioned he was keeping tabs on me."

"Don't even get me started on how furious I am at him for not telling me."

Part of me is thankful he didn't. I needed to do this on my own terms and being away from her allowed me to prove to myself that I can do things on my own. If she would've found me early on, we would've ended right back where we were. Me dependent on her.

"Why did you stay away for so long though?" I shrug, embarrassed to admit my reason. Her brows furrow. "I just don't understand. I get you were in pain and having to deal with the unimaginable. But I, of all people, understand that." I stare out across the living room, away from her questioning eyes. What Addison went through, being kidnapped, beaten, and raped, makes me feel ashamed of going away.

"At first, it was easier to forget about everything living out there, but in the process, I lost a bigger part of myself. I kept thinking I would find myself if I stayed just a little longer. And, in a way, I did. I just regret what I sacrificed to get there." She stares at me, waiting for me to explain *why I stayed away from her.* I wring the tissue around my fingers, casting my eyes down. "I hate admitting this, but I was jealous. You had everything. I was left with nothing."

She gasps. "Really? That's how you felt?"

Pinching my lips together, I nod and finally look at her. "At the moment, yes. But my mind was filled with desperation to be needed during a time of distress."

She leans back into the cushions and cast her gaze up to the ceiling. "And I wasn't there for you." She rolls her head over. "Do you hate me?"

"Oh my god, no! I thought you hated me."

"Never."

She pushes forward and swings her arms around me in a tight hug.

Warmth from my heart mending flushes through me. I know it's just the beginning because my breaks are deep, but I haven't felt this at peace in a year.

CHAPTER SEVEN

SYDNEY

W hen the front door flies open, we both turn our heads. A toothless smile spreads across Lulu's little face. "Sydney," she squeals, running at me with arms wide open. Her overzealous hug knocks us both back into the couch. Hearing her excitement alone makes me regret not doing this sooner.

"Oh my gosh, you're getting so big."

She pulls back and looks at me. "I missed you so much. I didn't think you were ever coming back. Mom kept saying you were, but it's been forever."

I hold her face in my hands. It's the first time I've ever heard her call Addie mom. Lulu deserves the best after witnessing her parents' murder and she got it with Aiden and Addison. "I missed you too."

"What have you been doing?"

"I've been teaching singing lessons to little girls just like you." I missed teaching kids but didn't want to go back to teaching while I was performing at nightclubs most nights, so I taught a few lessons during the week. I still had money I received when my dad passed away, so I lived comfortably, but it wouldn't last forever if I didn't help offset some of my bills.

"I'll be right back." She jumps off the couch and runs out of the room.

I glance at Addie and she shrugs. "You never know with that one."

"I bet she keeps you on your toes."

"Oh, just wait until you see Jett. For a six-month-old, he's a busy guy." I chuckle, but it comes out more bitter than I had meant. "I'm sorry," she says quietly.

I expected the baby would bring out feelings I had locked away months ago. But that's why I'm here. To release these stored up feelings, free me to live again. It's okay for me to be sad that I lost a child. I accept that.

"I'm all right. Don't be sorry. I can't wait to meet him." The awkwardness that has never been there before, weighs heavy between us.

Lulu comes back into the room carrying a kid's radio with a microphone attached to it. "Let's sing," she cheers.

I swallow, remembering the last time we sang together. I can't do it. I play with my hair, pulling it back and into a twist. I've compartmentalized my singing. Singing for a job, I can do without feeling, but singing for enjoyment, I've yet to find my voice. I bite my lip, trying to think of what to say. What excuse I can give her.

"Sweetie, Syd's tired. She's been traveling all day. How about you get your homework done first?"

I breathe a sigh of relief.

Once she's out of the room, Addie looks at me. "I'm here anytime you need to talk. I know this is hard for you, so anytime it gets to be too much, just say... *Magic Mike.*"

I purse my lips, trying not to laugh, remembering our night in the wild club. "I still can't believe he went up the ladder with you riding him." I burst out laughing.

Addie laughs, falling on the couch next to me. This feels so good, us laughing together. "I was going to kill you. *But it was kinda hot.*"

"I'm going to choose to ignore the fact that *my wife* just said riding someone was hot," Aiden grates, walking in carrying an adorable little boy with large green eyes identical to his dad's. His gummy smile shines as soon as he sees Addison. She walks over and takes him from Aiden.

"You're so hot when you're jealous." She pushes up on her bare toes, kissing him on the lips and he slaps her on the ass as she walks away. I love that their dynamic hasn't changed.

I glance behind him and sigh. "Where's Max." I'm sure he was happy to drop me off and run. He did his job. I'm not his problem anymore.

Aiden studies me for a beat, making me rock back and forth from his intense stare. "He's staying at a hotel. Said to call him when you're ready to go back to LA."

"What?" Addison clips. "Are you leaving soon?"

I wince at her disappointment. "I told Graham I'd only stay a week."

"Wait a minute, Graham DeLong?" I nod, wondering if she would've remembered him. "He always adored you in college. So, are you ready to meet your nephew?" She takes a couple steps toward me. "JD, this is your aunt Syd." He grins and claps his hands while drool spills from his mouth. Addison wipes it off and laughs. "He's teething, so he's a slobbery mess."

I reach out and shake his plump hand. His fingers wrap around mine. "Hey JD." I glance at Addie. "What's JD stand for?"

She swallows and looks around the room for Aiden. I tilt my head, surprised by her hesitancy. Aiden stands behind her, squeezing her shoulders. She finally answers. "Jett Damon." My hand drops to my side.

Oh.

That hurts. *It shouldn't.* It makes total sense why they would do it, but knowing it, doesn't stop the sting. I shake the unwanted feelings from my thoughts, and manage a smile, holding my arms out. "Hey Jett, can I hold you?" He comes to me easily and I have to adjust him on my hip. He's a chunker with some serious chubby legs. *What are they feeding this kid?* I sit with him on the couch and slap his hands together, playing patty-cake. When giggles fill the room, they tickle my soul with happiness. Tears well up in my eyes. I glance at Addie and she's biting her nails watching us, trying to read my reaction. "He's perfect. Y'all did good."

When he falls asleep on me not long after, I'm disappointed when Aiden takes him from me. I tell Addison to tell me about him, wanting to know everything I've missed when Aiden disappears into a bedroom with Jett. It's surreal to think my baby would be the same age.

As Addison is telling me about the birth and Aiden's attempt to cut the cord right before he passed out, Lulu comes running into the living room. "Sydney, is that you?" She's holding my LA Now magazine that she must have snatched on the way to her room. It was next to my purse on the counter. She squeezes in between us on the couch and points to a picture. Addison and I both lean in to see.

I gasp. "Oh, my gosh." It's a picture from my concert the other night. I pull the magazine out of her hands and read the article next to the picture. My eyes widen and a few squeals escape my lips.

"What does it say?" Addison asks, trying to read over my shoulder. I'm done reading it, but I can't stop staring at it. Addison gets impatient and rips it out of my hands.

The smile on my face is ridiculous. "Syd, this is amazing. *While we have always thought Sky Owen was something worth watching, tonight she showed her raw side, singing 'Lost Boy' by Ruth B, and let me just say... she blew us out of the water. Her soulful voice mixed with rawness had everyone in the bar hypnotized,"* she reads out loud. She sharply inhales when she keeps reading the rest to herself. Laying the magazine down in her lap. She places her hand on mine and says, "Is this why you came home?"

Of course, the magazine covered my fainting too. I blow out a heavy breath. "I want to say no, but I can't. It made me realize that I had to mend my past before I could move forward." I squeeze her hand.

"I'm glad you did. So, should I call you Sky from now on?" she teases.

"Don't you dare."

CHAPTER EIGHT

SYDNEY

"I can't believe we're doing this," Addie says as we walk through the blacked-out doors.

We've spent the last couple days catching up on everything. Aiden kicked us out of the house, tired of hearing us talk. He cheerfully volunteered to take care of the kids as long as he didn't have to hear us laugh again. My heart is happy being here, but I miss Los Angeles. I was afraid coming back, I'd fall back into the same mentality that I had to be close to Addison. I realize I can have both. Addison and my singing career can coexist in my world.

"I know. Remind me why again." I shake my hands to stop the trembling. Pain makes me a wimp.

The walls are painted red with black-framed artwork pinned to them. We move from picture to picture admiring the inked tattoos.

"Hey ladies, what can we do for you?" A grizzly bear of a man approaches us. The only thing soft looking about the guy is his rosy cheeks you can barely see under his shaggy black beard.

"Um… we're here to…" Feeling out of place, I have a hard time finding my words. The sound of a buzzing noise comes from somewhere in the back and I can feel it in my teeth when I open my mouth.

"We're getting tattoos," Addison says confidently. *Easy for her to say.* She's never been afraid of pain. "Max Shaw recommended we come to you."

His eyes land on me and he cocks his head to the side. "*Hmm.* You wouldn't be Tink, would ya?"

I'm taken aback by his question. Only Max calls me that. I look at Addison and she does a small shrug. "That's Max's nickname for me, but I go by Sydney." I let out an awkward chuckle. After the shock of him knowing who I am dies down, I narrow my eyes at him and plant my hands on my hips. "If Max paid you to do some crazy tattoo on me, like a dick or something, I will hurt you."

He roars with laughter, holding his belly. "He told me you were a little spitfire. But I promise" —he holds up both his hands— "no dick tats. I'm Jay." He holds out his hand. I take a couple seconds to register that I'm supposed to shake his hand because I'm in shock at how large it is. How the hell is he going to do a dainty tattoo with the hands of a giant? If Max hadn't recommended him, I think I would back out. Instead, I put my trust in him and slip my hand into his.

I pull out a piece of paper from my jeans pocket, unfold it and hand it to him. "This is what I want, right here," I say, pointing to my inner wrist. I'm waiting for *this tattoo is too small for me to do.* I would totally understand why.

Instead, he nods and says, "Looks easy enough."

Addison and I scoured through hundreds of pictures last night on the internet. I knew what I wanted. A treble clef with wings. The treble clef represents the beginning of my song. My future. The wings represent my past. A reminder of those I loved and lost.

Another guy comes out and takes Addie back to his room. Panic flutters inside my belly. I was hoping they would let her hold my hand while I had it done and vice versa.

"Don't be scared. I'll go easy on you," he says, walking to a small room.

I bet he tells everyone that.

With the tip of his head, he motions to the dentist-style chair beside him and I slide in it while he scribbles on a pad and redraws the tattoo, changing a few things. Beneath the scent of disinfectant lay the faint smell of pot. I stare at him, thinking it's not too late to leave. But when he shows me his version, the wings more defined and feathered, my smile reaches my eyes, excitement stirring inside me. Maybe he smokes it for medicinal purposes. *Who am I to judge?*

"I love it. It's perfect." I relax a little, obviously he knows what he's doing. Max wouldn't send me here if he didn't trust the guy. "So, Jay, I'm sure you've heard this question a bajillion times, but entertain me… *does it hurt?*"

He turns his head, cocks a brow with an amused expression. "Nope."

"Really?" I say, sitting forward, the possibility giving me life. He chuckles, shaking his head as he returns to setting up. Hope dies a million deaths. "That wasn't very nice."

"You told me to entertain you. I could've told you it won't hurt as bad as Max."

I gasp, shock robbing me of words. Did Max tell him about us? My face flushes from embarrassment. He doesn't seem like the kiss and tell kind of guy, but there's no way Jay could have guessed that just by Max telling him I was coming. Jay rolls his chair over and I'm still too flabbergasted to do anything other than hold my hand out, wrist up on the arm pad. He rubs a cool pad over my wrist.

Jay chuckles. "Relax, Sydney. I was kidding. But the way your face is lightin' up like a firefly, says a lot. So, what's up with you and Max?"

"Nothing," I reply quickly. He slowly nods, with an unconvinced expression. "We're just friends."

I watch in silence as he places the transfer on my wrist, leaving the design on my skin when he pulls it up. "Good?" I nod, already loving how it looks.

"So, what *exactly* did he tell you about me?"

He rolls back over to me, his large hand engulfs the tool. His round eyes meet mine for a beat as if he's deciding what to say. "There were no specifics. Just how he met a beautiful woman and let her go."

I snicker. "That isn't quite how it went. It's more like he was never interested." The needle makes contact and I flinch, blowing out a long breath. *This isn't too bad,* I tell myself. Mind over matter, right? I stop talking to not distract him. The last thing I need is a permanent *oops.* My eyes water, so I hum to distract myself from the shocking sensation that isn't going away. I imagine myself on stage, playing in Central Park. Thousands of people scream my name. Except no matter where I look in the crowd, steel-blue eyes stare up at me. Without thinking, the words from "Mercy" by Shawn Mendes bubble up out of me. I'm singing directly to Max, spilling every emotion into the words.

As the words fade away, the buzzing noise interrupts my dream, and I'm back in the small, dreary room. It takes a couple seconds to realize his tool is no longer touching me. "Are you done already?" I ask, meeting chocolate brown eyes without looking at my wrist.

He shakes his head, and I arch a brow, wondering if something's wrong. I peek down, afraid of what I'll see, and only one wing is done. "Wow," he says to himself, shaking out of whatever trance he's in. "… he said you were good, but that was sick."

My cheeks warm again. "Sorry, I didn't realize I was singing out loud." This time I don't flinch when he begins again. The mixture of nerves and my week of healing has my emotions on a whirlwind.

"It's not a bad sound. Sing away, girl. Do you always sing when you're nervous?" he asks without looking up.

I bob my head. "Sometimes."

"Well, I can't wait to say I did your ink when you're famous."

I laugh out loud at the sound of that. *Famous?* My first single will probably bomb or I'll be a one-hit-wonder. It's easy to imagine myself on stage, yet it's difficult for me to imagine I'll make something of myself. The odds are not in my favor. A lot of singers sign with a producer, but they'll drop you quicker than cash if you're not selling and move on to the next hot thing of the moment.

An hour later, Addie and I are staring at our forever artwork on our wrists through clear plastic wrap. My skin looks pissed, red and raised. Jay hands us our healing instructions and says, "Sydney, it was great to meet you, finally." *Finally?* When did Max tell him about me? "And always remember, not every tattoo is exactly one of a kind. So, you can't get mad at me if you see it again." I tilt my head, confused.

"I'm sure there are millions of wings and music notes out there. I promise, I won't hold you responsible for not giving me a one of a kind." He glances over from the cash register, a mischievous grin playing on his lips as he nods.

I eye him for a beat before Addie and I leave; the bell dinging behind us as we walk out onto the street. "Is it me, or was he hiding something?" Addie is the queen of reading situations. I'm usually the one that tells her she's imagining things.

"Definitely hiding something."

I inspect my tattoo again, making sure he didn't *add* anything. It looks exactly like the drawing. I shrug, not giving it too much thought. So what if someone else has this? They won't have the same story behind it, that's for sure.

CHAPTER NINE

SYDNEY

I tap on the door lightly with my knuckles, a small part of me hoping he's not here. Blowing out a breath when I hear noises on the other side of the cream-colored door, I get ready to face Max. Folding and unfolding my arms, I settle with them by my side. My stomach flip-flops at the sight of him. He stands tall, holding onto the door and stares down at me.

"Hi," I say, my voice barely a hushed whisper.

"Hey."

I sigh from his lack of words. "Can I come in?"

After two quiet awkward beats, he nods and pushes the door open. He stays quiet as I walk under his arm and shuts the door behind me. The couch in the living room is an ugly light orange color with two yellow chairs next to it. When I found out where he was staying, it surprised me it wasn't a higher-end hotel. I sit on the stiff orange cushion and watch him swing a kitchen table chair into the room, sitting on it backward.

"Why are you hiding out?" *And in a shitty hotel like this?* I keep that thought to myself. Now isn't the time to bring up his terrible choice of hotels.

"You're fighting your demons, Tink. I'm fighting mine." He looks away from my questioning expression.

"I guess... I'm your demon then?" I swallow, surprised by his words and reaction.

His lips crack a small smile and he shakes his head. "No, you are definitely not a demon."

"Then what is? Talk to me, Max."

For every time he's been there for me, I'd like to think I can return the favor.

He pops out of his chair and takes quick strides to the fridge, grabbing a beer out of it. As he leans against the counter, his gaze finally meets mine. "The *idea* of you. Of us." His fingers run through his hair haphazardly and my thoughts go back to when my fingers did that. *Dammit, Sydney. Stop.* It's been two years since we've been together. And now a river of guilt that flows over a dead man runs between us. Words have escaped my mind. Deep down, I wondered if I was the reason Max was staying away this week. Yet, here I am, questioning him. Punishing both of us when we can never be.

"I couldn't do it," he responds, pausing for a quick drink. His arms straight as boards as he leans against the counter and drops his head. "Even knowing how your absence was killing Addison, I still couldn't tell her where you were. I'm a selfish bastard because as soon as I told her, she would have dragged you home, and I'd be right back where I was when you left me in LA."

Nervously, I lick my dry lips, unsure I want to know the answer, but I ask anyway. "Which was?"

He looks up, the raw hurt glittering in his blue eyes. "Broken from guilt."

I shove off the couch and move toward him. The counter divides us and I grip the edge. "Max, you did nothing wrong. Why did you feel guilty?"

"Someday I might tell you, but not today." He downs the rest of his beer and slams the empty bottle on the counter causing me to jump at the sharp sound. When he passes me, I reach out, grabbing his arm, halting him. The air grows thick with desperation. Frustration. Uncertainty.

He stares down at my wrist, the tattoo shiny from the ointment and his jaw tightens. "Sydney." The unspoken demand to let go should frighten me, but it doesn't. I squeeze tighter in defiance.

"Don't walk away," I whisper. His bicep twitches. It was the wrong thing to do. I should have let him walk away. Why do I keep doing this? The uncertainty of us doesn't need to be defined. Not now. Not ever.

It can't be.

He finally lifts his gaze from my wrist, meeting mine. In a quick spin, he has me pinned against the counter; the edge digging into my back.

"What do you want from me, Tink? Does knowing that I dreamt about your glacier blue eyes every night make a difference? That I owned you. *That you owned me.* That my dreams became my worst nightmare because you weren't mine, you were one of my best friend's fiancée? That I wished it was me instead of him, you said I love you to? And now he's not here, I'm drowning in guilt because I. Still. Want. You. I can't compete with a ghost. Nothing I say will make this right, so *please,* tell me what you want to hear."

His forehead rests on the top of my head, his emotions vibrate through my body. The erratic beat of my heart pounds against my chest, making me question why. Is it from his words or my guilt?

I swallow, my words barely a whisper. "Why didn't you tell me?" He shoves off the counter and walks away, taking my vulnerability with him, annoyance taking its place. "You made it clear we were a one-night stand, so where is this coming from, Max?"

He told Damon we were nothing. It hurt at first, but I dealt with it. We were two friends who got together after an emotional night. Even though I saw his jealous looks, I pushed them aside, thinking he wanted me *because* I was with Damon. Screw that. I wasn't about to entertain his brooding ways because he changed his mind after the fact. It was too late.

Max lets out a humorless laugh, pointing to himself. "I made what clear? Tink, I'm not the one who said it was nothing. It was anything but."

"What are you talking about? When Damon asked me out, I didn't want to say yes because of you. When he told me you gave him your blessing, saying we were both drunk and you couldn't even remember it, I didn't see a reason to say no anymore. In fact, it pissed me off so much, I said yes in spite." I never told Damon that, but he knew.

He falls back into the cushioned yellow chair, throwing his head back, talking to the ceiling. "And here I was, heavy with guilt for having feelings for your woman. Asshole." His words aren't for me, so I stay quiet. He lifts his head and blows out a breath, meeting my gaze. "I never said that." I narrow my eyes in confusion. "I could never forget the night we spent together. I didn't know what to do. I'd never experienced that intense need for a woman, it scared the hell out of me, so I didn't call you. When Damon said he had asked you out, and you said yes, I had lost my chance and it was my own damn fault. He wanted to make sure I was cool with it." He runs his hands through his hair again and groans. "What was I supposed to say? If you wanted something more, you would've said no, so I told him to go for it."

I should've said no.

At least he'd be alive.

I back into the barstool, sitting, stunned by his words. Only, they're a couple years too late to act on. I can't be mad at Damon for what he did. At least he took the initiative to go after what he wanted.

"It's my fault he's dead." The words slip out before I can stop them. Heat courses through my body as I admit the one thing I'll never forgive myself for. Max sits forward, his head tilts like he's trying to make sure he understood me correctly. *You did.* I wring my fingers together and cast my eyes down. I need to get this out and since we're airing everything else, I might as well finish. "Right before he left, we got into an argument." I close my eyes momentarily as the tears burn. "The last thing he said to me before he walked out was *'I'm not Max'*."

Max's body stills as he stares at me. He doesn't look like he's breathing as my chest heaves to catch my breath. "Why would he say that?" His eyes flicker across my face searching for answers.

"God, I hated you." I cover my eyes with my hands, embarrassed I'm saying this out loud. "You unlocked something inside me. There was always something missing when I was with a man. *Until you*. You made me feel like I've never felt before. I craved that feeling again." I sigh, ashamed that Damon wasn't able to achieve it, yet I agreed to marry him. A nervous laugh slips from my lips. I can't believe I'm telling him this. "I remember the first time I asked Damon to tie me up. He was furious."

I jump when Max's fingers touch my chin, lifting it until our eyes meet. A slow smile tugs at one side of his lips as if he's trying not to air his approval of my words. "It wasn't your fault, so stop thinking it was."

"But if I hadn't—"

"Tink, we're men. We compartmentalize things, especially when it comes to women and work. What happened could have happened to any of those guys. They were ambushed and none of them saw it coming."

I tug my chin out of his grip and slide off the stool, walking past him, not wanting his sympathy. "I still feel guilty he died thinking I would rather be with you. I loved him, Max," I plead, not sure if I'm trying to convince him or myself. No, I did. But I had already decided I wouldn't marry him, I just didn't know how to end it. When he left that night, his words stung, but they made me realize I couldn't keep living a lie. Damon was wrong about one thing though, I didn't want Max. That door was bolted shut.

Two freaking years ago.

"Where do we go from here?" he whispers from behind me, his chest barely touching my back. His words confusing me.

A hand glides down my arm, leaving a trail of goosebumps. "We can't do this, Max." I swallow hard and tell my feet to walk away from his touch, but my body screams back by leaning into him. "We'll drown in the river of guilt that divides us," I whisper, turning to face him.

"Just give me tonight." The intensity in his eyes bore into me. How can I give him tonight when my heart wants tomorrow and my mind won't forget yesterday?

I open my mouth to decline, but the words don't come out. For a hot second, I want to give in to the desire. It's been over a year since I've been with a man and I know Max can give me what I need. But will he be able to walk away after? Will I? I shake my head, answering myself. *No.* Max changed me and I changed him.

He didn't ask for forever. We can't be casual friends with benefits.

With that final thought, the chains of guilt lock back around my heart quicker than it took to unlock them and I back out of his grip, reach for my purse off the table and rush to the door feeling horrible that I'm once again leaving him. The irony that I just asked him not to walk away. "I'm sorry, Max, I can't. Thank you for everything you've done," I whisper.

As I'm shutting the door, I hear, "Anytime, Tink," and then the sound of glass shattering against the wall. Pain funnels through my heart knowing I'm hurting him by walking away. *Again.* This will be the last time.

Max doesn't need to save me anymore.

CHAPTER TEN

SYDNEY

"You left that hot hunky man in the hotel room?" Graham bellows, his voice echoing in his office.

I glare at him, sitting smugly behind his desk, knowing how Addison felt because that would have been my exact response. He's like the boy's version of me. I rehash my visit, and he focuses on one thing. "Of course, you'd only comment on that."

He shrugs, smiling. "It was the last thing you went over. It was fresh in my mind." He taps his temple a couple times.

"If it would have been in the middle, you'd still pick it out."

He waves a hand around, stands and struts around his desk to where I'm sitting. "Let me see that tattoo since you're avoiding my question."

I hold out my wrist and I can't help but grin at the perfect design. He holds my wrist in his palm, his thumb grazes over the wings. Without letting go, he sits in the chair next to me. "You ready to tell me *everything*?" he asks in a hesitant tone, knowing I kept out important parts. *Like how I lost my baby.*

He's never asked and I've appreciated that he never did. But after everything he's done for me, I owe him an explanation. I close my eyes and nod, gathering my wits again to repeat everything I told Addison. The weight of the words comes out lighter knowing I'm not hurting Graham with them.

As soon as I reach the part where I end up on his porch, he rises and pulls me up into a tight hug. Tears run down my cheek, not sad tears, more like relief tears.

"Thank you for being there, G." I sniffle into his chest. He pulls back, his eyes glisten, and he grins as he cups my face in his hands.

"Sky, even if you sang like the Cookie Monster, I would have dropped everything to help you." I chuckle at the image. "Thank you for telling me."

"It feels good to get it out. I wanted to tell you, but I couldn't find the right words, so I buried them with a new life. Max brought everything back."

"Aww, and now we're back to Max." He releases me, leans against his desk and crosses his arms. His spiked eyebrow makes me roll my eyes.

"No. We're not back to Max. He's a friend. End of story."

"Your story is ending in a huge cliffhanger and you know how much I hate those." He playfully scowls and walks back to his chair.

He's wrong, it's more of a happy for now ending. Our story isn't unresolved, it's settled. Like oil and water. And they don't mix.

To move the conversation away from Max, I ask about the article. Graham's eyes light up as he opens a manila folder on his desk. The article lies on top of other papers. Giddy butterflies tickle my stomach as he reads the article, and I read along with him to myself, already having memorized the entire piece. I might have read it a *few* times.

The next couple of hours, we go over my schedule for the next week. I'm buzzing with excitement as we talk about meeting with a few songwriters. But first, we meet with our attorney tomorrow to go over the contract.

GRAHAM SQUEEZES my hand right before we walk into Jude's office. He could crush it and I wouldn't notice with the amount of adrenaline running through my body right now. *I feel sick.* Taking a couple deep breaths, Jude's assistant opens the door for us and we step into the executive office. Floor to ceiling windows overlooks the city. Platinum and gold records neatly display on one wall with a TV on the other. I glance at a few records and swallow, wondering how I'm even here. These people are greater than great, and I'm… nobody. My stomach tightens and I fight the ill feeling I have. *Don't lose it now, Sydney.*

"Sky, please sit down. You're looking pretty ghostly," Jude says, pulling out a chair for me.

If only I could go *poof* and disappear.

"I know it's overwhelming. But you'll do amazing. I foresee you having one of those yourself." Jude points to one of the platinum records. Pinching my lips together, I nod slowly, not accepting his confidence. He laughs at my dim response. "Wait and see. You'll be the next Taylor Swift." He swipes his hands in the air like my name's on a banner.

An unbelieving laugh escapes my lips and I cover my mouth with my hand. "Sorry. I… this is all a little overwhelming." I push my foot off the floor to spin my chair until I'm at the table, staring at Jude and Graham.

"I understand. But trust me, I'll get you there." I nod as he flashes his perfect white veneers. I'd follow that man into a burning house if it leads me to a famous singing career. "Okay, so let me introduce you to Shane Witt." I glance at the attractive middle-aged man on the couch, one arm stretched out across the back, with an ankle resting over his knee. He eyes me carefully and stands, walking over. "He's one of our amazing songwriters and we know the pair of you will create magic."

"Nice to meet you, Sky," he says, his voice rich and warm,

reaching his hand out. I wipe my damp palm down my jeans and slip it into his. An easy smile plays on the corner of his lips. "Don't worry. I'm with Jude, I've heard you sing and you're amazing. I can't wait to hear you sing the song I wrote specifically for you."

My whole body tingles with excitement. *Someone wrote a song for me to sing.* How is this my life? I squeeze my hands into fists under the table so I don't get up and dance around.

"I'm ready," I blurt out. The three guys chuckle. "I mean... whenever you're ready. Tell me where to go and when." I lean back, stuffing my hands under my legs to contain my enthusiasm.

Shane leans against the wall, glances at Jude and then back to me. "We can start tonight."

"That's perfect." Jude claps, standing up. "The quicker we can cut a single to get your name out, the better."

The next hour Jude discusses timelines and the ins and outs of recording. Thank god Graham is here because by the time the meeting finishes, I only remember bits and pieces of it.

"So Sky, tell me a little about yourself," Shane says, sitting across from me. It surprised me when he told me to meet him at his house, but Graham reassured me it's normal practice that a song-writer has a studio in his home.

I stare at the white wine in my glass for a moment. "I'm a southern girl trying to make it in a singer's world."

He smiles, staring at me. My gaze darts around his modern home. Silvers and whites set the tone, the only color in a framed piece of artwork above the fireplace mantle. "Don't be nervous." He gets up, stands in front of me with the wine bottle in his hand. "Like some more?"

I pull back my glass. "No, I'm good. The last thing I need to do is drink my nerves away. But thank you." He nods, placing the bottle on the table and sits beside me on the couch. My leg is bent and tucked under my other leg. I pull it out from under me to give him more room, but he grabs my knee and squeezes.

"I want you to be comfortable around me. We'll be spending a lot of time together."

I stare at his hand for a beat, a tingle wrapping around my spine paralyzes me momentarily. Is he coming on to me? But just as quick as he placed it on my knee, he removes it and stands back up. I adjust so both my feet are on the floor and run my hands down my jeans.

No. I'm just nervous and he's trying to help calm me down. Get a grip.

"How about we get started?" *Yes, please.* He takes his place back in the chair opposite me and picks up the guitar leaning against his chair. "Do you play?"

I nod, blowing out a nervous breath. "I'm better at the piano."

"Good to know."

The next couple of hours, we dig into the song. All my anxiety washes away as Shane leads me through the piece. He's good. And I love this song. A girl growing up without a father, searching for the one man that can protect her. Her journey moves through man after man until she finally meets him.

I lie to myself that I don't love it because I can relate to it, but the truth echoes in my emotions as I sing. My father loved me, but the feeling of abandonment from my mom led me to search for it from men and women. I feel this song deep in my bones.

"Wow," Shane whispers after my voice trails off, singing the last note. "That was… brilliant."

My cheeks redden. "Thanks."

It's midnight, and it feels like I just woke up. My body is buzzing with an adrenaline high. I tug my shirt a couple times so air can blow over my overheated body. "That was insane."

Shane jumps up and sits next to me again, his smile reaching his eyes. "It was. That's a hit." He drapes his arm against the back of the couch and his fingers brush against my temple, moving the couple tendrils of hair sticking to my sweaty face away. It takes effort not to jerk away.

"You're so beautiful." His eyes bore into me.

My smile fades.

Things just got awkward.

To defuse the situation, I hop up, focusing my eyes on anything other than him. "I can't believe we created that." I boast, ignoring his advance, walking back and forth in front of his coffee table. "I mean, that song is amazing, Shane." He stays seated, his arm still stretched out and his leg resting on his knee, sitting there like he's relaxing from a long day at work rather than a man that was just shut down.

Maybe he said *that was beautiful*. Meaning the song, *not me*. I tend to be great at reading men, especially ones that want to get in my pants. But I'm confused. One second he's eye-fucking me, the next he's just someone I'm collaborating with. It has me doubting myself, wondering if I'm just imagining what's happening.

He grabs my attention when he rises and takes two long strides to where I'm standing. I step back. Not far enough away that he can't reach out and tug on some of my hair. "I could take you to the top. My word goes a long way with Jude."

My eyes widen. Nope, not imagining this.

Another step back and my hair slips out of his fingers. A flush of heat spikes through me. "Um…" I'm speechless. We were working so well together. Why is he doing this?

He flashes a wicked smile. "You know the old adage, do something for me, I'll do something for you."

Words stick in my throat and I have to swallow the knot to speak. "So, you want me to…" I can't finish the sentence. I want to believe I misread him.

He chuckles and runs his finger under the strap of my pink tank. "You're smart, I think you can figure it out." When his finger moves to right above my breast, my heartbeat is pounding in my ear and I take another step back out of his reach again. This is the first time he doesn't follow my lead. I take in a couple ragged breaths. My mind too stunned to form a coherent response.

Instead, I hold up my finger and whisper, "Can I use your restroom?"

He nods, pointing down the hallway. "I'll be waiting."

After grabbing my purse, I risk a quick glance over my shoulder to make sure he isn't following me, rather he's downing his glass of wine, paying no attention to me. He's not concerned at all that I won't come back.

I won't, right? The voice in my head screams as I walk to the bathroom.

The bathroom door snaps shut and I lock it. Staring at myself in the mirror, the voice inside my head starts screaming again. *Don't do it.* I wrap my fingers around the porcelain sink and I drop my head. If I leave, I'm taking the once in a lifetime chance with Jude and throwing it away. I really want this, the taste of success is at the tip of my tongue.

It's just sex.

Shane's a good-looking guy and I've had a one-night stand before. Just keep my eyes on the prize. Stardom.

I can do this.

Digging through my purse, I grab my lipstick and drag it across my lips, the red tint bringing my face alive.

It's just sex.

I keep repeating those words to drown out my subconscious telling me I'm making a huge mistake. The soft sound of music floats past the bathroom door as I reach for the knob.

My breath snags on something deep in my chest. Anger and realization. The thought clicks in my head. I'm not the first person he's done this to. He's not hoping I'll stay. The arrogance in his actions speaks louder than his words. He knows I'll stay. How many more women has he blackmailed into sleeping with him? How many have stared at themselves in this same bathroom mirror telling themselves that it'll be okay? Or worse, stared at themselves after they sold their soul to the devil.

Anger fuels my body and I swing open the door, marching past his shocked expression, straight to the front door.

"You'll regret this." A shadow of annoyance crosses his face as he places his wine glass down on the coffee table.

I snort with derision, holding a finger up. Nodding my head, I pin my stare on the douche bag. "You know what? You're right."

The arrogant bastard smiles as I cross the living room floor to where he stands. For a man who thinks he can control women, he doesn't read them very well. As soon as I approach him, I let every ounce of anger out, swinging my knee up to his dick, connecting hard. I hope I broke it.

His groans and curse words fill the air as he drops to the floor, drowning out the music. Proudly, I turn back toward the door. Looking over my shoulder once more, I say, "Now, I have zero regrets. You fucked with the wrong girl. Or should I say, *didn't fuck?*"

Not until I'm parked in front of my apartment, does the significance of what I did weigh on my chest. Silent tears flow down my cheeks, the darkness outside blurs. I did the right thing, yet I feel like I did something wrong. Somehow this is my fault.

I pick up my phone, sniffing as I search for a name. Addison answers, her sleep-filled voice fills the air through the Bluetooth in my car. It's past three a.m. there, but I know she won't care. She's the one person who will make me understand what I did was worth the turmoil. The guilt filling my head makes me wonder if I'm a horrible person.

"Syd, what's wrong?"

I sniff and try to chuckle. Instead, it comes out a strangled noise. "What, don't I always call you at this time?"

"Shh, it's Sydney," she whispers.

"Is she okay?" A deep voice vibrates through the phone. The sheets ruffle in the background.

"I'm fine," I answer loudly, knowing Aiden's listening.

He grumbles and I hear Addison moving around. She whispers for me to hold on while she goes into the living room. "Okay. Talk," she says firmly, once settled.

I run my hands through my hair, gripping the ends, letting out a slow sigh. "I need you to promise me you won't tell Aiden." That's all I need is to make this bigger than it already is. And if Aiden knows... Max knows.

"I won't say anything..." She pauses, changing her mind. "... unless you're in trouble. Then I can't promise shit."

My lips twitch. "I'm not in trouble. But I just destroyed my career before it even started."

CHAPTER ELEVEN

SYDNEY

Hulk: **Hey west coast, how's it going?**

I stare at the text and sigh. *Seriously?* Can't anyone keep their mouth shut these days? Maybe the text is just a strange coincidence and my best friend didn't go behind my back. Dropping my hand to the couch, gripping my phone, I shake my head. There're no coincidences with Max Shaw.

Curiosity has me searching his name, my finger hovering over the call button. *I'm calling to help save a life,* I tell myself. *Shane's.* I press send and place the phone to my ear. My pulse races as I wait for him to answer. Sending a text is one thing, but talking to me, he might not want to after how I left.

"Well hell, this is a surprise," he quips, his deep voice instantly making my heartbeat race.

"You texted me," I retort. "It shouldn't be that much of a surprise. So, who told you?"

"Told me what?"

I roll my eyes. Why does he always have to be difficult?

"Shane? The reason you're texting me."

"Who's Shane?" he asks, his voice is flat making it hard to decipher by his tone if he's being serious. "I was just wondering how you were doing." *Mmm-hmm, sure.*

I rub my temple, debating if I should make an excuse that I have to go or continue talking. "He's just a guy they had me working with. Nobody important." I pause, waiting for a hint of disapproval, but he stays silent. "I'm doing good. How 'bout you?"

"Been busy with work, but same old shit. Have you recorded any songs?"

I narrow my eyes. This is his way of getting me to talk about Shane. Nice try, but if he wants me to talk about what happened, he needs to admit he knows. And who told him?

"I've been working with a couple songwriters." If only that was true. Nope, just one bastard that'll destroy me in this business. "But, I've yet to record a song." *Probably never will.*

"You sound disappointed."

"I just wonder if I belong in this world. I'm like a balloon floating in the vast open sky, just waiting to be popped. Self doubt is a killer," I admit, my fears getting the best of me. Singing on stage at a local bar is uncomplicated and effortless, but becoming a star might take the rest of my fractured soul.

"Sydney," he says sternly. "If anyone should be in the spotlight, it's you. I know how much fight you have in you, use it to control what you want and don't let anyone stop you from what you deserve."

His pep talk brings a smile to my face. I want to ask why he's always my cheerleader when I've been nothing but ungrateful by walking out on him. Instead, I say, "Thanks, Max."

My phone dings in my ear, so I pull it back real quick and see a text from Graham.

G-love: Meet me at Starbucks in an hour.

I dread hearing what he has to say. He was Team Sky and ready to set up the firing squad. With him, it's all bark. Max, I'm afraid of his bite. Graham had a meeting with Jude this morning. One thing is for certain, I'm not working with the douchebag, Shane, anymore.

"Well, work is calling," I reluctantly say, enjoying hearing his voice. "Thanks for checking on me."

"No problem. And hey, Tink…" He pauses for a beat and I hold my breath, waiting for him to continue. "I'm proud of you for standing up for yourself."

He knew.

"Thanks," I whisper. "Did Addison tell you?"

I glance at the phone when I hear nothing, confirming he hung up. Holding it to my chest, I release a puff of air. His words boost my confidence that I did the right thing, but didn't answer my question of who the rat is.

"WHY ARE you staring at me like I'm a Rubix Cube?" Graham says, setting his black, nothing added, coffee on the table. "I can already tell you, you'll never match all the colors of this cube." He waves a hand in front of his body and laughs.

I bite my lip to stop from laughing. It'll only encourage him to keep going if he knows he's entertaining. "I *am* trying to figure something out." He lifts his brow. "Do you like Max more than you do me?"

There's a slight tic at the corner of his mouth. "Well, that depends."

A small gasp slips from my lips. "On what? You're supposed to always be on my side. It was you, wasn't it?"

He holds his hands in the air. "Hold up there, love. Don't get your panties in a ruffle. I'm on your side, always. But if I'm going to pick a lover, *let's say*, it won't be you. But that's not what you were referring to, was it?"

I shake my head. "No. Someone told Max about Shane."

Graham sits up tall, eyes wide open, with his hand on his chest.

"You think I did?" He opens his mouth and then snaps it shut, acting like I insulted him. "You need to be asking your other BFF."

"I don't think it was her. She's still upset that Max withheld where I was for a year. She has the one-up knowing something Max doesn't. So, if it wasn't you or Addie, who?"

Graham's lips twist as he thinks, his gaze set on the ceiling. "The only people aware of the Shane situation is Jude, me and your security team. We needed to make sure they were aware to never let him near you again."

I slap my forehead with my palm. That man is relentless. "I bet one of the guys is moonlighting for Max."

Graham slams his hand on the table, making me jump. "What? They signed a non-disclosure agreement when working for me. This is unacceptable." He doesn't know the extremes Max will go to get his way, which includes killing people.

A few people glance our direction. "Shh." I put my finger to my lips. "Don't worry about it too much. You can't stop Max. If he wants to watch over me, he'll find a way."

He's done it for the last year. He won't stop now.

Graham plops back down in his seat. "The power that man has, slightly concerns me. At least he's on our side."

I smile at his resignation, not sure why I'm okay with this. It should make me furious that Max needs to have control in my world. What will happen when I start dating? Am I going to get a text asking how my date went? A small part of me likes how protective Max is. It means he thinks of me often. And that right there is why it's best we stay thousands of miles apart.

"Then let's move on to something I can control. Like your music career."

Jude was very receptive after Graham met with him. They're pairing me with a woman songwriter. After the disappointment that their train of thought was to assign me to a female, Graham assured me Tristan Weiss was a good fit for me and my music.

"She was at the meeting and is crazy excited to work with you."

"What'll happen to Shane?"

Graham dusts off some lint on his brown blazer with his long fingers. "Let's just say the only songs he'll be selling won't be worth the pennies he's selling them for."

I close my eyes as a flush of guilt smacks me in the face. Max's words come back to me and I focus on them. I stood up for myself. Shane doesn't deserve my sympathy. He made a choice and I shouldn't take responsibility for the consequences that came from that choice.

"Sky," Graham clips.

I hold up a finger and blow out the guilt. "I know. This is not my fault. It still doesn't negate the feelings I'm having."

"You weren't the first. But because of you, hopefully you'll be the last. That should make you feel better."

I manage a small smile. It does.

"Beverly Hills is calling our name. Let's go drown out all these feelings with a day of retail therapy." He beams, picking up our cups and throwing them away. I take one more deep inhale of the coffee aroma, debating if I should get another drink before leaving. There's nothing therapeutic about Graham's retail therapy. I'll be sweaty from trying clothes on by the first stop. I roll my shoulders and put my hair up in a messy bun.

Let's do this.

CHAPTER TWELVE

SYDNEY

"**P**inch me!" I yell at Graham, dashing to him when he steps into my dressing room. "Is this happening?"

After the Shane ordeal, I was hesitant to work with Tristan. But she changed my life. The last four months have been a whirlwind of coffee, interviews, promotions, and more coffee. Her songs were extraordinary and my first single landed me in the top twenty countdown. Which led me to open for a major headliner and go on tour with them. It starts tonight. For the next two months, I'll be in twenty-nine cities. This is absolute craziness.

He wraps his arms around me. "It's really happening." He draws back and eyes my attire. I snicker, shaking my head. Typical Graham and his clothing rules. I whirl in place, showing off my white shorts and a black tank. Kicking up my foot to make sure he notices my boots makes him chuckle. He touches my hair, which hangs past my shoulders now. I swear I dropped ten pounds with the extensions cut off. "I guess I like it."

Narrowing my eyes, I huff. "I love it."

"I'm kidding." He grins. "I love it too. You look like a star."

"Sky, this came for you," Brett, our stage manager, says as he strolls into the room. He's carrying a bouquet of exquisite red roses. Placing them on my dressing room table, I smile wide, glancing at Graham.

"Don't look at me, sister. It's your other admirer. You know, the one that's brawny, brooding with eyes that can cast a spell on you, and a beautiful smile when you catch it."

Not likely. I hadn't spoken to Max since our phone call months ago. Addison talks about Max every few times we talk, giving me updates as if I asked for them. I'll never admit I like hearing them though. I tug the note from the plastic holder and open the small envelope, pulling out the card.

Roses are red
Violets are blue
You're goin' to kill it
With your voice, it's true.
~ Your Best Friend

I TILT MY HEAD, reading it again. "Who's it from?" Graham asks, stepping up to my side. He reads it over my shoulder and I shrug.

"I *assume* from Addie." I'm not sure who else they would be from, and she's always been lousy at poems. My eyes water from a happy heart. We visit at least twice a week on the phone and text all the time. I told her after the tour, I'm taking some time off to spend with her and the family.

"Stop. That." Graham points to my eyes and shakes his finger in front of my face.

I blink back the tears. "I'm sorry. Everything is just so perfect. And it's all thanks to you." Pushing up on my toes, I lay a fat kiss on his cheek.

"This is all you, sweet cheeks. I just pointed you in the right direction." He peers down at his watch. "And now, it's time for me to show you again. *It's time.*"

Butterflies flutter in my stomach. I squeal and dance in place; the excitement rushing through me. Preston Scout, the headliner, pops his head into the room. "Hey Sky. Good luck out there." His deep twangy voice reminds me of home.

My eyes twinkle over and I dreamily say, "*Thanks.*" He winks and leaves.

"You need to stop that too," Graham whispers into my ear. I slap him in the chest with the back of my hand, still staring at the spot Preston just left. I can't get over I'm *his* opening act. "Okay, dreamy eyes, it's time for you to shine." He guides me by the elbow out into the hallway.

"Oh, wait," I stop, lifting my finger. "Be right back." I rush into the dressing room and text Addie thanks for the flowers. She'll worry I didn't get them if I say nothing. I toss my phone back in the bag, take a deep inhale and exhale. This is it. My dream is about to come true.

———

"Here's to the first show going off like fucking fireworks," Jay, my guitarist, declares, holding up a shot glass filled to the brim. My band and Preston's band are all gathered in the green room, winding down.

"And to Sky for killing it on stage," Preston says. "I even heard some people chanting your name when I got on stage." I almost fall off the arm of the chair I'm sitting on.

"Shut up! They were not. But thank you." I lift my drink and all the guys follow suit. I'm the only woman in the room and it surprises me. I always had these images of major partying with drugs and orgies going on in every corner backstage. I chuckle to myself when I glance around the room at all the guys sprawled out in their chairs relaxing.

"Is it always this tame? After a show?"

"Is our little wild cat looking to party?" Phillip says. Preston's bass guitar player pours himself and me another shot.

I shake my head fast and down the shot, the taste barely a burn. "No. I'm about to fall over dead from coming off my adrenaline rush. I thought... backstage would be... crazier."

"It can be sometimes, but not most of the time. If we want to party, we'll go find one before taking off on the buses," Preston explains. Everyone continues to inform me what I should expect the rest of the tour. I soak it all in, feeling out of my league. One minute I'm fainting on stage and the next I'm on tour with one of the hottest country music singers.

I will kill whoever wakes me up from this dream.

"So, Sky... inquiring minds want to know, are you single?" Chaz, Preston's drummer, asks.

I awkwardly laugh when all eyes turn on me. I can't tell them my fiancé died last year and now I can't stop thinking about his best friend so I keep it simple. "Yes." Chaz opens his mouth, but I cut him off. "But, I don't date people I work with."

He flashes a wicked smile. "Who said anything about dating?" Preston smacks him upside the head. "What? You can't blame a guy for trying. Look at her. She's hot." He waves his hand in my direction and I can feel the blush of heat on my cheeks.

"She was trying to be nice and tell you she doesn't want your ugly ass," Preston jokes. They burst out laughing when Chaz flips him off.

I'M PICKING up my dressing room, packing everything when I see the flowers, reminding me about my text. I bet Addie texted me back. When I find my phone in my bag, there are a few text messages, but I scroll right to Addie's.

Addie: I wish I would have thought to send some, but those aren't from me. I can't wait to live vicariously through you. Love you!

Hmm. If they're not from Addie, who could they be from? They're not from Graham, so that eliminates everyone that I would label my best friend. *So weird.* I answer my question when I continue reading the other texts, sort of. I stare at the text from a number I don't recognize.

Unknown: You should say thank you for the roses. Xoxo

I lean against my vanity, debating what to do next. On one hand, I want to thank whoever gave me the roses, but the whole thing seems off. Who would demand a thank you through a text?

Shane comes to mind that he might want to screw with me? He is not going to kill my excitement tonight. I'll deal with this later.

Walking onto the bus, a mixture of leather and pizza greets me. The sleek modern living room has orange leather seats and shiny metal accents everywhere. The band rushes in and plops down on the seats, digging into the pizzas, like a pile of ants on a sugar mound.

A few months ago, most of these guys were strangers to me, but now, I consider them my brothers. Tug lets out a long belch and my face twists in disgust. Okay, maybe the bus life won't be the most exciting part of this life. Sleeping with seven guys in a small confined space, I'm dreading the smells.

Oh, god. *The smells.* I wave my hand around, struggling not to gag, pulling my shirt up over my nose. "Seriously, y'all?"

"Sorry," Jay, the drummer, blurts out. "Beer and pizza are the worst."

"Don't make me ban pizza," I quip through my shirt, getting up and heading to the back of the bus where there's a sitting area that converts into my bedroom at night. I grab a slice of pizza and glare at Jay as I pass him. He shrugs, a smile plastered on his face.

Shoving the curtain closed so the land of smelly men can't reach me, I pull in a deep breath of fresh air.

My drained body protests as I transform the sitting area into a bed, but rejoices when I lay down. Movement from the bus gliding over the road rocks me to sleep. I barely register the first trill of a text, but when it goes off again, I grab my phone to mute it so it doesn't wake anyone else. I peek at the time—three a.m.

"Rule eighty-nine on a tour bus, turn your phone on silent at night," Jay slurs from outside my room.

I peek out the curtain, and even though I'm staring at closed up bunks, I whisper, "Sorry." I crawl my way back up the bed and touch the face of my phone. It lights with a text from the same unknown number as earlier. Unease rolls through me as I read the text.

Unknown: You need a lesson in gratitude.

The phone slips from my hands onto the bed and I stare at it, becoming instantly awake. Silence, except the hum of the road under the tires surrounds me. I focus on the phone, expecting another text to come through, but it eventually fades to black. My mind races with thoughts of who it could be. Again, Shane comes to mind. I don't know what happened to him after they fired him and I don't care. I'm certain the narcissistic ass holds me responsible. Falling back into bed, I sigh loudly and my gaze darts to the curtain, waiting for someone to say something.

The next hour, I toss and turn, my mind not shutting off. I give in and take a Benadryl, having brought them just in case I had trouble sleeping on a bus. It doesn't take long for my body to become heavy, like it's sinking into quicksand. I don't fight the fatigue, rather welcome it.

CHAPTER THIRTEEN

SYDNEY

"I need a new phone," I mutter to Graham while having our mid-morning call. He's already at the next city, in a hotel room. I'm lying on my bed. The Benadryl hangover is strong.

"Why?"

He doesn't need to know about the texts. I already feel like a burden with the Shane situation. I'm nothing but drama these days.

I dramatically sigh into the phone, the lie rolling off my tongue. "My aunt decided now that I'm famous, I'm worthy of her time, I guess."

He grumbles. "She's not worth the gum I stepped in today. Which, by the way, took me an hour to get out of my Gucci loafers." I sip on my Red Bull. I might need two of these. He continues to tell me about how he got the gum out and how inconsiderate people are. Finally, he finishes, redirecting his attention to what started this conversation. "Okay, I'll have a new phone by the time you guys get to Phoenix."

"Thank you." We go over my calendar for the next week. In between concerts, he's set up more radio station interviews. I groan. "I hate when they talk about my personal life."

"I'll reiterate to them they are not to ask if you're single."

It won't stop them. That's what the people want to hear about. It's annoying that everyone is so invested in my dating life, then it's almost inevitable I'm asked out by the time I walk out of the studio. Not without trying to back out a couple times, I agreed to go on a date a few months ago. One of Tristin's friends, whom she said was perfect for me. *He was nice.* But it seems nice isn't my type anymore. That's all I used to date, the artsy guys, in college. My taste has changed, thanks to Max. I need someone to take control of the date, not ask me five times where I want to eat. After going home that night, I decided I don't have time to date.

WITH MY NEW phone in hand, I glance around the locker room, transformed into my dressing room. I imagine the gorgeous football players walking around in their towels after a game. I don't want to admit how many times Addie and I tried to sneak into the Cowboy's locker room when we were in high school. Pulling out my phone, I snap a picture and send it to Addie.

Me: I finally did it! Minus the hot naked guys, ha!

Addie: Oh! And I'm missing it.

As I'm typing out a response, another text comes through.

Hulk: If you're looking for hot sexy men... I can show you the way. Why new phone?

A blush spreads over my cheeks, tingling sensations strike my core. How does he do that? We haven't talked in four months and any other guy would say that and I'd laugh them off. I wish I could turn off the visceral reaction my body has whenever Max speaks.

Addie: Sorry! Aiden is sleeping on the couch tonight since he can't keep his eyes off my texts. We're at Max's. Lulu wanted to ride the horses this weekend.

Me: LOL. It's okay. Tell Lulu I said hi.

I hop up on the director's chair, staring at my reflection in the mirror. A response to Max comes to mind. The thought sends a mischievous grin to my lips. What's the harm in a little flirting? I light up my phone again, opening Max's text.

Me: Certain family members decided I was worthy, and I said hot NAKED guys.

Graham slaps his hands together from behind me, the sound echoing in the silent room, making me jump. I glance up from my phone and spot him and Zoe, my makeup artist, in the mirror. "Well, isn't this lovely?" He walks up next to me and does a quick scan around the room. "Large and comes with its own gorgeous sweaty man aroma." I pull in a deep whiff and shake my head, not smelling anything. Thank god for small miracles.

"Sky, ready to get this party started?" Zoe says, laying out all her brushes.

I snap my fingers, swaying from side to side as I belt out the song *"Get the Party Started"* by Pink until Graham covers my mouth with his hand. "Save your voice for the stage."

I scowl at him, pushing his hand away and sing the intro to *"Shut Up"* by The Black Eyed Peas.

Zoe laughs under her breath. "Don't encourage her," Graham sighs. I could do this all night. My phone dings in my lap, halting the song next in my mental playlist to piss off Graham.

I gasp at the image.

"Well, hello," Zoe purrs over my shoulder.

Graham looks down. "Oh my. I just had a heart palpitation."

I slowly nod, licking my lips as I stare at the picture of Max in nothing but a white towel hanging dangerously low on his hips. My eyes roam over his hard muscular body to his fingers holding up the towel. The slight upward curve of his mouth, flashing a sexy smirk, sends butterflies fluttering in my lower belly. Places tingle to life that haven't in months.

"Dayuum," Graham mumbles in my ear, holding his hand to his chest. My thoughts exactly.

"You know him? That's not just a picture of some model?"

Graham snickers. "She knows him. *Very well.* You're a stupid, stupid girl."

I slap him on the chest, finally able to pry my eyes away. "Be quiet."

Despite my head reminding me why it's a bad idea, my body is revolting, remembering how that body heats me up, those fingers had me on fire and that mouth destroyed me. Two and a half years, you'd think I would've forgotten, but the buzzing going on down south, it feels like last week.

I cross my legs, trying to ease the ache building and fan my face. My phone buzzes again and I glance down to see it's another text from Max. I hold the phone to my chest and both Graham and Zoe whine.

"Y'all, what if he's..." My words trail off.

He's sending these texts to me, not knowing I have an audience. And I don't want them to see him naked. I'm not gonna lie though, I kind of do. It's been too long since I've been with a man. It's not like I don't fantasize about Max already. This will be a refresher.

"Exactly," they both say together, loudly.

I shake my head at both of them, sliding off the chair leaving the grumbling behind me. When the coast is clear, I open the text.

Hulk: One second from being naked. Ask me again.

I swallow back the desire burning inside my throat. My fingers hover over the keyboard itching to type *yes, please.* I peek at his picture again. Nope, this is enough for my sexual desire to blow up. Seeing him naked, on display for me, will only bring regrets.

Me: So, you're assuming I think you're hot?

Hulk: lol. Touche

Hulk: Thanks for killing my ego.

Me: As if that was possible...

Knowing no one will see naked Max, I return to my chair. The horny duo is at my side instantly. "Sorry guys. No dick pics."

After makeup, Graham walks out with me to the meet and

greet. Preston joins us right before we step outside. Cheers erupt, hundreds of fans scream our names. Goosebumps pebbled my skin. This never gets old. I wave my hands as we make our way to the table set up for us. A young girl, standing on the metal railing, has my face planted on her shirt and when we make eye contact, her emotions get the best of her and her eyes water. She reminds me of myself at that age when I went to my first concert, N'SYNC. I glide over and give her a hug.

"O-o-o-oh my god," she cries. "I love you, Sky."

"What's your name?"

"Isabelle," she says, her voice reaching a high octave. It's a good thing because it's hard to hear over all the screams.

"It's nice to meet you, Isabelle. Wanna take a picture?"

She almost drops her phone, handing it to her dad. He shakes his head, smiling at his daughter. He doesn't get it, but that's okay. He's a great dad for bringing her. We take a quick photo before I'm whisked away to do the same thing for two hours. It's still hard for me to believe I have fans. People pay to come see me. I always make it a point to be there for them, one hundred percent. Even when they tell me about their dogs humping to one of my songs.

"If they have babies, let me know." I smile, autographing a picture of her dog.

"You have an hour," the concert manager yells down the corridor as Preston and I head back to our dressing rooms. As much as I love the meet and greets, it's draining. You're in the spotlight, and your switch is on the entire time. I always take this time to turn off, decompress. Writing songs, or writing in my journal helps me get back in balance. I open my notes app on my phone to see where I left off on the song I've been working on.

"That looks tragic." I look up from my phone, following Graham's gaze. I freeze when I notice the dozen black roses on top of my makeup station. "Who gave you the death roses?"

"They are not," I snap, hoping someone just thought the color was cool. Graham strides over to them, plucking the card off the long stem plastic holder. His eyes widen and they lift to meet mine.

He waves the card in the air. "What in the hell is this?"

"What's it say?" I wince, walking over to him, afraid my suspicions are correct. He holds it out for me to read.

Roses are black
Violets are blue
Who's an ungrateful bitch?
It might just be you.
~Your enemy

I LET OUT AN AWKWARD LAUGH, pinching the card out of his fingers. "Someone's just playing a stupid prank on me." Panic flickers in my chest, rattling me at the core, obliterating the confidence I had this person was no longer an issue. I turn away, but he blocks me with his arm.

His gaze hardens as he towers over me. "Sky, I'll ask you one more time. Who sent those?"

I swallow the panic clawing its way up my throat. "I don't know." He narrows his eyes. "It's the truth. Remember the flowers I got at my first concert? From my *best friend*?" His head bobs up and down. "Well... after the show, I received texts from the person who sent them. They were expecting a thank you. It was weird, so I just ignored it. Then while on the bus, I got another one. It said maybe you need to learn a lesson in gratitude."

"Is that why you wanted a new phone?" I drop my head in shame. So much for handling it myself. "Sky, I need to know this stuff. Especially when someone is threatening you."

My eyes jerk up to his. "That's a little extreme, G." There hasn't been an actual threat. Right? Whoever it is, they're just trying to scare me. "They're probably all talk. I mean, don't all musicians have to deal with crazy fans?" I throw my hands in the air.

"In this business, you can never be too sure." I sense his disappointment as he calls a guy from my security team to come in. Whoever this asshole is, they are not ruining my night. Or my career.

"Don't say anything to Jude," I beg, squeezing his arm while we wait for security to come in.

"Sky—"

"G, please. Just tell my security guys to check things delivered to me. Jude will regret bringing me on, if he doesn't already. I don't want some flowers to ruin my career." He eyes me, twisting his lips. "I'm low man on the totem pole and you're right there with me."

"Don't do that," he sneers, pointing his skinny finger at me. "Your safety is more important to me than any career and I'm a little offended that you would think otherwise."

"I'm sorry," I mumble, walking back and forth in front of him. Why is this happening to me? I'm a good person. I treat people like I want to be treated so why does karma have a bullseye with my face on it? And why does it seem to want to destroy my music career?

After Graham informs my security team, they form a plan to not have deliveries sent to my room anymore. Security will intercept the delivery before I ever receive it. The rest of the conversation, I ignore, sticking earbuds in my ears, plopping on the couch, and clearing my head as the music drowns any fears that might cause me to have a horrible concert. I've got plenty of time to think about this *after* the concert.

CHAPTER FOURTEEN

MAX

S lamming the phone down, I wonder if I'll ever get over this feeling of needing to rescue her. For such a small person, the grip she has on me is iron-clad. She has a security team, one employed by me and Knox just checked in with news I didn't expect.

Sydney has a stalker.

I remind myself, she's not my job.

She's not anything. She made that perfectly clear.

The lie sours in my mouth. Why can't I hate her? I've never wanted a woman who has told me no, yet this time, it's only made the want that much more intense. By keeping tabs on her, I'm doing this to myself. Self-deprecation at its finest.

"Hey Max," I hear, followed by a knock on the door. Kase, the new guy on my team, leans in the doorway to my office. I motion for him to enter. An interruption is exactly what I need.

"Have a seat." He sits down and wipes his hands down his pants. Fuck, he looks uncomfortable. I hope he doesn't plan on quitting already. I like him. His resume is like Bill Gates in the security world. A SEAL Sniper. When I found out he was getting out of the military, I offered him a position before another team got to him. Good thing for me, he wanted to work with me as well.

He tells me about him and Ell, the girl he's dating and how he used some of my resources to find out information on her. Come to find out her real name isn't Ellie. Listening to his story how they were highschool sweethearts about to get married until she was in a car accident and lost all her memories makes me feel sorry for the guy. At least Sydney remembers me.

"Why did she change her name?"

He shakes his head and sighs. "I'm not sure. I haven't seen her in ten years. She doesn't have her old memories. It's possible she wanted a clean slate."

What is with women running from their past, changing their fucking names? "Sounds like someone else," I grumble, running my hands through my hair, frustrated that I'm back to thinking of Sydney.

I pointedly stare at him when he asks, "Does this have to do with the woman in California?"

He doesn't shrink back, rather he stays in a relaxed posture. I sit up taller and square my shoulders, proud and irritated at the same time. "She's not up for discussion."

He nods slowly and I blow out my irritation when he doesn't continue his questions. I get enough of that shit from Stone. Although, my relief doesn't last long. After telling him I'm okay with him dating someone as long as he does his job, he shoots back with, "Well, if that isn't the pot calling the kettle."

Damn, this boy has a death wish. All I can do is chuckle at his audacity. I think I need to remind him who his fucking boss is. If I want him to scream *my name* when he has sex, he better make sure the whole fucking neighborhood hears.

"Max, I shoot straight, and you respect that. That's why you hired me. I have an idea why you went to California. One look at you when someone mentions her name, it's obvious how you feel about her."

I tent my fingers, deciding the best way for him to die. I despise that he can read me like that. Even more so that Sydney makes me act this way. Kase is right, I respect that he tells me how it is, but when it's at my expense, it fucking stings.

Maybe I can rig his parachute.

"I didn't hire you for your humbleness." I laugh, standing and grab the car keys out of my desk. "Feel like jumping out of a plane?"

He stands at attention. "Fuck yeah."

As soon as the car engine roars to life, and he slides into the passenger seat, he glances over, smiling wide. "I don't know who packs your parachutes, but I'll be repacking my own."

I nod and laugh out loud, backing out of the drive, expecting nothing less from him. *Trust no one.*

"WHEN ARE YOU LEAVING?" Stone asks, sarcastically.

"When am I firing you?" I drop my pencil and cock my brow.

The guys chuckle around the table and I turn my glare toward them. We're in our weekly team meeting and I just got done telling them Knox's report on Sydney. Stone's question hits home because I've picked up the phone at least ten times to call my pilot to get the plane ready. It's the knot in my stomach — that Sydney put there when she walked out of the hotel — that tightens, reminding me why I can't. "Sydney has a security team, we're not it. *I'm staying.* But, since I probably have a *slightly* better computer hacker than they do, Stone, I need you to dig into Sydney's phone records and find where the calls are coming from. Also, the security footage of who is delivering the flowers."

"Slightly?" He snorts, his ego taking a hit, right where I intended. "Maybe I'll take my *slightly* better skills to someone who appreciates them." He's only saying it cause he's butt-hurt. He knows how much he means to this team and me. He's irre-placeable.

"I could give you a recommendation," Hudson jests.

Everyone laughs again, except Stone. "Fuck all of you. You guys wouldn't know what to do without me." He crosses his arms, scowling.

"He's right, guys. I definitely wouldn't have someone to test my new paint gun on," Kase says, adding fuel to the fire. Stone's face turns red and I'm fairly certain he's about to pop. Sure enough, Stone shoots up out of his chair, pointing at Kase.

"You fucking cheat. You're a damn sniper. No one has a chance to shoot you when you get all high in your hidey spot on roofs."

I chuckle. "I did." Our team building day was a game of paint-ball. I was proud of myself that I took out Kase. Stone glares at me. "Okay, guys, let's get back to business." Stone remains standing, still pissed. "Stone, sit. You know you're a crucial part of the team."

He swings his pointer finger around the table. "Crucial," he says, slowly sitting. Thankfully, the guys let him have his say without egging him on anymore. "Get me her phone numbers and I'll start looking into it."

And just like that, we're back on track.

I love my fucking team.

CHAPTER FIFTEEN

SYDNEY

K   *ill them with your voice.* ~*G*
        I pluck the sticky note from Graham off the box of chocolates. Smiling, I open it and gaze at the wonderful pieces of chocolate heaven, the scent alone takes me to a happy place. He knows me so well. But damn him for knowing I can't eat one until I'm done singing. I press the lid back on and give myself a once over in the mirror before leaving the dressing room.

The energy of the crowd is electric, one of the largest I'll have sung in front of. People talk to me as I stroll toward the stage, but I'm in my head, searching for the one thing that will calm my nerves. This doesn't get any easier. New crowd, new critics, new fans. Each concert is its own being. Has its own heart. It's up to me to pump it to life and bring it to its feet. I'm the opening act.

And I'm ready to shock this heart into overdrive.

"Chicago, how y'all doing tonight?"

The cheers reverberate all around me, driving the rush to keep going. The songs create an orchestrated atmosphere, the ups and downs of the melodies create a whirlwind of exhilaration.

Words come out of my mouth, however it's the crowd singing back to me I hear. My heart races, my voice chokes from the intense awe. *They know my words.* Holding my hands over my heart, a couple tears escape down my cheek before I can regain my voice to keep singing.

THE HALLS FILL with congratulatory words as I walk back to the dressing room. Sweat beads on my forehead and I blot it with the towel handed to me as I exit the stage and gulp down a bottle of water. Another successful night. The dressing room is lit bright yet quiet when I shut the door behind me. When I sit on the director's chair in front of my mirror, it creaks as I get comfortable.

"You did good, Sydney," I whisper to my reflection.

A few cleansing breaths help calm my hyperactive nerves. My reality is this moment. Tomorrow, I'll feel like an imposter. It tends to happen when I read the one reviewer who didn't like me. Everyone tells me to ignore it, that it's part of the business when you're in the public eye. But it's easier said than done.

Which is why I'm having a pep talk. If I've learned anything this last year, it's that I can survive whatever is thrown at me and I'm stronger than I think.

"You did so well, you deserve a chocolate," I continue talking to myself. I wiggle the top of the box off again and study the chocolate. "Hmm. I bet you're caramel." Picking up one that has golden piping across the chocolate shell, my mouth waters anticipating the taste. Sure enough, the hard chocolate crunches as gooey caramel explodes in my mouth. I lean back as my eyes roll back in my head. "Okay, you deserve two."

A knock at the door interrupts my chocolate induced orgasm. I grumble, walking to the door, opening it with an exaggerated swing and an icy stare.

"Sorry." Stella, my assistant, winces. "I know you like to have a chill moment, but Graham wanted me to advise you that the bus is leaving right after the show."

"Right. I forgot we need to be in Ohio tomorrow night. Thanks for reminding me." She flashes a quick smile before she walks away. Well, so much for quiet time. As soon as Preston finishes his set, chaos ensues to get us out of here as soon as possible. These back-to-back city concerts are exhausting.

An hour later, I'm packed and hanging around backstage, watching Preston finish his set.

"He's amazing on stage," Stella says behind me. I nod, my eyes never leaving him. The little girl he pulled up on stage to help him sing his last song, has a smile plastered on her little round face as he lowers her back down. The cheers are deafening. For the next half hour, we watch the rest of the show. Preston calls me out on stage and I run out for my last appearance. He wraps his sweaty arm around me and we take a bow before the lights flicker off.

"HERE'S to another fucking epic night," Chaz says, handing me a shot glass. He grabs the tequila tucked under his arm and tips it over to pour the golden liquid into my glass. This seems to be our ceremonial after concert tribute.

I cover the top of it with my hand and shake my head. "No thanks, Chaz. I'm not feeling too well." A tight stomach cramp has been happening off and on since we exited the stage. The last thing I need is alcohol to make it worse. Chaz glances at me with a worried look.

"You all right, Sky? You're looking kind of pale."

I slap him on the arm. "Stop making fun of my white skin," I tease, but then wince when the cramp intensifies. Digging my hand into my side, hoping it helps stop the pain, Chaz grabs my elbow.

"I'm not kidding Sky. Maybe you should sit down."

"I'm f—"

As the cramp becomes almost unbearable, my stomach convulses, and I put my hand over my mouth to stop what I know is coming. It happens so fast. I barely register the curse words coming out of Chaz's mouth as I continue to empty my stomach all over the floor. A large trash can is placed in front of me, my throat burns as I can't stop. Sweat runs down my back and tears cover my face.

I spit a couple times before attempting to stand up. Although as soon as I stand upright, my stomach gets angry and convulses again, sending me right back over the trashcan.

Someone pulls my hair back and wraps it in a tie. They blow cool air on my neck and I close my eyes relishing in the slight relief. I rise on shaky legs.

"Here, hun." Graham hands me a Kleenex. I wipe the tears and blow my nose.

Sniffing, I rasp, "Thanks."

"Wow. You look like hell."

I glare at him even though it's the truth.

"Come on, let's move you to a chair." He dips his head under my arm and brings me to a chair in the hallway. Security has closed off the end, but I notice a few people on the other side of them, glancing my way. Not two minutes go by and I'm already throwing my head into the trashcan. Graham stays by me the whole time. "What did you eat tonight?"

My arms drape around the trashcan like it's my best friend and my head rests on it. I don't want to move. It takes effort for me to think about what I've eaten. "I had some veggies from the green room and then I had a couple pieces of the chocolate you left for me."

"What chocolate did I leave for you?"

The mention of food is the last thing I should talk about because my stomach twists again. But I turn my head to peek at him moving no other part of my body. "The chocolate in my room. With the sticky note?"

His eyes widen. Panic floods his eyes.

Oh, shit.

"Someone call 911, NOW!" he screams down the hall.

CHAPTER SIXTEEN

MAX

"Hey boss." Stone's sleep filled voice fills the line. I fist my shaking hand. It's midnight and I could give two fucks that I just woke him up.

"Wheels up in two hours," I quip, anger strangling me as I attempt to keep my cool. "Round the guys up too."

"Yes, sir."

It's time to go to work.

And save the woman who continues to stomp on my heart.

Again.

What the fuck is wrong with me?

CHAPTER SEVENTEEN

SYDNEY

The hospital bed squeaks as I roll to my side, the muscles in my stomach ache. I moan, bringing my legs up to my chest. When I manage to open my eyes, steel-blue eyes meet mine. And they're burning through me with anger.

"Max," I whisper. He takes a deep inhale and lets it out through his nostrils, leaning forward, he rests his elbows on his knees. "I guess I shouldn't be surprised to see you." The rasp in my voice from the stomach acid and the tube to pump my stomach burns. The early day sun brightens the room, lighting up his stern expression. I'm thankful I'm alive to see the sun. There were moments I questioned my mortality during the night. Some moments I begged for it. The sound of my heart drums in my ears as Max stares at me, the sudden feeling of weakness and vulnerability overwhelm me.

He finally breaks his silence, raking his hands through his hair, leaving it in disarray. "Fuck. I don't even know what to say, Tink. How are you feeling?" His forehead creases with worry.

"Like I gave birth to an alien. Through my mouth."

He nods once with a slight tic to the mouth. "The police found the chocolate you had packed in your bag. They're running it now."

I wince as I sit up. Despite any apprehension I have of him being here, I'm safe with him around. The reality that someone poisoned me is terrifying. "Max, I had no idea it wasn't from Graham. It was *his* handwriting. He leaves me little notes all the time. There wasn't any reason for me to question where it came from," I say in my defense. This morning, I've done nothing except go over the entire night wondering if I missed something out of the ordinary. I didn't.

"Why'd you get a new phone?"

I swallow the lump in my throat. He's not going to believe the lie about my family contacting me anymore. "Someone sent me some flowers. They became aggressive wanting a thanks through texts. I thought it was just a crazy fan that would go away," I explain, dropping my hands on the bed.

"But they didn't, did they?"

I release a harsh sigh at his persistence. "No. Then they sent me black flowers with a not very nice message."

"So, don't you think it would have been a good idea not to go eating random things sent to you." The aggravation in his voice pisses me off.

"I'm sorry I made a mistake," I snap, straightening my back and squaring my shoulders. "I don't find the bad in everything, Max. I don't go around questioning life, living in fear. It's not like I don't have a security team. I never thought someone could get to me."

The chair scrapes across the shiny floor as he pops up and paces the room. The internal conversation he's having with himself is clear by the shaking of his head and the clenching of his fists, the muted growls. He wants to tell me *I should*. But that's not me.

Finally, he talks himself down and leans against the wall, arms crossed. "I'm sorry." His gaze drops to the floor, shifting his feet.

"Someone *shouldn't* have been able to get to you." Leave it to Max to take responsibility.

The brown wooden door swings open and Graham walks in with a couple uniformed officers. Max pushes off the wall and shakes hands with them.

"Oh, sweet cheeks, am I happy to see you not throwing up." He glides over and wraps me in his arms. "Even though you still look like shit."

"Hey, at least I'm alive," I tease, then wince when I regret the words. It's not a laughing matter. I shoot a glance at Max and by his scowl, he agrees.

Graham pushes back, his hands grip my shoulders, and he glares at me. "That. Is. Not. Funny."

Okay, so I won't win an Academy for Comedian of the Year.

"I'm disgusted that whoever did this used my note to trick you."

Snapping my finger, I point at him. "That was a note from you then." I jerk my head at Max, lifting a brow, but direct my attention back to Graham so he can't rebuke my smug expression.

"It was. I left it for you during the last show. Was that the first time you saw it?"

I nod, fear prickling my body, a frightening realization washing over me. Whoever did this is close to me.

"Ms. Owen, do you mind if we ask you some questions?" The officer steps to the end of my bed and pulls a notepad out of his front pocket.

It's official.

I have a stalker.

They tried to kill me last night.

"RICIN?" I jolt upright in my bed. I've been waiting all day to hear something. "Isn't that what people send in the mail and is crazy dangerous to touch?" Max nods with a death grip on the rail to the side of me, his knuckles white. "How does someone even get a hold of something like that?"

"There are ways," Max replies dryly.

"I'm just glad they pumped your stomach. Hopefully, they got it out of your system without damaging things internally." Graham stands on the other side of my bed, holding my hand.

"Yeah. Me too." Although, the moment of having my stomach pumped, I had wished for death from the poison. That is one experience I never want to have again. Graham breaks the bad news that I'm stuck here for four days under observation.

"I'm so sorry. I let everyone on the tour down." Tears well up in my eyes, the emotions of everything building up inside me. Between Shane and now this, maybe the universe is telling me I'm not supposed to be a singer.

"Stop it. Right now. This isn't your fault." Graham squeezes my hand and the bed dips as he sits down beside me. "Jude is furious someone was able to access you. He's setting up more security."

"He wants me back?" I sniff, rubbing the tears off my cheek with my fingers. "What about Preston? He probably doesn't want to deal with all of this while he's on tour."

"The team met this afternoon. They want you there. They're afraid you'll not want to come back."

The decision to stay is mine? How is that even possible? I'm the opening act. I'm replaceable as quick as the polish on my nails. The thought of returning to the tour excites me, yet scares me at the same time.

"Nobody has stated the obvious, everyone is skirting around the fact that my stalker might very well be someone on staff."

"That's where I come in," Max states. My eyes dart between Max and Graham, wondering what plan they have concocted without me.

"The security Jude hired," he tilts his head toward Max. "Meet your new security detail."

I swallow, hesitating to look at Max, torn by conflicting

emotions. Graham smirks like he just stole a cookie behind his mom's back. It's one thing coming here to see if I'm all right, but being by my side for the unforeseeable future... it's not a good thing.

All day, I've yearned for Max's touch, but talked myself out of it, knowing he's headed back home as soon as I get out of the hospital. I don't want to set either of us up for disappointment again. But now, he's here full time. How do you tell the guy that wants to save you to save himself? His hero complex has always been stronger than his feelings.

"Can we have a sec," I whisper to Graham.

His lips twist with a raise of a brow, expressing that I need to lighten up. Of course, he's excited Max is here. He blows out a resigned breath, knowing he doesn't get a say in this, before he pushes off my bed and glides out, with one last pleading glance. I roll my eyes and shoo him out with my hand.

"You know he likes you, right?" I say, avoiding what I really want to say.

Max chuckles and shrugs a shoulder. "It's good to be liked."

The sheets crinkle as I adjust my sitting position, tugging them off my legs. My body's heat increases as Max pins his eyes on me. The decent sized hospital room closes in around us. It's like the universe is pushing us together. The question is, can I fight the pull if he's right next to me?

"Max," I sigh. "You know security teams all over the freaking world. Why are you taking this job? Especially with how I left New York.."

He clicks his jaw. "Because you almost died. I already had a guy on your current detail that works for me." The bite of his tone has my attention so I skip out on telling him I already figured that out. "It's just until we find out who did this," he adds quickly. Despite the sting of his last words, I nod. The faster we can get back to normal the better. Him on the east coast, me on the west.

"Everything will be all right, Tink."

I flash a hesitant smile knowing my heart and my life are on the line. The words to the song *Everything's Gonna Be Alright* by David Lee Murphy and Kenny Chesney escape my nervous lips. Max chuckles as I snap and sway in my bed.

"Seems your wings are straightening out." He flashes a sweet smile and I tilt my head, his previous words about my twisted wings coming back to me. I hadn't realized what he meant until this moment. *The music.* It's in my heart and soul, part of my inner being. But during that year, I tuned it all out. My voice created it, but my soul was deaf to the melody. Does he know it's all because of him I can hear again? Feel the rhythm of the music? "Get some rest. I'll be right outside the door if you need me."

My thoughts leave me reeling as I watch his large, muscular body stroll out the room.

Focus on the music.

Not on Max.

CHAPTER EIGHTEEN

SYDNEY

"Oh, hey," I say to the good-looking guy standing guard outside my hotel room door. I thought I heard room service, but this guy is not room service. He's wearing all black and his eyes are intense, but they never leave mine.

"Ms. Owen." He holds out his hand. "I'm Kase Nixon."

"Nice to meet you. You're one of Max's guys?" I tilt my head, studying him, knowing full well he works for Max. There has been a guy stuck to my side for the past week. Although, I'm surprised I don't recognize him. Max never mentioned a new team member.

"I am."

Great. He's about as talkative as Max.

"Well… nice to meet you." I back into my room and shut the door when it becomes clear he's not into small talk.

My nerves are getting the best of me. Being back into the mix of things, knowing there is someone out there that wants to hurt me is giving me spikes of panic. Tomorrow night is my first concert since being released from the hospital. I eye my cell phone on the coffee table. *He can make me feel safe.* Fear of walking through that door makes me pause. He wasn't supposed to come running to save me, dammit. This is his fault, he's opened the door again and now I can't stop thinking about him.

Oh, screw it.

"What's wrong?" he answers the phone.

Reality hits me, my cheeks heat from embarrassment. "I hate that your first concern is something's wrong when I call." He remains silent on the other end, I'm sure wondering why the hell I'm calling. "I just want to talk."

"Anything specific you want to talk about?" The deep timbre of his voice, vibrates inside of me.

I need to hear your voice.

"No."

"Tink, are you okay? Do you need me to come over?"

No, and *definitely no.* I don't have the energy right now to walk away.

"I'm okay. Wound up a bit. Being back is making me nervous."

"I can…"

"Just talk to me, Max," I reply, frustrated that he's not under-standing what I need. *Do I even know what I need?* "You've always been able to calm me down. I need your voice right now."

He chuckles. "My voice is here for you." I smile and settle on the couch, already feeling at ease. "I didn't know you hired someone new. Tell me about him."

He groans and the phone rubs against his rough jaw, like he's moving around. He mumbles something under his breath about talking to Addison. "Max? What are you doing?"

"Hold, please," he bites out. I pull the phone back and stare at it, surprised by his tone. A few moments later, he comes back. He exhales loudly and I wonder where the sudden irritation came from. The line stays silent for a few more beats. "His name's Kase, started working for me a few months ago. Anything else you were wondering about him?"

Snappy much?

I open my mouth to ask what his problem is but shut it when I overhear talking outside my door. My eyes narrow as I get up and walk to the door. Peering out the peephole, I see Hudson standing guard.

"Max Shaw, you did not just do that?"

"What are you talking about?" he answers with a trace of humor in his voice.

"Ugh. I don't *like the guy*, you jealous ass."

He laughs and unapologetically says, "I needed him to do a perimeter check."

"Liar."

Our chuckles die down, but the tension between us is felt through the phone. I close my eyes and place my hand over my heart, it thumps against it like Morse code. I know what it's saying, but can I mentally act on it?

Can we move past the demons of guilt keeping us apart? Sometimes, our demons are just truths trying to be set free. When I look at Max, I'd rather him be in my life than not. But is it too late? Have I pushed him away too many times? Since he's been here, he hasn't given me any sign that he's here because he still wants me. He's here to do a job that he was hired to do.

"Tink?" he says, pulling me from my thoughts.

"I'm here. What's your favorite ice cream," I blurt out. I smack my forehead, shaking it.

Can I be any more random?

"Hmm… vanilla, I guess."

I stifle my laugh with my hand.

"What's wrong with vanilla?"

"Nothing. You're just not the *vanilla* type."

"Sydney." His voice is a deep rumble mixed with heat as he calls me by my real name. "We're talking about ice cream."

Heat that pierces deep inside my lower belly, making me take a deep breath.

"What's yours?" There's struggle in his words, our conversation making him squirm too.

"Cherry Garcia."

The memory of having the ice cream for the first time pops into my head. I had broken up with a jerk boyfriend in high school. Addison thought it was a great reason to try a dozen different Ben N' Jerry's ice cream flavors. Addison's aunt came into the kitchen, the table covered with the pint-size ice cream containers. She joined in and we spent the whole night picking the asshole apart and eating ice cream. Cherry Garcia replaced him. The love of my life that never disappoints.

"You want one of the guys to bring you some?"

"That would be ah-mazing. But, I can't have dairy the night before a concert."

"*Hmm*. I'm learning so much about the life of a singer." The fear fades away the more we talk. "Oh, funny story you'll get a kick out of." I sit taller, surprised that Max is sharing. "The other day we had a paintball game at my house. I took out the last man standing."

His ego can't get any larger.

"Oh, of course," I laugh.

"Unfortunately, I didn't account for any of the women left. I figured they would've been out long before the end."

Women. A pang of jealousy welling up inside of me catches me off guard. "So, Addison shot you?" I say, trying to mask the emotion.

"Nope, she wasn't there."

My gaze darts around the room as I push off the couch and pace. Why is this affecting me so much? What did I expect? I'd tell Max no, and he'd stay single for the rest of his life? Is this why he doesn't seem interested? He's already dating someone?

"Oh," I muster, eyes closed.

"Oh?"

I clear my throat. "I'm surprised you're sharing your demise with me."

His laugh is heady and I'm fairly certain I heard it through the wall. "That's a bit overstated there, Tink. It was only a game."

I let out an awkward laugh, *hating* myself for being insecure. For no reason.

"It was Kase's girlfriend," he *finally adds*. "You'd like her."

Max wouldn't be telling me all this if he had a girl there. The one thing Max wouldn't do is hurt me even though he has every reason to. My mind stops wreaking havoc on my emotions and I blow out a calming breath.

"I like her already. I mean, any woman who can knock your ego down a couple notches is a friend in my book."

"I was just off my game."

"Really? That's a lame excuse. I have a hard time thinking anything could throw you off."

"There's definitely something," he mumbles, his voice trailing off.

The words get caught in my throat. I want to ask, but I can't. My heart wants to hear that it's me. That he still thinks of me. But my head is screaming at me not to open that door. *Again.*

CHAPTER NINETEEN

SYDNEY

"Stone!" I run into his arms, surprised to see him standing on the side of the stage instead of Max.

"Hey, short stuff." He wraps his arms around my sweaty body in a tight hug. "You rocked it on stage."

Out of Max's guys, Stone is my favorite. He's definitely the most personable out of the group. The rest are broody and intense and when they stare at me; I feel like I've done something wrong.

"Thanks. It's crazy, huh?" I turn back to the stage and watch as it's transformed for Preston. Stone throws his arm around my shoulder and watches with me.

"It's fucking cool. Someday when Max fires me, it'd be dope to run the boards for a show like this." I stare up his tall body, shaking my head. He smirks and shrugs cause he knows as well as I do, Max would never fire him. "I can have pipe dreams."

"Speaking of Max, where is he?" I glance over my shoulder, expecting him to be behind us.

"He's checking some things out."

My body stiffens as I wonder if I received another package. "Did something happen?"

"Sy…" He clears my real name from his throat and pulls me to a quiet corner and his eyes dart around. "*Sky*, calm down. Nothing happened. He's running checks, inspecting and scanning everything to make sure it's safe. *Not that I already did that*," he says sarcastically. "It seems he doesn't trust me these days."

His joking tone helps calm my frazzled nerves. "Nice catch," I quip about his slip with my name.

"Yeah, sorry 'bout that. That'll take a little time to get used to."

"Here you go, Sky." I turn around to Demi, the backstage concierge, handing me water. Stone grabs it before I can, inspects the clear liquid and the lid before twisting it open. The seal breaks, which is enough reassurance for me.

"Where did this come from?" he demands. Demi's green eyes widen at the abrupt question. I snatch the water out of his hands and roll my eyes. Stone's jaw tightens.

"Chill, Stone. It's fine." I turn toward Demi and smile. "Thanks, Demi."

"You're welcome. And just so you're aware, I got it from the barrel of water over there." She points to a rolling barrel and then pins her eyes on Stone, squaring her shoulders. "The same place I grab all the waters for everyone."

In a slothful move, I bring the bottle to my parched mouth and stare at Stone while I take a painstakingly slow drink, all while trying not to laugh. Everyone got the memo that *anything* delivered to me needs to go through security first, but this is a little extreme. It's water. I drink water all night and while I am more cautious about who hands me things; I trust Demi.

When she walks away, Stone leans into me and says, "Don't be naïve just because you like someone."

"I'm not," I huff. "Stone, I can't live in fear of everyone. I was driving myself insane this week. I'm around hundreds of people every day. I've worked too hard to become a strong, independent woman for someone to rip that away from me in the blink of an eye. He'd have to tamper with all the waters in that barrel if that was the way he wanted to get to me."

Stone releases a heavy breath, softening his intense gaze. "I know how hard you've worked." He crosses his arms, tilting his head. "But why do you assume it's a *male*?"

I contemplate it for a beat and can't really come up with a valid reason. "I just assumed, I guess. Aren't stalkers usually men?"

He bobs his head a couple times. "Statistically, yes. But there are some catty bitches out there, so you can't rule out the female population."

My body deflates with the new revelation. I never imagined it was a woman. The new fear wraps around my spine, just as Zoe walks up. "Hey Sky, let's get you touched up before you head back out." I stare at her, my mind reeling with our past encounters. *Did I ever piss you off? Have you ever seemed upset with me? Would you be able to kill someone?* She waves her hand in front of my empty stare. "Sky?" I shake the thoughts from my head.

"Sorry. Yes, I'm ready."

Dammit. Just when I had control back.

MY IMAGINATION HASN'T STOPPED the full throttle of females that could be out to get me as I stomp on the bus. I head straight to the back. The guys have already figured out I'm not in the mood. I don't even care they assume it's that time of the month.

Jerking to a stop at the door leading into my space, I stare at the large man sitting at the table, working on his computer. He glances up at me and smiles. No. He can't be this close to me—all night.

"Max," I murmur. "Why are you in my room? Or even on the bus?"

The bus shakes to life as the engine turns. I jerk around. No, don't go—*we have a stowaway.*

"What did you think would happen when you demanded you stay on the bus versus flying to your next concert?"

It wasn't this!

Blowing out a hard breath as I turn back, I toss my bag on the couch that wraps around the back of the bus in a U-shape. My butt hits the hard bottom frame from the impact of dropping onto the cheap cushion. I sigh in defeat.

"Sooo, this is cozy."

He nods, glancing around the room. "It's actually nice. It's the first time I've been on a tour bus," he says, ignoring my sarcasm.

"I'd give you a tour, but you had it walking all the way back here. To my room. Passing the multiple places you could have sat and done work."

He leans forward, his fingers laced on the tabletop. Silence hangs between us, and I fidget under his scrutinizing stare, shifting one leg over the other. Finally, he calmly says, "I needed privacy, and everyone was coming on the bus soon. But me being back here isn't what has you acting like a bitch. So, what's wrong?"

My gaze jerks to his as his words shoot spikes to my raw nerves. "If you really want to know, calling me a bitch isn't the way to get it." He shrugs but stays quiet. I don't expect a sorry to be crossing his lips — especially when it's true. I fold in half, covering my face with my hands. I'm the one that should be apologizing.

"I made a list. Of everyone that I come in contact with daily, except this list only has guys' names on it."

"You should—"

"Shh," I clip, holding a finger up. "Stone enlightened me. I worked all week to cross off every name on that list. It made me feel better about being around them again, like I was creating a false sense of security between us to manage my paranoia."

Max closes his laptop and shifts in his seat like he's about to get up, except he thinks better of it and stays where he's at. Disappointment drags its feet on my heart only to be kicked with confusion in my head. Leave it to Max to have my emotions dueling against each other. One minute I'm pissed he's in here only to be wishing he was sitting by me the next. "Tink, I want you to feel safe. That's why we're here."

I lie back against the cushion, mentally drained. Pulling my legs up under me, I nod. "I do. But I'm tired of looking at people, wondering if they hate me enough to kill me. And now, my list just doubled."

"I can go out there if you need some alone time."

A flash of loneliness makes my insides ache. I fix my attention on the drapes covering the window. Pushing aside the heavy black polyester, highway lights brighten the darkness every few seconds. This week, I debated if I could put myself back out in the public. But being on that stage made me realize it was exactly where I belonged. The drapes slip from my fingers, but I continue to stare at them, mindlessly.

"No. I'm glad you're here," I say without looking at him.

My whole body jerks at the sound of a phone. *Is it him? Or her?* I frantically search for my phone, but Max clears his throat and holds up his ringing phone. I squeeze my eyes shut in relief and embarrassment. I'm losing it.

"Hey Ma," Max says, his voice naturally deep but with a sweet undertone. It grabs my attention. He's never mentioned his mother. He chuckles. "He shouldn't have said anything." I glance at him and stare in awe. Is Max a mama's boy?

"I am."

I giggle to myself that he answered my unasked question, certain I didn't ask the same question his mom did.

"Ma, we're not talking about this right now."

He flashes me a mischievous grin. *What is that about?*

"Yes, I'll tell her." *Her?* Are they talking about me?

He laughs again. "Enough. Now, tell me why you're really calling me at midnight your time."

The sweet undertone does an about-face when his voice hardens. "What the fuck did he do now?"

His cheeks redden as he winces. "Sorry. What the *hell* did he do now?"

I roll my lips between my teeth to stop from laughing. Max just got put in his place by his mom. A taunt of a smile crosses his lips when his eyes flash to mine. He points at me, teasing.

"You're gonna get grounded," I whisper.

Max can't help but laugh out loud. "No. I'm listening. Sky's just being obnoxious."

I unfold my legs and kick him under the table.

"Yes, she's right here."

"Absolutely not. You don't *need* to talk to her."

I jump up and reach for the phone while nodding. Yes, let me talk to her. He smirks, grabbing my hand so I can't get to the phone. "Another time, Ma. Finish telling what he did."

Our eyes lock as our hands stay connected. His warmth awakens parts of me and I inhale sharply. We both pull back busying ourselves, him talking to his mom and I look through my bag for nothing in particular. Settling on my iPad, I pull it out and open the book I started yesterday. I sense Max's eyes on me, but I force myself to stare at the empty words. It might as well be a blank page because I'm not retaining any of it.

"I can't bail him out every time. He needs to learn."

He lets out a small groan. "Fine. I'll do it for you. But I can't promise anything."

"Love you too, Ma."

I flinch when he slams the phone down on the table. "Be glad you don't have any siblings," he grates out.

"You have a sibling?" I ask in utter surprise.

He leans back, lifting his hands behind his head and stares up at the ceiling. "A half-brother," he murmurs. The level of disappointment in his voice is probably a clue why I didn't know about him. Although, he's never mentioned his mom either.

"Tell me about your mom," I say. A lazy smile crawls up one

side of his face as he brings his attention back to me. It's sexy as hell.

"She's a fan of yours."

I sit up taller, placing the iPad on the table and cross my legs. "Really?" I prompt, smiling ecstatically. "Where does she live? You've never talked about her." Learning about his mom has piqued my interest, I have so many questions.

"She's in North Carolina." Figures he doesn't offer any other information until he senses I'm about to ask more questions. "She lives there with my step-father, Brad and Rex is their kid."

Hmm, Max and Rex.

As if reading my mind, he says, "My mom has a thing with the letter X."

Him rolling his eyes makes me chuckle. "It's cute."

"It's not," he responds flatly. "He's younger by five years and a total fuckup. Every time he gets into trouble, my mom calls and guilts me into helping him out. It's getting old."

I wrinkle my nose. "Sorry. I'm a pro at having fucked up family members."

"Let's not go down that road. I'm still pissed about your aunt." I sigh, dropping my head, hating that he witnessed my aunt straight-up lie that she didn't know me. But that's been my life of being discarded so easy. "Tink, look at me," he softly commands. I lift my head. "It's their loss, not yours. They don't deserve you."

If only it was my aunt that felt that way. *But it's my mom.* That's probably why hearing that Max's mom likes me gives me life.

"Look." He picks up his phone, searching for something and then hands it to me.

A small gasp escapes my lips as I stare at a picture of Max and his mom standing in front of a lake house. "Max, she's beautiful." The gorgeous petite blond, who's arm barely reaches around Max, is peering up to her son, the love she has for him evident by her bright smile. I can't stop staring. Especially the part where Max is smiling down at her too. It's the perfect picture. The feelings I have for Max jump to a new level and it startles me. I tear my gaze away and hand the phone back to him. "Was your dad tall? Because you tower over your mom."

He nods as he eyes the picture and then puts his phone down. "He was six foot."

I wonder if his dad had a hero complex too. Is that why they like petite women? The need to feel superior in the relationship because they can protect their woman. Seeing that picture, it's obvious he takes after his dad in type. His mom is my size. Petite.

"What's going through that head of yours?"

I wave my hand around. "Nothing." As if I'd tell him I was stereotyping him. "How long were your parents married?"

"They never married."

"Oh."

He shrugs. "I'm the result of a one-night stand. My dad was too busy building an empire to make time for a wife, so my mom never pursued a romantic relationship. And he never tried to change her mind."

I swallow, folding my hands in my lap and bite my tongue. *The apple doesn't fall far from the tree.*

Both our attention turns to the door where music floats in from the guys messing around. We both chuckle when we hear Tug butcher my song. That's why we don't have him sing. It surprises me when Max continues. "My mom met Dan when I was three, Rex came five years later."

"Have you and Rex ever been close?"

"Not really. He's always been the annoying little brother. He's an entitled punk ass who acts like life handed him a shitty hand because he's not me."

My eyes widen. "Why don't you tell me how you really feel," I joke. "Is he really that bad?"

I wanted a sibling so bad growing up; I prayed every night that my dad would accidentally get my mom pregnant again. We'd be so close because we would have each other. I was eleven when I found out my mom had her tubes tied right after she had me. Talk about a dream killer. Which is why it's hard for me to understand the distaste Max has for his brother.

Max lets out a sarcastic laugh. "Yes. When he was ten, he started stealing. A candy bar here, a bag of chips there. It started small. His ill-gotten gains increased in worth over time. He honed in on his craft and *became* great at stealing without being caught. Might be the only thing he's ever been good at." Max disappointedly shakes his head. "Then he put a team together."

I lean on the table, snap my gaping mouth shut. This is crazy. "Like a legit Ocean's Eleven team?"

"I guess," he mumbles, not impressed. "The first time he was caught, he was seventeen, and I was already in the FBI. My mom called freaking out because they wanted to try him as an adult. He had stolen around ten grand worth of electronics. I helped get him out of it. Paying off the homeowner. Instead of learning a lesson, that's when he formed his team and decided they needed to think smaller, things that were easier to steal, which led them to jewelry heists. I had heard nothing about his endeavors lately, so I was hoping he found something else to do with his time."

"Holy shit. Did he get caught again?"

He shakes his head. "Not sure. No one's been able to contact him for a couple weeks."

My heart hurts for his mom. She has two sons that are on different sides of the law, but both chose paths that risk their lives daily. "I bet your mom is going out of her mind."

Max runs his hand against his five o'clock shadow. "She is. But, you have to know my mom, she's always making drama about something."

I kick him under the table but quickly pull my legs back under me so he can't grab them. "Consider who her sons are. Can you blame her?"

"Shit, I'm the good son." He puffs his chest out, his massive shoulders squaring and he flashes a roguish grin. I've never seen his brother, but I can bet Max is the sexiest of the two. I bite my lip at his playfulness.

"And yet, she has probably lost more sleep worrying about you."

"Pshh. I can handle myself."

His cockiness irritates me. Damon had the same superhero mentality, thought nothing could hurt him. It's like he was daring the universe. The universe proved him wrong. Not liking the direction my head is going, I scoot over into the corner, prop up a couple pillows and stretch my feet across the back cushion. I don't think I could handle another heartbreak like that. I close my eyes over the wetness, the unfounded fear creeping up on me. *I'm not even with Max.*

"Hey." His voice is soft. I open my eyes when I hear him move. He scoots to the other corner, lays his hand across the back and asks, "Why are you upset?"

I blink back the tears, rubbing my temple. My body is tired. "Nothing. My emotions are all unhinged right now with every-thing going on. The smallest thing can trigger them."

He surveys me for a few minutes. "Tink, nothing will happen to you. I won't let it."

My brows furrow and I blow out a ragged breath. "Max, you can't promise that. If it was meant to be, it'll be."

His eyes darken and his chiseled jaw tics. "That's fucking bull-shit." His bite catches me off guard. His nostrils flare as he takes a few calming breaths.

I realize both our fears are of losing each other.

"Sorry," I whisper, regretting my words.

He reaches out, grabs my bare foot and gently starts massaging it. I start to pull it back until he digs his thumb into my arch. Ohhh! That feels amazing. My eyes roll back and I melt into the pillows as he continues his therapeutic assault on my foot. A small moan escapes and his hands freeze. Shit. Knowing where his mind just went and afraid he'll stop, I blurt out, "I didn't know foot masseur was part of your resume."

He chuckles, adjusting his shorts and position by bringing a knee up on the cushion. When his fingers move again, I refrain from throwing my hand in the air like I just won bingo. "I just want you to relax. Don't think about anything."

The only thing I'm thinking about is how fan-fucking-tastic your fingers feel — and not in a sexual way.

Music is no longer coming from the galley, leaving only the sound of tires pounding the road underneath us. With the sway of the bus and Max's strong fingers taking turns on both of my feet, my body feels heavy, pulling me under.

CHAPTER TWENTY

SYDNEY

"This is insane," I squeal, peering out the window at the sea of limos. Ours moves forward only to stop again. Paparazzi lines the street to capture the perfect shot that will skyrocket their career in the land of tabloids. Earlier, when I was here for rehearsal, this place was like a ghost town compared to the zoo it is now.

I sit back against the black leather and peer at Max. He winks at me. My smile grows as I admire him in his tux. He looks down-right sinful, the black jacket outlining his muscular build. The second he walked into the hotel room, my heart did cartwheels and tingles fluttered in my lower belly. After the foot massage night, Max tasked Stone with riding on the bus with me. It stung, realizing he didn't feel the same way about me. Since then, he's always been around, but he's kept to the background. Interactions kept to a minimum.

Nothing has happened since someone poisoned me. I tried to convince Graham that Max scared the person off just by being here, but neither of them is letting up on my security. Especially since no one around us has disappeared, they think the person is just lying low. So, here we are.

Max escorting me to the American Music Awards.

Last week, Graham told me a country artist had to drop out last minute due to a family emergency and they asked if I'd be willing to take her spot as a performer. We were off this weekend because Preston is attending. I screamed. *Really loud.* Max came running into my room, ready to kill. He was less than thrilled when I told him it was a happy scream. "I'm happy for you," he grumbled as he stomped out of the room.

Movement from the limo brings me back to the present. When it slows down, I roll the privacy window down so I can peek out the front. One, two, three... ten limos away from our destination. *The red carpet.* My nerves kick up a notch and I roll the window back up. "What if I fall while I'm walking down the carpet," I moan, leaning back again. I fan my face as the nerves continue to mess with me, my forehead starting to glow. Clicking my Roger Vivier clutch open, I pull out a compact and start blotting powder across my face.

Max chuckles and I glare at him over the mirror so he stops. "I'll be right there by your side."

"While I appreciate that, I'm still surprised you're escorting me. You're not an in the spotlight kinda guy." I wonder what Addie will say when she sees the pictures of Max by my side. I can already imagine the gossip that'll spread like butter on warm toast. Quick and easy.

"When duty calls, I'll do anything." His smile turns down. Here we go again. He's about to lecture me, for the umpteenth time, what I should do if anything looks, seems, or smells suspicious. *Go inside immediately.* He's crazy if he expects me to leave the Red Carpet early. This might be a once in a lifetime opportunity. They'll have to drag my dead body off. Of course, I didn't share that tidbit with him. Knowing Max, he'd throw me over his shoulder and walk me off himself if he knew I didn't plan on following his rules.

"Max, nothing will happen tonight. This is a very publicized event. You can't pick your nose without someone snapping a shot."

"Then don't pick your nose." I laugh at the serious tone in his voice. *Oh, I won't.*

After makeup touch-ups and a quick peek at my nose, I smack my red lips together and take a sharp inhale, letting it out slowly. I've been counting each stop and we're at seven now. We have to be close. Right as I'm about to ask the driver, Max sits forward and tells me we've got five minutes. My brows draw together. He taps his ear at my confusion. Ah, the hidden ear mic. Max, in his tux and gadgets, could be the next James Bond. *He'd be the hottest of them all, that's for sure.*

Max watches me fidget. I run my hand over my dress, trying to straighten the creases. "You look gorgeous, Tink." I halt my hand and glance up. Worry creeps up my spine that I won't be able to hide the feelings I have for Max. It's easy when I'm busy. But there are millions of cameras. Pictures that catch the perfect moment when I peek up at him adoringly are bound to happen. I close my eyes, searching for personal restraint.

He's your bodyguard. Nothing else. Nothing more.

I jump and my eyes fly open when his hand covers mine. His touch throws me off balance, my fingers tingle under his hand. Why is he choosing *now* to touch me? I'm in the middle of hunting for self-control and he *touches me*?

The car stops and the door opens. My heart beats against my chest, not because of the crowds' screams drifting into the car, but his gentle touch. We both stare at our connected hands for a beat before we're instructed to get out.

"We're here," I whisper, removing my hand. I sigh when he doesn't say anything. Not the time, Sydney.

Lights flash around us as we begin our trek down the red carpet. The smile plastered on my face is a true reflection on how I'm feeling on the inside. The excitement is hard to contain. My publicist, Aleena, flares out my dress and directs Max to stand next to me for the perfect shot. Then it's rinse and repeat every two minutes during the photo op.

I bite my lip to suppress my laugh when Max has enough of her and snaps, "I got this." She steps aside as he takes his position like he's done the last ten pictures. My reaction amuses him. He smiles at me with a slight shake of the head. He leans down, his lips a breath away from my ear and whispers, "You think this is funny, huh?"

The heat of his voice sends prickles of goosebumps up my arm. When I draw back, our eyes lock. His eyes soften as they trail down to my lips causing my heart to turn over in response. Our bodies so close, his tux jacket brushing against my breast as I take in a heavy breath.

"It's time to move," Aleena says, pulling me out of my daze.

"But..." I spin around, mindlessly following because my head has yet to catch up to what I'm supposed to be doing. "Wait, we didn't take pictures back there."

Her smile widens as she glances at Max and back to me. Leaning in close, she answers, "They definitely got a lot of pictures."

My eyebrows shoot up and I pin my glare on Max. The devilish smile plastered on his face makes it hard for me to maintain an even calm tone when I say, "You did that on purpose." Seeming very pleased with himself, he motions for me to move forward, ignoring my accusation.

Max and his hurt ego go to the wayside with all the commotion on the carpet. After the pictures portion, Aleena directs me to the Radio Booths. She already has a list of the ones I'm stopping at. Max continues to stay by my side as we get closer to the booths, stepping back whenever a DJ interviews me. Even through all the commotion, the couple times he's placed his hand on my lower back guiding me, the slight pressure feels heavy on my heart. I haven't wanted him to remove it, but he does. Like he catches himself doing it and takes it away like I stung him.

In between reporters, I'm waving at screaming fans when my shoe snags on something sending me into Max's arms. My whole body heats from embarrassment. Max lifts me to my feet without fuss, leaning down so his lips are a breath away from my ear. To the public, it might seem like we're having a moment rather than me being clumsy.

"You all right?" he whispers.

I run my hand up his lapel, gathering my wits but when I put pressure on my left foot, something's wrong. It lowers farther than my right. Oh no. No, no, no, this can't be happening. I squeeze his lapel and let out a nervous whimper. Max pulls back and looks down at me, concerned.

"My heel broke," I whine. "Max, what am I going to do? I can't walk the red carpet with a broken heel." I hold stock still, my hands grip his jacket out of desperation. Behind Max, fans scream my name, so I release a clenched fist and wave, managing a smile, but return my focus back on Max, hoping he has a fix. He can fix anything, right? He shrugs, shattering all my hopes. I drop my forehead against his shoulder.

Max's large hand tilts my chin until we're staring into each other's eyes. "I've never known you to care what people think. Don't start now."

"But it's—"

"What's wrong?" Aleena says, stepping up to us.

"My shoe broke," I grit out the words quietly as my irritation grows. "These stupid shoes cost more than my dress. How could they have broke?"

"I'll have you new ones within fifteen minutes." She hustles a few paces away from us, whipping out a phone.

"I can't stand here for fifteen minutes." My glare returns to Max and he hides a smile, pinching his lips together. "Oh. Now, who's laughing at who?" I swat him on the arm. "You're not helping."

"What... Max," I snap as I'm swooped up into his arms, and I have to throw my arm around his shoulder to sit higher. "What are you doing?" A few yells and whistles come from the crowd.

"Helping."

Smart ass.

"This isn't quite what I had in mind." He shrugs with a smirk. "I just figured you had some superglue or duct tape with you."

With a lift of a brow, he chuckles. "Sorry. The penguin suit doesn't go with my tool belt."

"Okay, shoes will be here momentarily," Aleena states walking up to us, still typing out a text. When she lifts her head, her eyes widen as she notices me in Max's arms. Her eyes dart around, not amused by Max's *helping.*

"Where to?" Max asks, not seeming to care about her or the million cameras snapping pictures of us.

Kill me now.

I pull in a deep breath, searching deep for that girl that didn't care what people thought of her. By the time I exhale, a resigned energy fills me and I let out an awkward laugh. Max exchanges a smile with me and I shake my head at the ridiculousness of right now. Addison and I will laugh our heads off in a week, but at the moment, it's tragic.

"Um…" she hesitates, torn by what to do. Tapping her phone against her palm, she glances at the next booth and then back to us. She's never dealt with Max. He's not putting me down so she might as well just go with the flow.

"Aleena, let's just move on. My shoes will probably be here by the time we're done with the next interview."

She nods with a vague hint of disapproval and spins on her toes, sauntering to the booth like she's about to be executed. I don't know what she's worried about. I'm the one in the spotlight, being carried around.

To make things even worse, we're doing TV interviews now, so the cameras catch Max setting me down. He tries to adjust my dress, but Aleena shoos him away. I place most of my weight on my right foot, trying to achieve looking graceful in front of the camera.

"Sky Owen, so glad you could talk to us," Gwen Stark from Entertainment News says into her mic. She stands next to me, at least six inches taller than me, so I have to look up at her. "What an entrance though." Her mouth twitches with amusement, glancing at Max.

"I mean, don't you have your own personal escort to carry you around everywhere?" We both laugh, but I have an overwhelming need to tell her why. "He's actually helping me since my heel broke." I lift my dress, flashing my left foot and the broken heel hanging on by the backside stitching. The red silk fabric slips from my fingers, covering the shoe disaster.

"Oh, no. Well, I like your solution." She wags her brows. "Let's talk about you. You've been touring with Preston Scout and your first single hit the top twenty on the Billboards. And now, you're performing tonight. You're already being crowned the up-and-coming star of the year."

My cheeks burn as I nod, listening to her run through my last few months. Every time someone reiterates my accomplishments, it makes me uncomfortable. I clasp my damp palms together to prevent fidgeting.

"It's been a surreal ride so far. I'm humbled by the support I've received from everyone. I still can't believe this is my life." My gaze sweeps across the red carpet. Cheers grow louder and I glance to see who's coming. An excited squeak from the back of my throat escapes my lips. "Seriously. There's Taylor Swift." I regain my senses and turn back with a slight shake of my head. *Graham is going to kill me.*

Gwen laughs at my fan-girl moment. "You're such a doll. You came out of the shadows, guns blazing. Let me tell you, I'm a huge fan. I can't wait to watch your growth in the industry."

"Thank you."

"One last thing. I have to ask because you're trending on

Twitter and our viewers are *very* interested." My brows pinch together. *I'm trending? Please don't ask me who the designer is for my shoes.* My mind reels with responses other than outing the designer. Nobody would ever want to dress me for a future event.

"Everyone wants to know... who's your date?"

My smile freezes on my face, while my head switches gears. I glance over my shoulder at the gorgeous man standing behind me. He gives me a subtle wink, having no idea what was just asked or that he's the center of the social media frenzy today.

When I turn back, I'm anchored with Gwen's inquisitive gaze. "He's a good friend." As soon as the words pass my lips, I know I'm opening a floodgate. My chest tightens thinking about all the women that will search Max out since I said the *friend* word. She waits a beat for me to continue, but when I don't, she lets it go.

"Well, there you have it," she says into the camera. She turns back to me. "It's been great talking to you, Sky. Thank you for stopping by." The camera stops filming us and points down the carpet. Gwen leans into me before I can turn away and mumbles, "I wish I had a friend that looked at me like that. You better hold on to that one."

"It's complicated. But thank you for not expecting more."

"Like I said, I'm a huge fan. I don't want to be blacklisted already. When you get back to LA, let's have lunch. Without cameras."

I believe her genuine smile and that she just wants to be friends. "Yes, I'm always up for drinks with the girls."

She claps once, excitedly. "It's a date."

Right after she gives me a quick hug, Aleena runs up, with shoes high in the air. "I have new shoes," she beams.

Thank god.

Gwen allows me to change my shoes by stepping in front of me, talking to Aleena. I've never been so appreciative of putting two feet on the ground and walking around. Aleena stuffs my broken shoes in her bag.

"Ready for the next one?" she asks, her voice much more enthusiastic than before. I nod, saying one more quick goodbye and thank you to Gwen. Max takes his place at my side and everything is back to normal.

Until Max hears he's breaking the internet.

CHAPTER TWENTY-ONE

MAX

"Is the show that boring?" I ask, returning to my seat from using the restroom. Her eyes zone in on her phone as she scrolls. She jumps when she realizes I'm back, sitting up straight and pressing the off button on the phone, dropping her hand in her lap.

When Sydney gets nervous, she releases an awkward laugh. "I was just reading an article."

"What about?"

"I'll tell you later. The show's about to come off commercial break."

I let it go for now. I'm not a wait and see type of guy, but if it was important, Stone would have contacted me already. The show is almost over, anyway.

Tonight has been torture.

Keeping my hands to myself has been harder than I expected. The red dress that fits like a glove to her small framed body, accentuating her large breasts and dipping in the back to right above her ass, has given me heart palpitations all fucking night long. Sydney is my weak spot, and it pisses me off that I can't calm my emotions when I'm with her.

Walking beside her the whole night, I felt more like an ogling teenager than a bodyguard. The number of times I smiled like a goon is ridiculous. But every time Sydney found my gaze, I couldn't help it. And watching her light up on stage, I'm damn proud of her. She's come a long way from the broken woman I found on the floor over a year and a half ago.

But now, as we get closer to the end of the night, my mind won't stop stripping off the red dress, leaving her naked body standing in front of me. Ready and willing. I swallow back the fantasy, wiping my hands down my black pants. Focusing on the two people on stage presenting awards, I concentrate on every word they say. I'm relieved when I notice it's the last award of the night - Artist of the Year. As soon as they announce the winner, everyone stands and claps. I follow suit, sticking a hand in my pocket and adjusting my semi-hard cock.

"Ready to go?" I ask, placing my hand on her lower back. *Fuck.* I pull it back, shoving my hands in my pockets again.

She turns, her eyes jumping from my pockets to my eyes. She nods, her purse gripped in her hands. Another thing I'm doing, reading into everything. Her body language tells me she wants me to keep my hand there. But her body language also told me she wanted me in that hotel room and she still walked out. I can't do that again.

"I have to change before going to the after-party though."

Shit. I forgot about the after-party. She bites the inside of her lip, worry etched on her face. "Everything okay?"

I nod. "Yes. I just... never mind. We'll go back to the hotel and change." She lets out a relieved breath. Me, not so much. At least she won't be wearing the red dress.

JESUS CHRIST! Why can't she wear something in another color, like puke green?

She smiles from the doorway of her room. I went to my room and changed, figuring I'd have plenty of time to get back here and wait for her. I was right. I've been out here for fifteen minutes. Her tight red dress has nothing on the tiny, short red skirt and the sexy white sleeveless top that has a deep v-cut and shows off her gorgeous boobs better than the other number.

Fucking torture. I'm tempted to call Stone to escort her. I'll tell her I don't feel good. It'd be an easy lie since the pain from my ball sac is so intense I might pass out. Eyeing her up and down, I shake the idea from my head. Stone's a man and I don't need to be wondering if he's hard as hell all night long, staring at her. I'll just buck up and endure the pain.

"Ready?" My voice breaks and I clear my throat. She pops up an eyebrow.

"Yes," she says, slowly. "Are you feeling okay, Max? You're a little pale."

"I'm fine." She stands taller, my tone coming out harsh. I squeeze the bridge of my nose and lie. "I just got an update that Rex is still missing."

She lays her hand on my arm. "I'm sorry. I would understand if you needed to go search for him." Her sing-song voice is pure silk. Yet, I like the rawness underneath more.

"No. Cory is still working on it. For now, I'm not leaving your side. You never know when another shoe blow out will happen."

She laughs. "Oh god, I hope not anytime soon. Can you believe of all the times for that to happen, it happened then?"

"You handled it well, Tink."

She wraps her arm through mine - I think she's trying to kill me - and we make our way back to the limo.

Sydney's been quiet for a while, which is not like her. I clear my throat and she looks up from her phone and a moment of panic flashes in her eyes. "Tell me what's going on."

"I'm so sorry, Max."

I sit taller in my seat, folding my arms across my chest, waiting for her to explain.

"Has Stone called you? Or anyone else?"

I stare at her in confusion. Stone and I spoke between changes, but nothing was reported. I set my phone up to receive calls only from certain people when I'm working and I took out the earpiece. She hesitates, chewing the inside of her cheek and she passes me her phone. Glancing down at the bright screen, a picture of me flashes. I scroll through the Twitter feed, reading comment after comment until I've seen enough.

Fuck me.

My head drops and I'm shaking it when Sydney says, "At least they gave you a good hashtag."

"You think hashtag *AMAs most wanted* is good?"

Her head does a quick bobble. "It could be worse."

I hand her phone back, thankful I don't have social media accounts. I make a mental note to do something cruel to Stone for not warning me. One of the world's best hackers can't claim he didn't know. He fucking knew. I wouldn't have put it past him to give me the name.

"Do you hate me?" Sydney's voice cracks.

"Why would I hate you? I knew I'd be in the public eye escorting you." The tension in her shoulders release and a relieved expression washes over her face. "Tink, it's okay. It's not like I wasn't already known."

She's barely able to keep the laughter out of her voice when she says, "Oh, I forgot who I was with—the infamous Max Shaw. Although, the basic person doesn't know who you are." She shakes her hand, holding the phone in the air. "Well, at least not yet."

I open my mouth to ask her if *she* really knows me. But snap it shut. Why should I care? The limo stops at a light and a car full of teenagers hang out the window, yelling and trying to figure out who we are. Sydney gets excited and scoots to the window.

"Don't—"

She rolls down the window

"Open the window," I say in defeat, too late.

I scoot next to her as she reaches out the window, shaking hands with the excited kids. A blonde spies me and points. "Is that AMA's most wanted? You're so hot, what's your name?"

Thank fucking god the light turns green. I pull Sydney in and roll up the window as the limo rolls forward. She lands on my lap, laughing so hard, she's blotting tears from her eyes. I drop her next to me and glare at her.

"What?" she says, fanning her face. "It's funny. Never thought you'd be on a most-wanted list, huh?"

As much as I hate the direction this instant fame is going, her laugh reminds me of the old Sydney who was carefree and loved life. Her barriers are crumbling, but she's still holding steady a few parts of it. I'm sure having a stalker isn't helping.

The vibe is different walking into the after-party. There are still a million people taking pictures outside the venue, but they're now yelling questions at *me* as well. They're like turkey vultures and I'm the roadkill dinner tonight.

Unlike Sydney, who is searching for other artists to talk to, I'm searching for exits and security. Once I've surveyed the entire place, I relax a little.

I jerk my head down when a squeal comes out of her mouth, wondering where she's hurt. She leans into me close and I catch a whiff of her perfume. I pull in a deep inhale, her smell triggering memories of her in my arms. Of the night we fucked. Ice-blue eyes pierce me through the darkness, her perfect body molding to mine. My soul devouring every piece of her.

"Max." Sydney's voice pulls me back. Where we're just friends. I sigh at the thought before looking at her. Her brows furrow. "Did you hear anything I just said?"

"Sorry." I shake my head, shifting my weight from one foot to the other. "I was just remembering something I have to take care of tomorrow. What's up?"

"I said that I really want to meet Savanah Morris." She tilts her head in the woman's direction. "Someone told me backstage that she was a fan of mine. I about died. Savanah, a fan of *mine*?"

"Stop selling yourself short." I wish she could see how amazing she is like everyone else does.

She rolls her eyes at me. "You're just saying that cause you're a friend." *I'm starting to hate that word.* "But let's go over because she's with Preston."

She wraps her arm in mine and leads me to the group of people standing to the side of the stage. Savanah glances our way as we approach, and her smile widens.

As soon as Preston sees us he gives Sydney a hug and shakes my hand. He introduces us to the six people, including Savanah. Although, we've already met.

"Max." Her eyes bounce from me to Sydney, with questions in them before she walks over and gives me a hug. "I'm surprised to see you here."

Sydney's posture straightens, and she takes a step closer to me. I stop myself from looking down at her wondering what the hell. "You two know each other?" The excitement in her voice thirty seconds ago falls flat. Preston's brows rise. His confusion is on par with mine. Don't get me wrong, I may be confused, but I'm happy as fuck she's getting territorial with me.

"We do," I reply, wondering how Savanah plans on explaining our acquaintance. "It's been a long time, Savanah."

"Too long," she says in a sing-song voice. "I see you've given up your rule about staying in the background."

Every rule I've ever enforced is tossed out the door for Sydney. I shrug as if it's not a big deal despite knowing the repercussions that could happen from placing myself in the public eye. My business could suffer. Shaw Security has a reputation of confidentiality and covertness and I'm putting that at risk. Although, I've maintained that with my team being here. I'm the only one who's been by her side, making me more susceptible to the public eye.

"And Sky, I'm so excited to meet you. I love your song, *'Take Me Back.'*"

"Thank you, it's great to meet you too." I watch her paste a fake smile on her face. To everyone else, it looks genuine. Except, she's not happy. It's killing her not knowing how Savanah and I know each other. And since she was a client, I can't disclose that information. She hired my team because she was having issues with an ex-husband and worried about her safety. When Savanah doesn't divulge the specifics of our relationship, it only leaves Sydney to guess. And by her body language, her guess is not accurate. Girls are catty because I'm certain Savanah did that on purpose. When we walk away, I break another fucking rule.

"She was a client," I whisper.

"I figured," she says coolly, yet her body relaxes next to me. "She doesn't seem your type. She's too tall."

I throw my head back in laughter. "That's a big observation, considering you've never met a past girlfriend."

She stops and pins me with her gaze. "Am I wrong?"

I think back to the women I've been attracted to. "They *might* have been on the shorter side." None compare to the five-foot-two gorgeous woman standing in front of me though. So, if I have a *type*, it's not what they look like, it's Sydney. She flashes a grin and spins on her heel.

As I watch her float around the room, I question why I'm here again. The compulsory need to help her seems to be ingrained so deep inside me, it's jarring. From the first day we met in Aiden's hospital room to the day we jumped out of a plane, the effect she had on me differed from any other woman. But I couldn't pinpoint why. Why was I so attracted to her? She's beautiful, intelligent, sensitive yet feisty; I could list everything that I love about her and I'd still be left questioning why her. Although, it's all irrelevant because her guilt lies deeper than our attraction.

I'm stuck between being a hero and her *friend*, of which neither will make me happy because I don't have her.

"You've gone quiet," Sydney says with a slight slur, slinking up my arm. She giggles when I lift a brow. "Right. What was I thinking, you're a man of few words." Her eyes gloss over as she waves a hand around, spilling some of her wine on her shirt. Thankfully, it's chardonnay. "Oopsy." She grins wide, her perfectly white teeth reflecting in the dim room.

Grabbing the drink from her hand, I whisper, "I think it's time to go." The last shot of tequila is in full effect.

"I think you're right," she mumbles, wiping the small spill off her bare chest. My eyes dart away, searching for somewhere to put the glass so I don't offer to help. *With my tongue.* "I want to look like a fool."

"Huh?"

She shakes her head and chuckles. "I *don't* want to look like a fool."

"Good idea," I say, wrapping my arm around her waist and leading her to the exit. Before we walk out, I glance down and do a quick assessment of her before we meet the vultures. She looks gorgeous. "Hey, Tink…" When I have her attention, I continue, "… we're heading outside, say nothing to the paparazzi, just keep walking and ignore them."

"Okay, Mr. AMA's Most Wanted." A security guard overhears her and coughs to hide his chuckle when I glance at him.

"You want me to throw you over my shoulder, don't you?" I tease.

Her eyes widen and she places her petite hand on my chest, like it could stop me. "Max. I will scream your *full name* to everyone out there if you do. *Aaannnd* they'll love hearing that you're a millionaire."

Shit. My smile drops as hers grows. She wouldn't. Then again, she's drunk.

"Leverage, baby," she quips, walking out the door, swinging her sinful ass. At least I know she's capable of walking on her own.

She flashes a wicked smile as the paparazzi scream their questions.

"*What's my name?*"

"*Are we dating?*"

"*Boxers or briefs?*"

I tilt my head, staring pointedly at the guy who yelled the last one, and he cowers. Jesus Christ... these people have no limits.

"Co—" I slap my hand over Sydney's mouth. It wouldn't embarrass me for people to know that I sometimes go commando, but she'd be mortified in the morning. Her stomach vibrates under my hand from laughing as I lead her to the limo.

I shove her in and say, "I thought your goal was to not look like a fool?"

She shrugs. "Your fans were interested. And since I know..." Her words trail off and her eyes close. "You know what I want." She leans over and whispers in my ear, the smell of tequila lingering on her breath. She'll hate life tomorrow.

I chuckle as she tries to focus her eyes on my face. "I have no idea. But if it's more alcohol, I'm going to say no."

She shakes her head slowly. "Nope. That's not what I want." She touches my hand, and the buzz of desire immediately slams back as she drags her finger up my forearm. "I want..." she looks at me through hooded eyelids, licking her lips, "... you to tie me up." Her eyes glow with eagerness as she straddles me, her skirt bunching up around her waist.

My muscles tense under her body. Closing my eyes, I search for the restraint I've always had with her. I slowly open them. "Sydney," I grate out in warning. She fucking giggles.

"Yesss?" she purrs. Her fingers slide down my tie, stopping at my belt. She lifts her hips to run her hand in between us, over the swell of my cock. She lets out an approving hum. "You want me, Max."

There's a fine line between want and need. I'm in the gray area where they both intersect. The area is blurred which blinds me to my emotions. I never know which direction I should be going. Only, I can't let go.

I grab both her hands, pinning them behind her back. She pushes out her breasts, tempting me. Her blue eyes flash with fire and ice. My restraint slips as I growl, "Get on your knees." I release her hands and she slides off me, sitting on her knees on the limo floor in front of me. Waiting to be told what to do.

I could easily whip out my dick and have those red lips wrap around me, milking me.

I could easily do everything I've been fantasizing about tonight.

I swallow, looking out the moon roof.

Fuck! That's the problem. It's too easy.

She's drunk and I'm clearly thinking with the wrong head.

I roll down the privacy window and instruct the driver to pull over. Rolling the window back up, Sydney peers up at me with a questioning expression. I lift her back up to her seat, reach over to grab the seatbelt and stretch it across her body.

"Max, what are you doing?"

The car stops and I kiss her on the forehead before hopping out on the dim empty street. The driver rolls the front window down and I instruct him to take her to the hotel. I pace the street, hands behind my tense neck. Goddamnit, Sydney. Why did you do that? Pulling out my phone, I shoot off a text to Stone. He'll intercept her and make sure she makes it up to her room. We're only three blocks away from the hotel so I'm not concerned about her safety. My sanity is my top priority right now.

My feet pound the pavement as I walk in the direction of the hotel. Live rock music blares out of a dive bar as I pass it and I try to talk myself out of turning around and drowning my frustrations with liquor. I would never do that on a job.

Sydney's a job.

My fingers tighten into fists as I stare at the hotel, glowing against the dark sky, my mind stuck on ice-blue eyes. Fuck that, I can't go back to the hotel. Spinning in place, I take two long strides toward the open door. The bouncer looks me over, recognition flashes in his eyes. With a tip of his head, he motions for me to head inside without asking for my ID. Before, when someone recognized me, it was because they knew about my team. Now, I don't have a fucking clue. I'm not sure putting myself in the spotlight was a good idea.

Sliding onto an empty barstool, I pull out a hundred-dollar bill, pushing it toward the bartender. "Johnny Walker, neat. Keep 'em coming."

My phone vibrates in my pocket so I pull it out.

Stone: In bed and passed out

Good. I hope like hell she doesn't remember tonight. Shit will get awkward. My phone vibrates again.

Stone: You good?

Me: Never better

Stone: Fucking liar

I chuckle, bringing the glass to my lips. When the golden liquid wets my mouth, I can't stop from downing the entire drink. I slam the glass down, sliding it to the bartender. He nods, fills it again and slides it back. I spin the barstool, sitting back while I watch the band on the tiny stage. The small-framed brunette swings her hips and belts out a song. *See, she's short and I'm not at all attracted to her.* I sigh as her voice screeches through the air. I don't know if I'm more irritated that her voice is annoying as fuck, or if it's because it's not Sydney's. The past few weeks, my addiction to her has grown to an unhealthy level. And hiding it from her is becoming harder each day we're together.

Her stalker has nothing on me.

The only difference between the two of us... I'd never physically hurt her.

But I would kill for her.

CHAPTER TWENTY-TWO

MAX

"How much longer?" Stone asks, staring at me from across the table, weaving a pencil between his fingers. We're having our pre-concert meeting in my hotel suite. The word *forever* is on the tip of my tongue, but if I say it, he'll probably launch the pencil at my head.

Instead, I glare back at him, irritated he asked. Although, I get it. I shouldn't be using most of my resources for this one case. If this was a typical case, I'd have one person working it. But this is Sydney. I need all hands on deck. Typically, these types of people don't hide for long. They feel justified for doing what they do and won't stop until they are satisfied. I don't think they're satisfied.

I sigh out of frustration and relent. "If nothing happens this week, you guys can go home."

Stone rubs his temples. He's been frustrated with me over my feelings about Sydney ever since she was engaged to Damon. And now here I am, following her around the country, using her security as an excuse. I could pass this off to another team I trust, but fuck that.

I'm not leaving.

"If you want me to stay, I will," Kase states, sitting forward in his chair. Stone jerks his head toward Kase, the pencil gripped in his fist. Kase looks at Stone and shrugs. It's not that Stone doesn't want to complete a job, he just hates seeing the emotional warfare I'm putting myself through. If he had a say, he'd rather me leave and they stay. But since he's not the boss, he doesn't.

What can I say? I'm a glutton for punishment. I wish I couldn't read past the lies that came out of her mouth. Her truths flash bright in her eyes and body language. That's even before last weekend's drunk Sydney came out to play. She wants me as bad as I do her. But we've made our own hell. Or maybe I'm causing the hell we surround ourselves in because I can't stay away.

Aiden called me this week after seeing the tabloids with her in my arms making sure I was okay. Even though he'd rather see us together, he knows how I feel. Which is crazy because I don't even know how I feel from one minute to the next. I thought I could handle being around her. But the first night on the bus, it took every bit of restraint I had to walk out of that room and sleep five feet from her.

I glance at Kase and send an appreciative nod. "I'll decide what we're doing after the show. For now, we keep doing what we've been doing. Stone, have you found Rex?" I clip, still pissed this hasn't been resolved. Three weeks since I talked to my mom, and no one has yet to hear from him.

"No. He's dead or off the grid."

"Fuck." I hang my head, the strain gripping my insides. "There is no way in hell I could ever tell Susie her son is dead." My mom would lose her shit. "Have you checked all five homes?" A shimmer of hope that the bastard broke into one of my houses and is hiding out.

Stone shakes his head. "There's been no trip in the security alarms. And I checked the surveillance footage just in case he got around that somehow."

He'd never get around Stone's security, so the latter part was only for my peace of mind. I pinch the bridge of my nose. "I fucking don't have time for this." Thinking he was on vacation somewhere or just lying low, I didn't give it much attention before. "That fucker got himself into this, he can get himself out." My mom's voice ricochets in my mind, the guilt already creating a knot.

"Want me to get Cody to go check out the team?" Stone asks, knowing I can't let this go. Since I'm not leaving Sydney's side, the next best option is to send one of the guys. I shoot him a quick nod.

There, I did my part.

SYDNEY SHINES IN HER ELEMENT. Her body moves without thought, dances with reckless abandon. She's so fucking sexy. Watching her is like being in a cage with a tiger. The adrenaline inside me wants to tame her, make her mine, but the voice in my head is telling me I'll get eaten alive. The power she holds over me is a vice to my existence. I can't seem to break away. And since she hopped her hot body on top of mine, I haven't been able to get her out of my head.

"We're all clear up here." A voice rings in my ear. I shake out of the trance I'm caught in.

I take a deep breath. *Keep your shit together.*

"Clear down..." I stop mid-sentence, staring across the stage. Brett, the stage manager, is standing behind a speaker, his eyes pinned on Sydney. I glance around and while most people are watching her too, they are looking at her in awe. Brett's intense stare sends warning bells inside of me.

Son of a bitch. *It better not be someone this close and we missed it.*

"We need to look more into Brett McDonald." I ran background checks on the entire staff, but no one jumped out at us.

"Got it, boss," Stone replies in my ear.

"Nixon, I need your eyes on him. Something's up with this guy."

"Found 'em."

When Sydney's song ends, the lights go dark to [change floor]. I keep my eyes trained on him as he works. When the lights shine back on, the crowd goes wild. I turn my attention back to Syd so he doesn't suspect anything, but I watch him out of the corner of my eyes. His gaze stays glued on her the rest of her time on stage. After her set is over, she runs to the side stage I'm standing on. Her black tank shows her gorgeous boobs off, her chest glistening with sweat. She wraps her hair up in a bun showing off her long neck. My mouth waters thinking how salty she would taste right now. She bounces on her toes as the endorphins rush through her body. I know that rush; *I crave it.*

"That crowd is insane," she boasts.

I peek out at the audience, the cheers and roars, I can see why she's so hyped up. Brett stares in our direction. *Fucker keeps watching.* I slide my arm around her small waist and pull her into me, my lips slamming against hers elicit a surprised expression. The second I taste her, I know this was a bad idea.

I pull back, trying to act immune to her body. I force my gaze to look for Brett, but he's gone.

"He saw," Kase says into my ear. "He wasn't happy."

"Keep track of him."

I flinch as a hand slaps my cheek. *Jesus Christ!* She needs to stop slapping me. I look down at a pissed off Sydney. "*Really?*" she sneers, her hands on her hips. "You're such an asshole, Max." She whips around and walks away.

I grab her arm and spin her around. "What the hell, little girl. What the fuck was that for?"

Her jaw tics and she growls. It's kind of hot. "Don't. Call. Me. That."

"Then stop acting like one and use your words." I get in her face, not caring that we're causing a scene. All my suppressed desire's about to snap.

"Oh, you're one to talk. *Use my words...* that's rich coming from someone who never uses them. Fuck. You. Are those words good enough?" she spits in my face. "Stop toying with my emotions." Her arm twists in my hand and she yanks it back.

I'm trying to keep her safe, dammit. I catch up to her again, pulling her back into my chest. "They haven't done anything in a couple weeks. I needed to light a fire," I whisper-yell in her ear. The rise of my chest hits her back.

"Yeah, you're all about lightin' fires but nowhere around to put 'em out," she says over her shoulder. She twists away from me again and walks off, leaving me there, regretting kissing her. She's right, I shouldn't have done it.

Because now, *I need more.*

CHAPTER TWENTY-THREE

SYDNEY

L *ight a fire*? I'm about to light a fire and burn his ass down. How dare he kiss me like he owns me and then pretend it was for the job. My whole body shakes with fury. "Ugh!" I scream out. That man infuriates me. I jump at a knock at the door. It's probably Hudson making sure I'm okay. Well, *no*, I'm not. I'm pissed.

I swing open the door to yell at him, because… well, he's guilty by association. When a hotel staffer greets me, I snap it shut and peek around him to a grinning Hudson. I exhale and paste on a fake smile. "Hi."

"Good evening, Ms. Owen. Here is what you ordered." He hands me an ice bucket.

My brows furrow as I stare down at the brown bucket. "I… I didn't order anything." I lift the lid, my eyes widen in disbelief. There's a small note on top.

Hope this makes you feel better. ~M

You have *got* to be kidding me. I smash down the lid and go to hand it back to the guy, but I only see Hudson. Sticking my head out my door, I glance down the hall and watch the staffer disappear into the elevator. I'm about to chuck the whole thing down

the hallway, but then think how bad that'd look in a gossip magazine if it got out. Turning my glare to Hudson, he winks at me.
"Your boss is an asshole," I scoff and slam the door shut. His laugh
carries through the door.

"Men." I smash the bucket on the kitchen table and scowl at it,
fuming. I can't believe he sent me *vanilla* ice cream. If this was his
way of trying to apologize, he should of *at least* sent me my
favorite flavor. *Not freaking his.*

Another knock on the door. I debate if I want another surprise
that'll make me want to hurl more things at Max. Whoever it is,
doesn't wait long until they knock again.

I swing the door open and say, "I don't wa—"

Max's large body fills the doorway as he leans against it. He's
sporting basketball shorts and a grey t-shirt that barely fits around
his muscular arms. Casual Max makes me forget my name as I
drink him in.

"I hear you're not happy with my gift?" he rasps, playfully,
reminding me about his thoughtless gift. His expression brightens
as my irritation grows. He takes a step inside and I back up,
leaving at least a body's length between us. The only sound in the
room is the click of the door closing.

"What are you doin'?"

He takes another step forward. "I came to have some ice cream."
My eyebrows pop up. He acts like this is freaking Dairy Queen.

I point to the table. "You can take your plain ass vanilla ice
cream and go back to your own room."

He gasps, mocking surprise. "You said you liked vanilla."

"No, that was your favorite. Not mine."

A wolfish grin pulls at the corners of his mouth. I'm confused
by the heated look in his eyes as he takes another step. The air
thickens around me and my body hums. *You're reading him wrong.* I
berate myself for thinking otherwise. Just like the kiss earlier… it
was strictly business.

"Max, why are you here?" I huff, throwing my arms out. "There's no threat in here."

"That's where you're wrong." His smile morphs into a serious expression. I swallow as he approaches me, rooted in my spot, I'm not able to look away from the wolf himself. He lifts his hand and runs his thumb across my bottom lip, goosebumps blazon my skin. "*You're* the threat. You always have been. My heart is in danger every time you're near me," he murmurs.

My lips part with a breathy exhale, heating his thumb. I hate how easy he can lift me up, because the fall is harder each time, but my body acts on its own accord when he touches me. His hand cups my neck and I lean into it, reveling in the warmth.

Enjoy it now, it'll be gone soon. This is our dance and when the song is over, we always go our separate ways.

Our eyes catch and the indifference usually reflecting back, isn't there. His confidence strikes a chord inside of me, like a record being scratched and something new plays. *Something promising.* Our song has changed, I just don't know the lyrics yet.

I shiver as his fingers graze my arm. "You have three seconds to tell me to stop if you don't want this."

Fear mixes with desire. *Three seconds.* This isn't a casual affair. This is Max. Does he know this will change everything between us? Is three seconds enough time to make that decision?

He lowers his face, dragging his lips across mine, kissing me lightly on the corner of my mouth.

"One," he murmurs.

I close my eyes and focus on the trail of kisses he makes to my neck. Fear is drowned out by heat and anticipation. He wraps his arm around my waist and pulls me into his hard chest. It's been so long since I've allowed my body to feel this way.

"Two." The warmth from his breath sends goosebumps down my arms.

My pulse quickens against his lips. The questions fade away.

Each touch sparks a new part of my body back to life until I'm fully charged. I want this.

I want him.

The muscles on his stomach tighten from my touch as I run my hands up to his chest. He pulls back so he can see my eyes. "Three," he rasps. He waits a beat, maybe to see if I'll change my mind, but when I don't, he adds, "It's about fucking time." He slips his gun and holster from his hip and then scoops me up and I wrap my legs around him. Our lips meld together in a heated, no holds barred kiss. He demands control and I willingly give it to him.

Clothes go flying everywhere until there isn't anything left to take off. Having Max stand naked in front of me, the epitome of strength and confidence, causes me to shrink back a bit out of modesty. His eyes narrow as he watches me react. I've never been uncomfortable in my skin until now.

"Get on your knees," he demands, his hand cupping the back of my neck. The memory of last week flashes through my mind. I might have been drunk, but the rejection stings nonetheless. The desire to make him happy courses through my veins, but I pause. His brow raises as he assesses me. "I don't ask twice, Tink."

"I... um..." I bite my lip and drop my gaze, staring at my cotton candy pink nail polish on my toes. Shivers run down my spine from the hotel air on my naked body. Max raises my chin until our eyes lock.

"What's wrong?"

I blow out a shaky breath. "Are you going to walk away again, if I do?"

His lip twitches as he nods in silent understanding. "Are you drunk?"

"No."

"Can you leave here on your own free will?"

"Yes."

"Then I'm not going anywhere." A simple, yet demanding kiss, reassures me. "You're beautiful, Sydney. Never question that. *Especially* with me because I think you're the sexiest woman alive." His fingers scrape up my arm and I watch them until they wrap around my heavy breast. Bending over, he takes the other one in his mouth and playfully bites my nipple before straightening back up. He pulls in a deep breath, releasing it with a growl. "Now, get on your knees before I lose the small amount of control I have."

Hearing him say he's losing control around me builds my confidence back up. I'm sure there are few people in this world that can make a man like Max Shaw lose control.

And I'm one of them.

I drop to my knees. My eyes widen when his cock is right in front of me. I remember feeling how big he was, but holy shit, I never saw it. And I didn't think it was this big. How the hell did he fit inside me?

"I know it's impressive, but are you going to stare at it all night? Have you never…" His voice trails off, raking his hand through my hair.

A slow smile tugs on my lip as I glance up. "Do you really want me to answer that?" I wrap my hand around him and glide along the velvety length.

He growls. "Fuck. No." *That's what I thought.*

His growl morphs into groans when I take him in my mouth as far back as I can. My eyes water working him with my hands, tongue, and mouth in a greedy desire to make him succumb to me. The grip he has in my hair tightens and his impressive size hardens and I slide him in and out faster.

"Syd," he says with a ragged breath. "If you don't stop, I'm going to come down…"

I work faster and hum my approval.

I want all of him.

And I get my wish.

He takes a couple seconds to regain his composure. I bite my lip, glancing up at him with hooded eyes. "That mouth of yours will be my downfall." He lifts me in his arms and I wrap my legs around him. His lips devour mine, the ache in between my legs so intense, I question if anything will dull it. He places me on the kitchen table by the ice bucket and I look up at him with a quizzical expression. Flashing a mischievous grin, he walks backward a few steps into the kitchen. Drawer after drawer, he searches for something. He holds up a spoon like a trophy when he finds one. A spoon? Is he going to eat ice cream right now? *Right after I...*

"Lay down on the table." His raspy voice interrupts my thought of untimely hunger. I do as I'm told, bending my knees up in the air so the hardwood table doesn't bite into my back. Max's tongue darts out to lick his bottom lip as he stares at my wet center. "You're going to ruin me, Tink." I glance at his hand and he pumps his already hard cock. "You're so fucking wet, all I want to do is sink into you." The way his eyes streak up my body, my insides shudder, almost orgasming. No man has ever looked at me and made me feel this sensual. I slide my hand over my breasts and down to my clit, moaning in pleasure. He grabs my hand. "As much as I want to see you pleasure yourself, that'll have to be another time." His eyes dart around the room, but I meet disappointment when they find mine. "Reach your hands up and grab the chair," he demands. I smile when I figure out it was because he couldn't find anything to tie me up with. After I find the chair, he says, "Don't let go. If you let go, I stop." I nod in anticipation. He'll have to pry the chair from my grip.

He pops the spoon in his mouth as he pulls a chair up to the table. I feel vulnerable as his eyes appraise my body in such an exposed position. I stare up to the ceiling, trying to calm my erratic heart. Hearing him open the ice cream, I peek down. He winks at me as he takes a spoonful of vanilla ice-cream, shoving it into his mouth.

My mouth opens to sarcastically ask if he plans on staring at me all night, but I snap it shut when he wraps his arms under my thighs and yanks me to him. His cold tongue darts out against my heated core and I cry out, my back lifting off the table. I grip the chair harder, afraid I might let go by accident.

God, he can't stop.

When he pulls back, I groan in frustration, the ache on the border of pain. "Patience, beautiful," he says, dipping the spoon back into the ice cream. This time, he spreads the cold ice cream against my clit to my entrance.

"Max," I whimper when he slips the spoon inside of me. The cold metal foreign object feels good. But it shouldn't, right?

He chuckles, pulling it out, replacing it with his mouth. His tongue expertly moves, sucking the ice cream off. My entire body convulses as he brings me to the edge. He plunges two fingers inside me and I scream out his name, over and over as I coat his fingers with my orgasm.

Holy hell. I pull in a couple breaths, calming my errant heartbeat. Max stands, leaning over kissing my stomach, trailing up my torso until he's at my mouth. His kiss is brutal, filled with need and possession. *I thought I was breathless before.* Squeezing my legs around his waist, his heavy cock pulses against my center. He reaches above me, without stopping his sensual assault and uncurls my fingers from the chair. I arch my back off the hard wood of the table when he grinds his hips into me.

"The need for you hurts. I've dreamed of this day for so long," he murmurs. "You're so fucking perfect." His hands slow their movement on my body and he crawls on top of me.

"Oh, no!"

"Fuck!"

We both say at the same time.

Suddenly, all desire seizes as the one thing holding us up, gives in and we crash to the ground with a loud thump. Max's hand protects my head, so it doesn't hit the hardness beneath us. Thank god, he didn't land on top of me, rather he pushed his weight to the side of me. The couple seconds of surprise and panic is washed away with my laughter. Max jumps off the destroyed table, holding his hand out for me to grab.

"I... I can't," I say in a fit of giggles, holding my stomach. We're both naked and we just destroyed a hotel table while about to have sex. The ball of desire and nervousness tickle my insides.

"At least you're not hurt," he says with a grin, squatting down to lift me up in his arms. With ease, he moves me to the bedroom, lowering me to the bed. Our bodies sink into the cool white down comforter. "I can say, that hasn't ever happened to me before."

"Really?" I say, eyeing his body, joking. My perusal stops short. "What the..." My words trail off, staring at Max's tattoo. Specifically, the one on his upper shoulder. Surrounded by other tattoos, this one stands out like a full moon on a clear night. Why hadn't I noticed it before? I trace the tattoo, the same way I've done my own. The path identical. Jay's farewell words come back to me. *"You can't get mad at me if you see it again."*

Max chuckles. "The bastard. I swear I didn't know. Not until you showed up at the hotel in New York."

"You didn't tell me."

He nods. "You were walking away from me again. What was I supposed to do? Would it have made you stay knowing we had similar tattoos? I'm certain, you would have been irate."

"Why do you have wings?" I ask, staring at the identical wings to mine in disbelief. He grabs my finger, still outlining them, and brings my hand to his lips.

"I got them after I came back to New York. After leaving you in California."

My eyes widen and I sit up on my elbow so I have a better view of his face. "What are they for," I ask, already guessing but needing validation.

"You."

The idea of him permanently marking me on his skin has emotions building inside my chest. He stays silent, his eyes flicker across my face. I open my mouth to respond, but I can't focus on one feeling because there are fragments of almost every one ricocheting in my mind. The overwhelming need to leave, to put some distance between us, burns at my core. I drop my elbow and roll to my back, taking in a deep breath, but finding it hard to pull in a deep enough one.

Max is on top of me within a second. His lips fused to mine. He kisses life into me, blurring the lines of all the fragments until they're just one piece of desire. His fingers play at my entrance and I grind my hips against them until he slips them inside me. I groan into his mouth as the tingling sensation in my core heightens from his expert fingers and I'm on the verge of release, my moans intensify, but everything stops when he pulls them out. My chest heaves and a few choice words are on my tongue until I notice him reach over and grab a condom out of his pants.

His eyes pin me in place, daring me to move. I'm not going anywhere. But it's been so long since I felt a man inside me. Damon was the last.

"Max, I haven't been with—" He stops me with his finger on my lips and nods in understanding.

Leaning over, he kisses the side of my lips. "I'll be gentle," he whispers, guiding himself inside me until he's fully sheathed. My body quivers, chills wrap around my spine and I gasp at the feeling of fullness, the slight sting twisting to pleasure. He entwines our fingers and brings them above my head.

Our bodies move in a fluid motion, my legs squeeze tight around his waist and his eyes never leave mine. Our souls are bared as we dance to a sensual rhythm. This time is nothing like the first time we were together where our sexual energies were riding high from emotions. Our hearts are leading this dance. The song, pure and simple.

I've never been so afraid for a song to end.

CHAPTER TWENTY-FOUR

SYDNEY

The silence between us is louder than a bull horn. The endless chatter in my head spurs panic.

What did we do?

Where do we go from here?

What will our friends think?

What would Damon think?

"It's just you and me in this room, Tink," he states as if hearing the damning questions. I press up on my elbow and meet his eyes.

"Is it?" I whisper, wondering if it could ever be just us. I dig my head into his hard chest and groan. I'm spoiling the moment. Why can't I let go of the past?

Max wraps his arms around my shoulders, kissing the top of my head. The sweet gesture helps me relax. I focus on his heartbeat. "We'll take this however you want. Slow or fast," he rasps into my hair. "The only option you don't have, is walking away. I'm not letting that happen again."

Before responding, I let his words sink in and close my eyes, turn off my mind and just feel. The once hollow core inside my heart is full, my soul is dancing, and my body has never been more alive than when I'm with Max. How can I walk away when every-thing *is* perfect?

"I don't want to run anymore," I surrender, lifting again. Tears blur my vision. It's freeing to say it out loud, the weight of giving a shit lifts off my chest letting me breathe easier than I have in a long time. His eyes flicker across my face. These are tears of relief.

He rolls us over and hovers above me, bringing his lips to mine, devouring my mouth with a desperate yet controlled need. The tension that always saddles us, dissipates. He pours his heart into it and I feel it. Every beat. Every emotion. Every want and need.

I gasp for air when he releases my swollen lips. Slowly, I regain my senses, and he raises a curious eyebrow. Seconds pass as I wait for him to tell me what's on his mind. Eventually, I ask, "What?"

"You didn't answer me. Slow. Or fast?" His question was regarding the speed of our relationship earlier, but the heat in his eyes and his hardness pressing into my hip suggests otherwise. My pulse quickens.

"Slow," I murmur, sounding out of breath as I watch his finger graze down the middle of my rib cage. "We should—" I swallow my words, whimpering when his finger skims my sensitive clit, sliding right inside of me. My back bows off the bed and I moan at the delicious, yet agonizing slow speed he moves in and out of me. "—take things slow," I mewl, the ache building in my lower belly.

Rocking against his hand, I groan as he takes my breast in his mouth.

"Slow isn't usually my style, but I accept the challenge."

STARING at myself in the bathroom mirror, I wait for the remorse. The guilt. Instead, a woman who's happy and thoroughly fucked stares back at me. My cheeks are red, my breasts still perky and firm, skin flushed from Max's stubble. And a heart that's full. For the first time, the thought of being with Max doesn't result in a storm of reasons we can't be together. *"Don't fuck this up,"* I whisper to my reflection.

"Tink, you okay in there?" Max calls from the other room, worry etched in his voice. His question pops into my head again. *Slow or fast?* A lazy grin creeps up my cheeks as I wonder if he thinks my answer was only about sex. Don't get me wrong, slow sex with Max was wildly hot.

I peek out of the bathroom, my full heart twists when I find Max sitting on the edge of the bed, elbows on his knees with a strained expression. His eyes dart to mine when he hears me coming out of the bathroom. His uncertainty devastates me. This fractured moment is my fault. I'm bringing this gorgeous man who doesn't answer to anyone to his knees. He hands me the power I don't want.

Standing in between his legs, he sits up tall, and I rake my hands through his hair. "Your question… we were talking about our relationship, *right?*"

With a slight tic at the corner of his mouth, he nods. His demeanor morphs in front of me to the confident man I'm used to seeing. "You're the boss."

I stifle a snort, pushing on his naked chest and he falls back on the bed. "As if."

Settling back, he puts his hands behind his head, flashing a lopsided grin as if telling me I'm in control. His jeans are unbuttoned, zipper down, flashing the top of his underwear. His ink on full display, I'll look at it thoroughly later. Laid back, Max is sexy as hell. But my dry lady parts were just oiled rigorously and need a reprieve.

We need to talk. But the way his gaze takes appraisal of my naked body, my engine buzzes to life. I fight the blooming urge to jump on top of him again, rather I spin in place and march to the bathroom. Maybe this will make him stop looking at me with sexy eyes. When I return, I'm wearing a white robe two times my size. It's so long, it drags on the floor. To reinforce my no-more-sex stance, I make sure I'm not within reach, leaning against the desk.

"Twenty-seven hundred miles didn't stop me from getting to you," he states, sitting up, a wicked gleam in his eyes. "You think three feet and that piece of fabric will stop me?"

Releasing an awkward laugh, I tighten the robe belt. "Expectations," I blurt out before he can stand up, knowing one physical touch would cause me to cave. Amusement fills his face. "Not *sexual* expectations, Max." His laugh echoes off the walls in the small bedroom.

"Okay, Tink. Let's talk logistics." He slaps his hands together, folding them in his lap.

I swallow, afraid he might take what I have to say the wrong way. "I'd like to keep our relationship on the down-low."

"Meaning?"

I clear my throat, my nerves getting the best of me. I've never had to put restrictions on a relationship. "I don't want to tell anyone." His expression remains neutral, making him hard to read. I wrap the robe belt around my fingers, over and over. "At least, right now," I add.

He scratches his stubble, nodding. *Say something.* I glance down when I feel the tingling in my fingers. I've wrapped the belt around my fingers so tight, they're turning blue. Releasing the belt, I hide my hands behind me to stop fidgeting—or cutting off my fingers.

"Max," I belt out. "You have to engage in this conversation."

"Why?"

Seriously? My eyebrows draw together. "*Why what?* Why do you need to be present in this conversation? Why do I want this between us only? Be specific."

And he tells me to use my words.

He cracks a smile at my irritation and I narrow my eyes at him, waiting for him to answer. "Why do you want to keep it a secret?"

I sigh, turning to the window worried if I tell him the truth, he'll think I'm running. I lick my lips, suddenly parched. "I don't want…" Drawing in a deep breath and letting it out slowly, I take a quick pause. "I don't want our friends to know until we're certain what this is."

He pushes off the bed and stops in front of me. "I'm certain what this is, so let me explain it to you since you're having trouble with it." His fingers swipe my hair behind my ear as his stare pins me in place. "We're two adults who like each other. We're exploring each other and seeing where this goes. There are no promises, no expectations other than *we try*."

"But what if we tell everyone and then it doesn't work? Reunions, friends, Lulu… everything will be awkward."

Steel-blue eyes bore into me and I shift my weight from foot to foot, wishing I hadn't said that out loud. He shakes his head, and I watch him storm away. The bathroom door slams.

How many times am I going to push him away before he doesn't return? Panic builds in my heart. I stare at the door, waiting for it to open. The air in the room must have followed him because I can't breathe. Like the tornado that just left here, it comes back full force when he charges back into the room. I wrap my arms across my chest, expecting the worst. Max towers in front of me again.

"I get it." My eyes widen at his declaration. It's his turn to distract himself with my belt. The white Terry cloth hangs in his hand. "One month." I tilt my head in confusion. "That's all you get to keep this secret. My team will know because it's imperative they know everything, especially since we're here for business. Graham will know as well." He quirks a brow up, waiting for an objection. I nod in agreement, not having found my voice yet.

He yanks at the belt, whipping it out of the two small hooks. Pulling apart the robe with his fingers, I shudder at the sound of his growl. The no-more-sex thoughts vanish. As soon as the robe falls at our feet, Max steps closer, dips his head into the curve of my neck, and with no warning, pins my hands behind my back with the belt.

"I choose fast. And hard," he rasps, his breath hot on my neck.

My eyes roll back.

Yes, please.

CHAPTER TWENTY-FIVE

MAX

Fuck, *I have to get out of here.*

I glance at Sydney sleeping, the wrinkled sheet only covering her from the waist down. Her soft tits on display. My dick pulses in pain, reminding me why I need to leave. I've been awake for the last hour, rehashing our entire night. I've tried to think of anything that can make my dick go soft, to no avail. My thoughts always take me back to being buried deep inside perfection.

"I'm going for a run," I whisper, leaning down to give her a quick kiss. She softly moans. I grind my teeth, squeezing my eyes shut. I fight the urge to touch her. The hunger I have for her is unrelenting. It's not in my wheelhouse to control my sexual appetite with a woman. I take unapologetically. But fuckin'-a, my appetite has never been this unsatisfied, craving more to the point of pain.

Walk away. Now.

I snatch my phone off the table, slipping out the door. As soon as the door closes, I breathe a sigh of relief. The wall between us helps me clear my head long enough to send Hudson a quick text that it's time for work. As soon as he steps off the elevator, I head in his direction. We pass with a couple nods. No need discussing what he already knows.

I glance down at my watch. Ten o'clock. The bus leaves in three hours and I need to run this sexual frustration off. Because if it's bad now, wait until I'm on a bus, not able to touch her for ten fucking hours.

First, I have a stop to make. The wooden door shakes under my knuckles. I wait five seconds before knocking again. He's in there; grumbling on the other side gives him away.

"If you work for me, you're fired," Graham mumbles, half awake, swinging the door open. His eyes widen when they meet mine. I stand there as his gaze works its way down and back up. It's a good thing I like the guy. "Max, to what do I owe the pleasure?" His voice softens.

Fucking, finally.

My smile widens at the relief in my pants.

"Thanks, G," I say, patting him on the back as I walk into his room.

"And what *exactly* are you thanking me for?"

I wave him off. "Just for being you. Grab your shoes, we're going running."

"Excuse me?" He runs his hand through his hair. "I didn't hear you right. You want me to go running after getting only..." He pauses, looking around the room for the clock. I point to the microwave and his head whips to it and back. "... Five hours of sleep."

"I only got three. I win. Get your shoes on."

"What if I don't like to run?" He crosses his arms.

Bullshit. "You ran the Los Angeles marathon three months ago."

His mouth drops open. "Many people do marathons just to say—"

"That was your fifth one this year."

"You are mildly invasive." I shrug a shoulder. *Yes, I am.* There is nothing mild about it. Especially for the people Sydney surrounds herself with. "Fine. But only because I had that extra dessert last night. *Not* because you're commanding me to." He mumbles to himself all the way to the bedroom. I survey the room as I wait. Shoes lined at the door, not one crooked or out of place; files stacked perfectly on the sofa table next to two pencils side by side. I glance at the closed door and chuckle to myself. I'm an asshole. Walking over to the table, I flick one pencil so it's resting in a V formation. Let's see how long it'll take him to see it. I give it less than a minute.

I lean against the wall, irritation grows the longer he takes. This was a dumb idea. "Graham, you don't have to dress nice to go running," I yell, tapping my head against the wall. "I don't have all day."

"Well, I don't roll out of bed looking like Thor," he says, walking out of the room, pointedly staring at me.

I chuckle at the Marvel character reference. It reminds me of my brother. He's called me that a time or two. Fuck! I didn't want to think about my brother right now. He still hasn't turned up and his team is clueless. It's like he's vanished. My next call is Aiden. Maybe the FBI knows something we don't.

"Are you just going to stand there all day?" Graham snaps, pulling me out of my thoughts.

I yawn and stretch my arms. "Yeah, I'm kind of tired. I'm gonna skip and go back to bed."

His expression is priceless. The vein in his neck pops out. "What!"

I shuffle past him, shaking my head. "I'm kidding. Let's go."

"Oh! You've got jokes." He laughs without humor as we walk down the corridor. While waiting for the elevator, he says, "Thanks for moving my pencil."

I turn in his direction. "I'm not sure if I'm impressed or disappointed. I had you pegged as a classic case of OCD."

"Why do you think I run?" He smirks as we step into the elevator. "And thanks to you, I'll be quicker today so I can fix the problem. Hope you can keep up." The challenge in his voice is everything I need right now. "How far we running?"

"At least ten miles." I hope that'll be enough to tire me the fuck out for the day.

His eyes snap to mine in surprise. "Aren't you ambitious."

Nope, I'm sexually frustrated.

As soon as my feet pound the pavement, the Sydney energy built up inside me, turns into fuel to keep me going. We don't talk the first half hour as we wind around a paved trail close to the hotel. The cool brisk morning air in Des Moines makes the run tolerable.

"Is there a reason I'm here, running with you?" Graham glances over at me. His lean body is made for running. Mine, not so much. But I'm keeping in step with him.

I shrug. "I needed a running partner, someone who would challenge me to go the distance."

Sensing his eyes on me, I look over. "You're so full of shit. Does this have to do with *the kiss*?"

It has everything to do with the kiss.

Turning my attention forward, I nod. "You heard, huh?"

"Who didn't?"

This makes me happy. That kiss had a purpose, and it wasn't to claim Sydney. But I'm definitely not upset that the purpose veered off course. Right to her bed.

"So, are you here to ask my permission to date her?"

Permission? Is he serious?

I have to slow down from laughing so hard. Sweat beads on my forehead and I wipe it off, stopping altogether. "Hold on," I say, holding up a finger, pulling in a breath. "I haven't laughed that hard in forever."

He stops, stands with his hands on his hips. "It wasn't that funny." His voice has an alarming notion of rightness and it rubs me the wrong way.

"I see that." I step closer to him, all humor drops from my face. He takes a step back.

That's right, back the fuck up.

He needs to understand his place in this equation, and it sure as hell isn't Sydney's gatekeeper. "If you think I need a blessing from you to be with the woman I have loved for over two years, you're fucking delusional."

Surprisingly, he stands tall, trying to mask his fear. The dilation in his eyes gives it away. Usually I would respect a man for standing up for what he believes, but he does not want to go toe to toe with me on this.

"It was nothing but a guess, Max. You wake me up to go running, yet we've never conversed except for business reasons. I don't know what to think."

Thunder rumbles overhead, pulling our attention to the skies. Clouds cluster together above us, threatening to release their wrath on us. I blow out a ragged breath, wondering where all this rage came from. And I'm not referring to the weather. Any threat to my relationship with Sydney, manufactured in my head or real, has me on guard.

Controlling my tone, I respond, "I brought you out here to tell you that Sydney and I are together. It's important you know since you're her manager. And a good friend."

He stares at me, lips twisted as he mulls over the new information. My eyes dart around at the people who jog past us rather than deal with the uncomfortable silence between us. I flinch from a drop of rain landing on my nose.

"Glad we talked," I say, slapping him on the back. "But we need to go."

I head in the hotel's direction, rain dropping rapidly now, but stop when I notice he's not coming. *What the ever-loving hell?* I spin around and he's still in the same spot. "What, Graham?"

He shakes his head, points my direction. "Why are you headed back? Scared of a little rain?"

My lips twitch. I didn't give the guy enough credit. I was going back for him, wasn't in the mood for some pussy whining about getting wet. Pushing forward, I jog past him and say, "I was giving you an out."

The sky never opens up to a torrential downpour, but enough to get us soaked. According to my watch, we ran for twelve miles, all in silence. The run is exactly what I needed to clear my head before meeting with the team.

Our shoes slosh and squeak against the tiled hotel lobby as we make our way to the elevator. People glance our way with sympathetic expressions at our drenched clothes like we were unfortunate to get caught out in the rain without an umbrella. A hotel staffer runs up to us with two towels in hand. We both mutter thanks. I wipe off my face and hair, hanging the towel around my neck.

For such a big hotel, the elevators should be quicker. I tap my finger against my leg, waiting.

"It's about time," Graham announces.

I glance at all three elevators, ready to jump on one, but none are even close to our level. "For what?" I say, turning my attention to him.

"It's about time you and Sky figured your shit out. I'm happy for you both." It took him all that time to say *that*? Is he blowing smoke up my ass? My brow cocks as I try to read him and his real intentions. He rolls his eyes and sighs. "I can't say I'm not concerned. I was there to pick up the pieces left of her when she lost..." He pauses and I nod in understanding. He doesn't need to finish the sentence, I was fucking there too. "You're in the same profession, *so to speak*, and I worry that next time there won't be pieces to pick up."

I get it. It's one of the many reasons I tried to stay away. It seems the power of a heart not only keeps you alive but decides without prejudice who to love. I was tired of fighting it.

"I can't promise things outside my control—"

His gasp stops me. "You're admitting you can't control everything?"

I narrow my eyes at his sarcasm. The elevator finally opens and we wait for it to empty before stepping into it. I press the buttons for the eleventh and twentieth floors. *"But* I can promise I'll do everything in my power to make sure we both stay safe," I say, ignoring his comment.

"Okay. You have my blessing." He smirks, walking off on his floor. *Smart ass.* "Time to go fix my pencil," he yells as the doors close.

A large hand slips inside just as the doors almost shut. The doors open again and Kase hops on. "Is that code for jacking off?" he jokes, pointing the direction Graham walked. I laugh.

"Nah. At least not this time." He chuckles but gives me a quizzical look after observing my wet clothes. "We went for a run. I need to change before the meeting starts so I'll meet you guys in the meeting room in ten."

"Got it, boss."

"What'd we find on Brett McDonald?" I ask, glancing up from my notepad. "We know that he delivered the first set of flowers."

The guys stare at me. *I swear I just asked a question.* Stone tilts back in his chair. Hudson crosses his arms and Kase lifts a brow as if waiting on *me* to say something.

It's clear as day, that's exactly what they're doing.

I throw my arms out. Let's get it over so we can move on. "Sydney and I are dating. Satisfied?" I pause for a beat, my gaze rounds the table meeting smirks and nods. I fight the burn on my face, dropping my eyes to my notes. There's never been a time I've had to announce my relationship with a woman. "Okay, moving on. What'd we find on Brett?" I steer the conversation back to business, leaving no room for questions.

"Nothing. No priors, a couple speeding tickets... on paper, he looks like an upstanding citizen," Stone states, holding up his record.

"Married?" I ask.

"Nope. Attended the University of New Mexico, where he grew up. I haven't found any link that would connect him to Sydney other than working for the tour company." I scratch my head, wondering if I misread him. It's possible he just has a crush on Sydney.

"I saw him," Kase says. "He was pissed. We need to watch him. Just because he's clean on paper doesn't mean he's not our guy."

"I agree. This is the last week of the tour, if he plans on doing something, it'll be soon." I sigh at my next bullet point. "Any updates on Rex?"

"Cody talked to the team. They're adamant about not knowing his whereabouts."

"Does he believe them?"

"He does."

"He didn't by chance ask about their last heist, did he?"

He smirks. "He did. They denied being involved in anything illegal." *Figures they care more about getting caught than their leader.* "He did some digging for any high-profile thefts in the weeks leading up to your mom's call. There was one - in Mexico." He slides over a printout of an article. I skim it, noting the dollar amount of the jewels stolen. 1.1 million.

Son of a bitch. Where the fuck you hiding, Rex?

"Tell him to get me all the info he can on the robbery."

I slide my phone over, search for Aiden's number and hit call. He answers on the first ring, "Hey hashtag boy." He will never let me live that down.

"Hey fucker, you're on speaker with the team."

He laughs. "Hey guys." They all return the greeting. "Any leads on Sydney's case?" His voice drops the humor. I fill him in on Brett, but the lack of anything else is disappointing to report.

"I'm calling for Rex. Know anything?"

"Other than he's an asshat little brother and has a questionable occupation?"

"Don't be bitter just because you guys can't catch him in the act." A slight sense of pride wells inside my chest. I'm not proud of what he does, but I have to respect that he has perfected his craft. If you're going to do something, do it right.

"Hardy har-har. It's just a matter of time." *That's if he's still alive.*

"He's missing."

The sound of a chair creaks in the background. "What? Why am I just hearing about this now?" Aiden grew up with Rex being around and as much as we both think he's a pain in the ass, he's like a little brother to Aiden too.

"Susie called a few weeks ago and said no-one has seen or heard from him. I figured he was just lying low for some reason." Guilt that I should have cared more stings. "I've had the guys looking, but he's vanished. I had an idea maybe the FBI had something to do with that."

"Not that I'm aware of. I'll look into it, brother."

"Thanks."

"You worry about keeping our girl safe. 'Cause you know if something happens to her, Addison will cut both our balls off. And I don't know about you, but I have eight more kids to have."

"Don't worry, she's definitely my priority."

The guys snicker and I shoot them a glare, shaking my head, holding my finger to my lips. After we hang up, Stone pipes in, "You didn't learn your lesson about keeping secrets from Addison?"

"Sydney wants to keep it on the down-low." My jaw tightens at the thought of her apprehension. I have to bite back the fear that her reason is she doesn't have enough trust in us. "I'm giving her a month. The only people that will know are in this room and Graham."

CHAPTER TWENTY-SIX

SYDNEY

Max knows how to keep a secret.

He also knows how to be sneaky. When I think of Max, romantic isn't an adjective I would use to describe him. Sexy, demanding, confident, and intense... *that* was what I expected. But staring at the small glass figurine of Tinkerbell that I found under my covers when pulling out my bed on the bus, I'm adding romantic to the list. The note attached to it reads,

Your flight path leads straight to my heart. ~M

Swoon.

Five days ago, we agreed we would give this a chance. It's been five days of misery. He's around me, yet we don't touch. And while he does these little things to let me know I'm on his mind, I think he's keeping his distance to make me want him more. It's working. *Max-1, Sydney-0.* Who's idea was it to keep this secret? Oh yeah, that would be yours truly. *That was a horrible idea.* I outline the wings on the figurine with my index finger and sigh.

In three days, we'll be in Phoenix and we sold out for two nights there. Which means a hotel. *And Max.* It's hard to believe the tour will be over in less than a week. Talk about a roller coaster ride. And I still love it. Other than the freak stalker, my stars are aligned, allowing me to see things I never imagined.

I fall asleep dreaming about the possibilities of tomorrow and every day after that. The sweet thoughts of music and Max. How they combine, I don't know, but it's the promise that kisses me to sleep tonight.

I roll over when I feel the bus stop and pull back the black heavy curtains. The light I expect to seep into my room doesn't come, rather it's still dark outside, and we're on the side of the highway. Worry has me sitting up, crawling to the end of my bed to peek through the drapes that separate me from the guy's bunks. Nobody is up yet. I crane my neck to listen for the bus driver and jump when my phone vibrates against the cup holder it's sitting in. My heart slams against my chest. What if my stalker is here? All the horror movies I've watched come to mind when the girl gets stranded on the side of the road, and almost always ends up dead.

"Stone," I whisper-yell, my nerves gripping hold. "Stone, wake up."

He rolls out of his bunk, only in a pair of sweatpants, holding his gun. "Wha… What's wrong," he says, fully alert, scanning the cabin of the bus.

"We're stopped. And I just got a text." I step back into my area and grab my phone, holding it out for him. He takes the phone, a smile creeps up one side of his face as he reads the text.

"I'm assuming you didn't read this?"

"No." I swipe it back, irritated with his mocking smile.

"Read it. I'm going back to bed." He yawns and crawls in his bunk. "Have fun," he murmurs, closing his curtain.

I glance down at the phone and notice it's from Max. Blowing out a breath; I attempt to release the crazy inside of me. *Why didn't I just peek at the text first?*

Hulk: Get dressed. Warm, layered, casual.

I stare at the text. He'll send another one with more info, right?

Because this is not enough. I shake my head. No, he's not. It's been five minutes since he sent this one.

Me: I need more info. Are we going to be outside? Public? Just us? How casual?

Just realizing how early it is, I groan.

Me: And why are we up at 4?

Hulk: Yes. Yes. No. Are there different ones? You'll see.

I match his answers with my questions and smile at his casual confusion. Yes, Max, there is. I decide on workout casual and pull out a pair of heather gray leggings with a long black v-neck t-shirt before I take a quick shower. The weather in Albuquerque is fifty-five degrees so I grab my thicker gray cardigan and my favorite slouchy beanie. It'll also help keep me under the radar of the public eye. *Hopefully.*

Thirty minutes later, I tread through the dark, quiet bus. When I slide the pocket door open to where Gus sits, Max is leaning against the dashboard, casually with his arms crossed, talking. My pulse picks up as I drink him in. Backward baseball cap, light washed jeans with a gray henley top that shows off his muscular arms underneath. *Oh, boy.* I squeeze the knit hat in my hands, wondering how I'm supposed to keep my hands off him while we're out in the public.

His lips part with a devilish grin. Gus turns in his seat. "Well, there she is. Good morning, Sky," he bellows, brightly.

I lean over to glance out the windshield to the pitch dark sky. "I wouldn't consider this morning yet."

He waves me off. "Just like they say, the early bird gets the worm." Memories of my dad saying that comes to mind. It was his favorite thing to say as I would drag myself into the kitchen before school started. He was always chipper and ready to start his day, but not without having breakfast with me.

"Aww, yes. But as Franklin D. Roosevelt said, '*I think we consider too much the good luck of the early bird and not enough the bad luck of the early worm*'." He hoots out loud, slapping his jeans. Max laughs, shaking his head as I close the door behind me so they don't wake everyone else up. My dad had the same response at my researched retort.

When I glance at Max, he winks at me. "So, are you the bird or the worm?"

I bite my lip, not able to keep the dirtiness of that question out of my mind. I will volunteer to be the worm if Max is the bird. Except, there's no bad luck when Max is doing the eating. My cheeks heat and I clear my throat, glancing down at my Nike shoes.

"We'll clear that up later," Max says with humor in his voice, pulling my attention back to him. "We need to go, though."

"You two have fun. I'll see you later in the afternoon," Gus says, opening the door.

I follow Max out of the bus, the crisp air hitting my face full blast. I pull in a breath, surprised by the coldness. Brrr. I put on my hat and tighten my cardigan around my waist.

"It'll heat as the sun rises," Max says, pulling me into his chest and kissing my cold lips. When he pulls back, he looks at my hat and tugs at the puff ball at the top. "Cute."

I huff, fixing the hat on my head. "You're like a five-year-old sometimes."

"You weren't thinking of me being a five-year-old a couple minutes ago." He flashes a knowing grin and then grabs my hand, leading me to the back of the bus where his black SUV sits. I shake my head as my cheeks warm. *No, I wasn't.* I slide into the passenger side after he opens my door, the inside air smells of leather and Max. Noticing a coffee cup in his console, I pick it up only to find it empty.

"We'll get some," he says, sensing my disappointment.

As soon as we pull out, I ask, "Are we going to watch the sunrise somewhere?" I glance out my window to the dark mountains where I assume we're heading.

"You'll see."

I narrow my eyes at him. "You know I have a concert tonight, right?"

He laughs. "Yes, I'm aware. Don't worry, I'll have you to the venue by noon. Graham already enlightened me what he'll do if I don't."

"His bark is worse than his bite," I snicker. Reaching over, Max grabs my hand and links our fingers. I revel in his warmth, loving how he makes me feel.

"I'm happy to see you."

"Me too," I say, staring at his profile. Can a guy drive sexy? Because, with one hand high on the wheel, his body in a relaxed yet confident position, his tattoo peeking out from under his henley, I want to crawl in his lap.

After driving fifteen minutes, when we pull into a VIP parking lot and park, my attention switches to the sea of cars parked and my nerves flip flop from desire to concern. "Um, Max. This is a little more public than I expected." He knows how hard it is for me to go anywhere without being flocked by fans.

He turns his hat around, low on his forehead, making him appear more youthful. "I have a plan. But you don't look like Sky without all the makeup and dressed up." I shouldn't feel offended by that, but I do. "You look beautiful. You look like Sydney. *My Sydney.*"

"Do you not like the way I look on stage?"

He drops his head. "You're the most gorgeous woman on this earth, no matter what you have on."

I eye him for a beat before saying, "Good answer."

The sky lightens to a cool blue, the transition from night to day right before the sun comes up. As soon as we're out of the car, Max holds my hand, not caring who sees and I don't either.

"Albuquerque Balloon Fiesta," I read the sign out loud. "I've always heard about this and seen gorgeous pictures. Have you been here before?"

"I haven't."

It makes my heart happy that we're both experiencing something together for the first time. I'm sure there aren't many things that Max hasn't done. Our first stop is coffee and a breakfast burrito. There are lines all around us and I relax when no one pays any attention to us.

"This thing is huge," I say, holding up the foil-wrapped burrito that has to be at least five pounds. "We could have split one."

He shakes his head. "Hell no. I'm eating all of this." He unwraps his. "You can't get a better green chile burrito anywhere else. Don't worry, I'll eat what you don't." His gaze moves to my burrito.

I pull the warm burrito to my chest. "Since you put it that way, maybe I don't want to share."

My response amuses him. "Spiteful and confident. Two of your sexiest traits, Tink."

I take a sip of my coffee and lift a brow over the rim. "You can sweet talk me all you want, you're still not getting my burrito."

Glancing around when his laughter is drowned out by a loud noise, we notice a crew of people rolling out a balloon, laying the basket on its side. "Oh! One is being blown up. Let's go watch before it's too late."

"Babe. There are over two hundred balloons that will take off during the first wave. We can miss one," he jokes.

My eyes widen. "How many waves are there?" He takes a large bite of his burrito right when I ask so he holds up two fingers. "Okay, then let's sit and eat." He nods in approval, taking another large bite.

When I've had all I can manage, I sigh, handing him the other half of my burrito. He smiles and accepts it. "Did you at least like it?" he teases.

"Yes. It was delicious, but it was a lot of food." I rub my full belly and take a sip of coffee, to wash down the spicy taste of green chile. He takes four bites to finish the last half.

Wiping off his mouth, he steps out of the picnic table. "Ready, beautiful?" God, I love when he sweet talks me.

I hop off the bench, nodding in excitement. I've been eyeing the balloons as they pop up for fifteen minutes. There are rows and rows of colorful balloons. We're able to walk right up to them. The heat from the blow torch thing they use blanket us in warmth. The anticipation builds, while observing them. We back up as one of the workers tilt a basket upright. The crew works feverishly to keep the balloon in one place so it doesn't take off or take out the balloon going up next to it. I tear my eyes off the impressive sight to glance around.

"No way! There's Smokey the Bear!" I point to the head of a bear that everyone learns about in grade school. "Only you can prevent wildfires," I say, repeating the slogan my students learned. Max chuckles at my teacher's voice.

There are rows and rows of balloons. Many kissing each other as the field overflows with the most vibrant primary colors. I cheer with the crowd whenever one lifts off. Max just stands back, enjoying my enthusiasm.

When he glances down at his watch, he says, "Time to go."

I freeze in place, my smile falling. "It's only eight. We have four hours before I have to be anywhere. Why are we leaving?" I whine.

"We're not leaving, Tink. We just need to keep moving."

"Oh." I shift from foot to foot. "Sorry. *Totally* misread that." I shrug, stepping into his chest. He wraps his arms around me.

"There's no way I'd leave now. I'm having too much fun watching all the different emotions cross your face." He slips his fingers through mine and we continue walking down a row. One by one, until the sky is filled with clusters of balloons. I wince when two of them seem like they're about to collide but blow out a sigh of relief when one operator pulls up, and the other goes down. Geez, it's intense up there. I hear Max chuckle next to me.

"That could have been a disaster." I pinch his arm for making fun of me. "I'm a little passionate."

"A little?" He quips, stopping at a balloon being rolled out. One guy from the crew stares at us. Oh, no. He recognizes us.

"Maybe we should keep going," I whisper to Max, knowing he saw the guy too. I turn to walk away, but Max wraps his arm around my waist, stopping me.

"Max, it's good to see you," a deep voice booms over the crowd.

My head jerks back around to see Max and the guy shaking hands. "It's good to see you, too. It's been too long. Brecken, this is Sydney."

His knowing eyes jump from mine to Max's with a questioning glance. "Now you know why you signed an NDA," Max states. He nods in understanding. I wish I knew what was going on.

"Got it." His gaze turns back to me. "Sydney, great meeting you." He holds out his hand and I slip mine into his leather-gloved palm.

"Brecken runs a security team here in Albuquerque," Max explains.

"You too. Is this your balloon?"

"Yes, ma'am. We all have our hobbies. Mine doesn't come with a plane and a parachute though."

Max chuckles with a shake of his head. "Breck, the invitation is always open."

"I'll take you up on that someday," he says, walking backward. "Don't go anywhere. We have to catch up." The smile remains on his handsome yet rugged face as he returns to work.

Standing there with Max's arms wrapped around me, we watch the blue and red balloon pop up. Brecken jumps into the wicker basket and yells at Max. "Ready?" My body tenses as Max pushes me toward the basket.

"Wait. What?" I say in shock. Max doesn't give me time to think as he pushes me forward. "Max!" I try to dig my heels into the grass, but Max has a firm grip on my waist and he lifts me an inch off the ground.

"You didn't tell her?" Brecken laughs.

I give up the fight because we're causing a scene. Rather, I wait till we're at the basket and turn around, slapping his chest. "Max Shaw," I grind out through clenched teeth. "What are you doing?"

His smile widens. "We're going for a ride. I thought you'd be excited."

"You haven't given me time to feel anything but surprise, you dominant ass." I pull in a deep breath, adjusting my clothes that went askew from being forced forward. His eyes stay planted on me as he shoves his hands in his pockets, waiting for me to gather my wits. My eyes dart from the balloon back to Max. "Are we really doing this?" My voice comes out an octave higher than I expected.

He nods, flashing me a lopsided grin. I shake my hands out, a thrill of frightened anticipation crawling up my spine. Nibbling on my bottom lip, I fist his henley. "If we drop out of that thing, you better land first to break my fall."

The four guys holding the basket down all chuckle. Max pulls his hands out of his pockets and covers mine. "I promise I'll land first."

"Okay," I say, swallowing the lump of nerves in my throat, looking up into the hollow balloon. I shake my head. Nope, don't look up into the piece of cloth that could deflate or pop. A squeal escapes my lips as Max scoops me up and places me into the basket. I grab onto the side when Max lifts himself in. With his weight, the guys have to work extra hard to keep it still. "See, I knew there was a reason you shouldn't have eaten the other half of my burrito."

"You have a funny one there," Brecken jests.

"Yep, she's a real comedian." He slaps me on the ass before sliding up behind me. "You don't have to have an iron-clad grip there, Tink," he says, peering at my white knuckles. "We haven't even left the ground yet."

"No, but we're about to. It's our turn." Brecken pulls the cord that fires the burner.

"Oh, my gosh," I shriek, jolting around, gripping Max's shirt again as I dig my face into his chest. The buzz of cheers mixed in with the crew's directions drown out the sound of my heart drumming in my ears. Max encases me with his arms and I focus on him.

"Are you scared?" he whispers into my ear.

I rock my head. "Nope, I'm just trying to become one with your shirt." His chest vibrates against my head. "Yes, I'm scared, captain obvious."

"Good. Because some of the best things in life are the ones you have to dig deep inside yourself to try." My shoulders drop as I try to calm down. "Tink, you were born to fly."

I pull back, humor flashing in my eyes. "That is not in the literal sense, Max. If I fall, I won't spread my wings and fly away."

"And if you're in a car accident, you're not promised to walk away either." He lifts a challenging brow. "You don't want to miss this, I promise." He leans down, brushes his lips against mine. The gentle kiss morphs into a passionate one as he pulls me into his body, one hand grips my ass, one in my hair. It's as if he knows the exact point when my body and mind submit to him, when everything else around us doesn't matter, that he pulls back reminding me where we are. And we're not alone. My cheeks flush in embarrassment.

I glance over my shoulder at Brecken. "Sorry," I say, feeling the need to apologize for our PDA.

He holds his hand up. "No need to apologize. I'm just over here, blown away that Max has a romantic side. Who knew?"

Max roars out in laughter. "She definitely brings out the worst in me."

I stab him with my finger in the stomach. "And you like it."

His eyes warm, finding mine, as he says, "I love it."

Oh! Butterflies flutter in my belly. *Did he just tell me he loved me?*

His gaze is focused behind me and the way his eyes glow with wonderment makes me turn in his arms. *No, he didn't.* Not wanting to miss the beautiful piece of artwork in front of me, I push back all thoughts of love and the hope that he said it.

There's still a bite to the early morning air as we rise higher. Leaning my head back against Max, I watch as we join the other balloons, all moving in the same direction, like a flock of geese. I begin to sing *"99 Red Balloons"* by Nena to tamper down some of my nerves. The basketweave tattoo on my palm will probably last for days. But that's okay, because I'm not letting go until we're safe on the ground. We float alongside a river, surrounded by luscious greenery. "What river is that?"

"Rio Grande," Brecken answers behind us. My stomach drops at the sound of swooshing. The balloon lowers closer and closer to the water.

I lean around Max. "I didn't want to go for a swim," I nervously say.

A smile dances on his lips as he shrugs a shoulder. "Just thought you might want a closer glimpse."

"Nope. I'm good, thanks."

The rest of the trip, Brecken behaves and we glide through the sky. By the time we land, I'm ready to go again despite my fears. It truly was a phenomenal experience.

And Max and I just had our first official date.

CHAPTER TWENTY-SEVEN

SYDNEY

"Don't you have a company to run?"

My red fingernail drags across his taut chest making random shapes. We're in Phoenix, our last stop on the tour. Nothing from my stalker for the three weeks Max and his team have been here. Yet, so much has happened in those three weeks between me and Max. Fear and uncertainty mounts daily the closer we get to me returning home. I've let go of the guilt, opening my heart to Max, but now I wonder if it was a bad idea. We lead two different lifestyles. *On two different coasts.* I tap down the negative emotions, wanting to live in this moment for a little longer.

"I'm doing my job right now. Keeping you safe."

"You're laying in my bed, naked. Is this how you keep all your clients *safe*?" I tease.

His hand lazily runs down my back, chills pebbled my skin and I yelp when he smacks my ass. "No," he chuckles. "I don't mix work and play."

Lifting slightly, I rest my chin on my hand. My thumb brushes over his nipple and he glances down at me with a lifted brow. "You're setting a bad precedent, boss man."

The room spins as he flips me to my back with ease. He looms over me and I shimmy up the bed to move away from his heavy thigh pressed against my core.

"At least you understand how this works." My brows furrow and he laughs at my confusion. "I am the boss. Always remember that." He says it in a joking manner, but he's not. His need for control is paramount in his daily life. I'm okay with that as long as he doesn't try to control *me*.

My eyes shine up to his. "You're the boss. Now go boss someone into getting us some breakfast, I'm starving. And you're super heavy." I wiggle underneath him until he rolls his massive body to the side of me. Watching him push off the bed, the sheets drape off his strong body until they slip off and I bite my lip, wondering if there was ever a better built man. When the shower turns on, I roll over and snatch the phone off the side table.

Ever since the night of the awards, the rumor mill has been going nuts trying to find out who Max is. His guys give him hell, reading all the comments from the various social media sites. The brazen comments women leave on posted pictures of him are crazy. An article pops up on my search I hadn't seen before. *Who is the real # AMAsmostwanted?*

I dart my eyes to the bathroom, making sure Max isn't standing there, and still hear the shower so I click the link. An article from Page six pops up. *Oh, shit.* Part of me hoped I would find a personal blog, or even a known paparazzi post that everyone knows is full of shit. But nope, this is a legit resource people read daily.

"Billionaire bodyguard, Max Shaw, is tall, dark and dangerous. And I'm not talking about his looks." I gasp, reading the article. Despite knowing it's about Max, it's like I'm reading about a stranger. Why didn't I know any of this?

Engrossed in reading, I don't realize Max is in the room until he says, "Food will be here in twenty minutes."

I jump and instinctually close out my phone. *Why do I do that?*

He caught me red-handed, yet I try to hide the evidence. With a cocked brow, he stalks to the bed. I sit up, lean against the grey tuft headboard and grip the sheets over my breasts.

"You're a horrible liar," he says, with an amused smirk.

I huff in defense. "I haven't lied about anything."

"What were you doing?"

"Nothing." The word falls from my mouth before I can stop it, realizing he just set me up.

His laugh echoes in the room as I stick my tongue out. "You tricked me."

I squeal as he grabs my blanketed foot and yanks me to a laying down position. The smell of soap and deodorant wafts in the air. I blow the hair that escaped my rat nest on top of my head out of my face. Max kneels on the bed, a white towel hangs low on his hips. He straddles me, gripping each of my hands and pinning them to my sides with his legs so I can't move.

"I should teach you a lesson about lying to me. I won't have it," he states, leaving no room for argument. I watch as his fingers loosen the towel, opening it to reveal how hard he is. "Still hungry?" he muses, inching up a little on his knees, bringing his cock inches from my mouth. My breathing quickens and my mouth waters as I lick my lips.

He deems this a punishment? I should be bad more often.

He hums as my gaze fixates on his hand, pumping himself a couple times. All my nerve endings tingle with desire in anticipation. Until he reaches behind him and snatches the phone out of my hand. I jerk to meet his eyes, disappointment meets disappointment. Although, mine is fueled by desire, his... displeasure.

When he rolls off me, I blow out a ragged sigh, irritated with myself that I'm angry. I'm the one hiding something. Ignoring his glances, I scoot to the side of the bed. "I hope your blue balls make your dick fall off," I spat before putting a shirt over my head. He pulls up a pair of basketball shorts and sits back down.

His smile is disarming, making it hard to stay mad. I shimmy into my panties and sit on the chair, bringing my knees to my chest as I watch him mess with my phone.

"Let's see what we have here."

I smile inwardly as he opens my phone and meets a password screen. He types in six numbers without so much of a pause. "How do you know my password?" I panic, thrusting up and reaching for my phone.

"It's entertaining you think you can stop me." He holds my phone away from me with one hand, pushing me back with the other.

"You don't play fair," I snicker, giving up the fight. "And we're going to talk about privacy."

His eyes dart up from my phone. "First, playing fair was never my game. Second, when your safety is involved, it's my business to know everything. No. Fucking. Secrets." I swallow at the intensity of his voice.

I plop back down on the chair. "It wasn't even about me," I mutter.

He stands and walks over to me, holds out my phone without looking at the article. "I don't like secrets, Sydney."

So you've said. The way my real name rolls off his tongue, it's punishment in itself. I don't unfold my arms from around my knees. Max's jaw tightens and his Adam's apple bobs as he swallows hard, staring down at me. "Sorry."

I grab my phone. "That *almost* sounded sincere."

He mutters a few curse words. "It was," he snaps, pacing the floor. "What am I supposed to think when I walk into a room and you obviously hide something from me? I'm just supposed to look the other way? Because if that's how relationships work, I can tell you right now, we're going to have a huge problem."

"I didn't mean to hide it. It was a knee jerk reaction." That's a slight lie. I'm worried how he'll react when he finds out everyone knows who he is. Max's job relies on him being a private person and his life was just put on the front cover of Page Six. Because of

me. I sigh, pulling up the article on my phone and holding it up for
him to take back. "It's about you," I whisper.

His brows shoot up and he takes it back. I watch for any reaction as he reads it. Typical Max, his face is set in stone the whole
time. When he's done, he turns my phone off, placing it on the
table next to me and sits on the bed with his arms crossed.

"I'm sure you have a lot of questions."

"Um, I guess," I hesitate, not ready for this conversation.
Instead, I was ready for him to be furious, call Stone to take down
their network, send Kase to threaten the journalists. Just not this.
Not yet. "Are you not mad?"

He shrugs a shoulder. "I'm surprised it took them this long."

"Oh."

"Tink, I was prepared to be in the public eye the night I went to
the awards with you. Nothing in that article is false or character
damaging. They didn't need to dig hard because it's not hidden."

My shoulders drop and I chew on my lip. "Except, I didn't
know." I've known Max for over two years and I'm dating him, yet
according to that article, I don't know a thing about him.

He observes me. "Did you learn anything that would make you
feel differently about me?"

"No," I say, throwing my arms out. "But your dad was Zachary
Lewis. Max, he built like half of New York City. The Lewister Hotel
is named after him. That article said that you were his only heir to
a couple billion dollars. Billions, Max!"

He chuckles, standing up and takes a couple long strides and
then squats in front of me. He tugs each of my legs off the chair
and nestles in between them. "You knew I had money, babe. And
do you introduce yourself to people by telling them who your
father is?"

I snort. "No, but all my dad left me was a mom who hates me."

I love you, Daddy. I glance up. Just in case he's listening. Don't
get me wrong, I miss him every day and wish he was still here to
see how I finally made it. He would be so proud. It's been three

years since I heard his laughter. Saw his face light up as we watched a Cowboys game together. Argued over whether peanut M&M's or plain M&M's were better. I drop my eyes and focus on the tiny freckle on my thigh, not wanting Max to see my emotions getting the best of me.

"My dad might have left me a lot of money, but what he didn't give me, your dad gave you in spades." I meet his eyes, wondering what he's referring to. "My dad loved me in his own way, but like my mom, he didn't have time for a kid either. I saw my dad maybe three times a year." That breaks my heart. A boy needs his father. He is right though, my dad had to love me enough for two people.

"Is that why you have your mom's maiden name?"

He shakes his head. "Shaw is Dan's last name. He adopted me when I was five at the request of Zack." I pull back, surprised the request came from his real dad. "He was afraid his life as a public figure would affect my life negatively, so they decided that was best for me."

I let out a sarcastic laugh. "And here you are, thanks to me, in the public eye."

"Again, let's not worry about that." His lips reach mine for a chaste kiss. "Any other questions?" he whispers and I shake my head. The simple brush of his lips makes me forget what else was in the article. I'll learn about Max organically like all other new relationships.

Not long after eating our room service food, we pack up to head to the venue. Max reaches for the door handle but doesn't turn it. Instead, he whips around and pulls me into his body. His grip tightens around my waist and he kisses me until I'm gasping for breath. When he lets go of me, I brace myself with a hand on the wall after our passionate exchange, needing to find my balance before I can walk.

His wicked smile and the gleam in his eyes makes my knees weak. No man has ever looked at me like Max does. Dominating, desire and genuine interest all wound up tight within steel-blue eyes. When he's with me, his attention never waivers making me feel worshipped. It's an addictive quality.

"That'll have to last me until I can sneak into your dressing room." He winks and walks out, leaving me still breathless. The thought doesn't help dull the craving, it just intensifies it. Thinking of him bending me over the couch in my dressing room, taking me from behind, fast and hard. I groan out of frustration.

"Dammit, Sydney. If you don't stop thinking about Max, you'll run out of dry underwear," I whisper to myself.

I grab my bag off the floor and meet Max's amusing smile in the hallway. "You can always go without." He wags his brows.

Slapping his arm, I roll my eyes. "You weren't supposed to hear that." He waits for the door to close all the way before we leave. "So, if I can't have any secrets, how am I ever going to plan a surprise party for you?" I joke as we walk down the long corridor to the elevator. His hand brushes against mine and I want to slip my fingers through his. The uncertainty of what happens after the tour always stops me. Except, our month is almost up and I'm positive he won't allow me an extension to figure it out.

Max presses the down button, staring at the silver doors in deep thought. The elevator dings and the doors open. Typical Max waits for me to enter before he does. As soon as the doors close, he answers without humor, "You don't."

CHAPTER TWENTY-EIGHT

MAX

"When you're settled back, we should have dinner."

I stare at the five-foot-nine, scrawny guy wearing a suit with pants that are too short. I remember when I was in school and guys would grow out of their pants, revealing what color socks they were wearing. Those are the kids that got made fun of. Since when did high waters and loafers with no socks become the *in* thing? And what the fuck is he asking Sydney out to dinner for?

She awkwardly laughs, sending me a quick glance back. I raise a brow, wondering what her next move will be. She breaks our contact, turning her attention to *Mr. Highwaters*. I'm standing a couple feet away from her because I'm supposed to be the body-guard. She has till the end of this week to fix that because this sucks.

"Digby, we should. I'll give you a call."

Digby? What the fuck kind of name is that? I'm surprised this guy made it out of high school alive. I glare at the guy, fisting my hands in my slacks as he stares at her with inappropriate thoughts. The quick drop of his eyes to her boobs might not have been caught by Sydney, but it sure the hell was by me. He might not make it out of here alive.

"It was great seeing you again. We'll talk soon," Syd says. *Over my dead body.* He leans forward giving her a kiss on each cheek.

"Ciao, Sky." He spins on his loafers and walks away, having no idea how close he came to losing those lips. I tinker with the small knife inside my pocket. Sydney turns, smiling at someone behind me, sending up a quick wave.

"Max," she says through a smile. "Please calm down. I can sense your anger."

I level my shoulders, releasing my fists and step next to her. "I wouldn't be angry if I was by your side," I say under my breath. *And dipshit Digby wasn't flirting with you.* She tips her chin up, a look of remorse flitters across her face. "Sorry," I sigh, dropping my head. This isn't the time to be having this conversation. Or the time for me to make her feel bad. Rather, she should celebrate her first successful tour. The label is throwing a party for Preston and Sky, welcoming them home. And she deserves the party, not my misplaced jealousy.

She'd never go for someone named Digby, anyway.

"I'll go get a drink at the bar." I motion to the cash bar at the other side of the party.

"I'd rather you be by me," she whispers.

Despite wanting to hear those words, they piss me off. "I can't be by you and *not* touch you. I won't be far." I flash a small smile and wink, masking my irritation. At the bar, watching her from afar, the night she got engaged to Damon slams into me. I try to swallow the distaste in my mouth, hating that I'm comparing that night to right now.

That night she was a regret. Tonight, she's my future.

I just need to find the right solution for both of us, considering our living situations are on two different coasts. There is no way in hell I'll let that put a wedge in between us.

"Stop brooding, Max. You should be excited, your girl is finished with the tour," Graham says, patting me on the back, then ordering a dirty martini. As soon as he gets it, he pops an olive in his mouth, putting two left on the toothpick back in the glass. He lifts his glass to toast and I clink my beer bottle against it.

"That I can drink to." Graham leans against the bar in his bright blue suit and yellow bow tie, scanning the crowd. It amazes me how much brighter Los Angeles is compared to New York City.

"So, what happens next?" he asks without looking at me.

I glance at him over the top of my beer, then wipe the excess off my lip. "I would think you'd be better equipped to answer what is next for Sky than I would." He gives me an incredulous stare.

"You know what I mean." I shake my head and shrug, not assuming anything. "You and Sky?"

"We haven't discussed the technicalities, but we'll make it work."

He pops another olive in his mouth. "I hope so. You're good for her. She hasn't been this happy since she showed up on my doorstep." Graham will always be in my good graces because of how he helped Sydney when I couldn't.

I find her in the crowd, surrounded by a few of her bandmates and more high-water wearing executives. Her laugh is contagious in the group, making me smile as she works her magic. Glancing down at Graham's pant legs, I'm not surprised at what I find. "Why, Graham? Why do men think that looks good?" I say, pointing down to his bare ankles.

His eyes follow the path of my finger and he laughs when he sees what I'm referring to. "It's called fashion, Max." He scans my black slacks — that go all the way to my black dress shoes — and white button-up shirt, humming to himself. "You should let my stylist take you shopping while you're in LA."

"What the fuck for? I look good." I tug on my shirt, daring him to disagree with me.

"You look damn good," a brunette purrs, coming up to my side. Graham's eyes pop open wide, watching her slide her arm around mine. "You should dance with me." The smell of cheap wine and perfume invade my nostrils.

I remove her arm from around mine, flashing her a fake smile. "Thanks, but I'm good." I cast my eyes at Sydney, finding her glaring at the woman before her eyes jump to mine. I take a long pull of my beer, wondering what she's thinking. She's not happy, but is she upset enough to come over here and claim what's hers? When the redhead runs her hand over my bicep and squeezes, Syd's petite body stiffens. I'm tempted to let her keep it there if it'll bring my beautiful woman over.

"Wow, are you a bodybuilder?"

"Lady! He's not interested," Graham snaps. She huffs, removing her hand, haughtily tilts her head back as she pivots and stomps off. Graham downs his drink and sets the glass on the bar. "It's a wonder why I like men." He makes me laugh out loud.

When another hand snakes through my arm, I open my mouth to tell whoever it is, *I'm not interested.* Again. Instead, I'm met with ice-blue eyes and a scent of vanilla that I'll never get tired of. Her smile lights up her face and I wait for her to do something, unsure where this is going. She's in the driver's seat and I'm the passenger holding on for dear life.

I hate being the passenger.

"Trying to get another hashtag?" she muses.

I shrug. "There's only one hashtag I want." Her brows draw together. Dipping my head so my words don't carry, I say, "Hashtag off the market."

She bites her lip, leaning into me and I take a deep inhale and groan. "I can help with that," she murmurs, slightly out of breath, lifting her face. Her lips brush over mine. When she pushes into me, deepening the kiss, I can't help but wrap my arm around her waist. The fear of her backing away too soon before I can get my fix of her overwhelms me. She might have started this, but I'm finishing. Hold on Tink, because I'm back in the driver's seat.

She moans into my mouth when I nip at her lip and my dick

jumps at the sound. Her sequined dress is rough under my hand as I palm her ass. It's not until Graham squeals in delight that I pull back.

"I need a man to kiss me like that," he says. "Know any?" Sydney and I pull apart and laugh. Not sure any of my friends fit his type. "So, does this mean the secret is out?"

I peer down at Sydney wondering the same thing. She nods, slipping her fingers through mine, sending a bolt of relief through my bones. "We'll tell Addison and Aiden tomorrow." She jerks her head over to Graham. "But G, don't say anything to anyone until after we talk to our friends." His lips turn down in disappointment.

"Fine. What's another day?" He waves his hand in the air. "I'm off to find me a hashtag *I'm off the market* boyfriend." We watch him disappear into the crowded dance floor.

"Are you sure you're ready?" I say, pulling her into me, concerned she might change her mind. Once she gives me the green light, there's no turning back.

My phone vibrates in my pocket, interrupts us. Her wicked smile from the vibration causes a deep-throated growl to escape my lips. "With that short dress, it wouldn't take too private of a place for me to put that imagination of yours to use."

Her body quivers against me at the suggestion. My eyes wander around the room, searching for a place as I pull the phone out of my pocket. It can only be Stone, which is the reason I'm looking. Otherwise, we'd be headed straight to the dark corridor I just saw.

Stone: call me asap.

The phone rings a couple times before he picks up. "Sorry to interrupt you, boss, but I think we found Rex. And it's not good."

Fuck. "Where are you?"

"Already outside."

I glance at Sydney, my lips puckered with annoyance as I hang up the phone. "Sorry. We need to postpone the tongue licking you were about to get."

She gasps, covering her mouth with her hand, her cheeks burn red. "Max Shaw!"

I chuckle, bringing her lips to my mouth for a quick kiss. "I have to meet Stone outside."

"I'm coming too," she says, readying herself.

"Hmm, I'm not sure that's a good idea."

She tilts her head with defiance, putting her hands on her hips. "So, you'll leave me in here without security?"

I scan the room, filled with hundreds of people, drinking and I'm sure a few doing drugs. Sydney's stalker is still out there and can be in this room. I growl, grabbing her hand and pull her along with me. I'd rather she not hear details, but her staying in here by herself is not an option.

As soon as we hit the cool crisp air, the window to a black SUV rolls down and Kase nods. Ignoring the flashes and the questions being thrown at us, I pull Syd in closer to my side until we approach the SUV. The door swings open and I hover over Sydney while she climbs in. The second the door is shut, Hudson drives off.

"Wait," Sydney panics. "I didn't know we were leaving. I can't leave my own party."

I rest my hand on her tanned thigh and she pushes it away as she shimmies her dress down. "We're going back. We just can't have paparazzi standing outside the door while we talk."

"Oh. Hey guys."

They all return the greeting. Stone turns in his seat, handing me an iPad. "We got word from a reliable source that Rex is in Mexico. That's where he's at." I glance at the map, the red dot representing the place he's supposedly at.

"Do we know if he's alive?"

Stone winces. "We haven't been able to determine that. The source hasn't seen him in a while." I want to ask who the source is, but not with Sydney around. Running my hands across my jaw, I'm at a loss what to do. That town, it's run by a cartel. It's not good news since Rex hasn't been heard from in over a month. I pinch the bridge of my nose, leaning on my elbow against the door. The danger I'd be putting my guys in because of the stupid shit my brother got himself into weighs on me. But so does leaving Sydney with her stalker still out there.

"Max," Sydney whispers. I turn toward her and she puts her hand in mine. The glow from the streetlamp lights up her face, outlining the delicate, perfect oval. "Go find your brother."

"I can't leave you. Not now."

"Your brother needs you. And I can't carry that guilt too." I bring her hand to my mouth, hating I have to make this decision.

"I'll stay with Syd," Stone says. I blow out a ragged breath and nod.

"You and Hudson watch her twenty-four seven." I stare at them until they both give me confirmation. I rarely demand a response, my guys know what to do, but I need it this time. "Kase, you're with me. We'll leave at five a.m."

"Hudson, take us to our hotel."

I jerk my head toward Sydney at her demand.

"Yes, ma'am." Hudson puts the SUV in drive and pulls forward.

"I thought we were going back to your party?"

"We are." She winks at me. "But we have a meeting that we postponed that needs to be addressed."

I lick my lips and nod, trying to hold it together in front of the team. "You're the boss."

CHAPTER TWENTY-NINE

SYDNEY

The stale air from the lack of life hits me when I step inside my apartment. I guess I should be thankful I don't smell cat shit. Glancing around, I'm half expecting Moxi to come prancing out of the bedroom before I remember she's at the neighbor's place. She wouldn't have welcomed me, anyway. Hopefully Gracie fell in love with her enough she won't bring her back.

"Hudson was just here, checked everything out," Stone says, standing in the doorway. I nod, barely able to wave my hand in the air. Max and I were up all night, a marathon of unadulterated passion. My whole body is deliciously sore. That man made sure I wouldn't be forgetting him anytime soon. "I'll be right outside in my car if you need anything. Hudson and I will alternate shifts. You have our numbers in your phone if you need anything."

"Got it. Thanks, Stone." He chuckles when I strain to open my heavy eyelids.

"Go get some rest," he says before he turns and walks away. "And lock your door." Yeah. Got it.

My bags hit the floor right before I make a beeline to my bed. As I pass the thermostat, I jab my finger on the down arrow until the air conditioner kicks on. Sixty-six. Perfect. Fully clothed, I snuggle into my comforter, my exhausting getting the best of me. Just as I close my eyes, there's a knock at the door. *Go away.* It better not be Stone. The only other people who know I'm home, wouldn't be knocking already so I ignore it and relax again. Except the knock becomes a pound. Whoever it is, isn't leaving. Throwing the covers to the side, I stomp toward the door and swing it open.

"Gracie." I stare at the teenager who has a fake smile plastered on her face.

"I thought that was you coming into your apartment."

I yawn and nod. I hope she hasn't sent out a massive text telling all her friends. I'm not in the mood to deal with fans right now. "You caught me. Did you need something?"

She looks down and I follow her gaze to an orange cat carrier placed on the ground. Green eyes glow between the grated door and a long, "meeeooowww," makes me smile. Seems I missed the spotted feline. I lift my head to meet Gracie's hard stare.

"Your cat is not very nice. She was mean to Dexter the whole time." I purse my lips to hide my smile. Dexter is a hyper labradoodle. I thought it would be good for Moxi to have an overzealous friend rather than stay at a boarding facility. At least, she'd be free to roam.

"I'm sorry. She can be a little turd sometimes." Gracie huffs and rolls her eyes. Turning in place, I grab my purse off the entryway table. "Here's some extra money for dealing with her. I really appreciate it." I hand her a fifty-dollar bill even though I had already paid her before I left. Her eyes light up and her smile turns genuine. Best thing to do for a pissed off teenager, *give them money.*

"Thanks, Sky. Let me know if you need me to watch her again." She beams, turning and jogging off. My mouth falls open as I watch her gleefully jog down the stairs. I turn my attention to the meowing.

"You know, you could at least be good while I'm gone," I say, picking up the carrier and bringing her inside. As soon as she's free, she continues to yell at me while pacing the room. "I hear you, I do. But you can be pissy by yourself, I'm going to bed."

She follows close behind me, hopping in the bed too. I'm hoping she shuts up soon. My eyelids turn heavy and I sink further into the therapeutic bed as I relax. Moxi kisses me on the nose and I grin knowing she missed me too.

"Ouch!" I shoot up, rubbing the bite sting on the tip of my nose. The spite filled cat walks to her pillow, circles a couple times and lays down. *You little asshole.* She closes her eyes, satisfied with herself. "You are a big meanie," I huff and lay back down. Well, I know where you're going next time. To see your best friend, Dexter.

My phone dings on my nightstand. I stare at it, debating if I have enough energy to reach over. After it dings a reminder, I muster up what little energy I have left and roll over to where I can grab it.

Hulk: Listen to *All to Myself* by Dan + Shay

The song is already on my Spotify favorites so it's easy to find. I press play, holding the phone to my chest, listening to every word as if Max is singing to me. My eyes close and I drift off to blissful sleep.

I OPEN my eyes to noise. My foggy brain can't place where the voices are coming from. Rubbing sleep out of my eyes, I sit up in bed and realize it's the TV. I glance at the empty pillow next to me. *Noooo, it better not be.* That four-legged jackass is going to end up locked in the bathroom. I stumble through my dark room and sure as hell, I'm met with green glowing eyes. Sitting right next to the remote. I growl at her, snatch the remote up and press the off button like it's at fault for waking me. "Are you done now? Can I get some sleep?" Her meows don't stop me from returning to my bed. Maybe I'll ship her to Max's house. She liked him.

I glance at my phone feeling like a bad girlfriend for not calling. The thought jars me. *His girlfriend.* Picking it up, the screen brightens, showing it's almost midnight. Nope, not going to call. He'll think something's wrong and the only thing wrong right now is I have an evil cat. I put it back on my nightstand, deciding I'll call in the morning and tuck myself back in.

I shoot up out of bed. "Fucking cat!"

The TV in the living room is back on. The glow casting shadows in the other room. That's it, you're going in the bathroom. I jerk to a stop when I notice her lying at the end of my bed. Narrowing my eyes at the heathen, she's not laying like she's been asleep and her tail is moving side to side. I shake my head, giving too much credit to my cat. There is no way she could keep turning on the TV out of spite. Once could be an accident. Twice, it wasn't the cat.

Spikes of fear pebbled my body as my eyes jump from her to the living room. *Hmm. Could it be the TV is just having a short?* I bite my lip, hesitant to go into the living room. Who would come into a house and keep turning a TV on? Trying to talk myself down from the TV watching boogie man, I glance at the nightstand where my phone sits. He wouldn't care if I called.

No. This is silly. I'm not calling him. He'd have Stone up here in two seconds for no reason. To prove to myself that I don't need to call, I rush into the living room and turn the TV off again, sprint back into my room, fly onto my bed in a ball so my feet aren't touching the floor. Just in case there's something under my bed.

I crane my neck to listen to the silence. Nothing. See, I'm being silly. I'll call a TV repair place tomorrow to make sure they fix this because I'm not doing this again tomorrow night. Laying back down, I groan, slamming my arms to my side. I have to pee. Max will get a kick out of this story when I tell him tomorrow.

Why is it when you're trying to pee fast, it feels like it's Niagara Falls and never ends? My sense of hearing is on overdrive as I listen for any noises. Of course, Moxi meows in the other room right as I'm wiping, making me flinch and my hand ends up skimming the pee filled toilet water. *Gross.*

I'm starting to hate that cat.

After washing my hands *twice*, I make it to bed. I mutter a few choice words at the damn cat. Not even settled in, I jump when the TV comes back on. *Goddammit!* The tingles come back, working their way down my spine as I stare at the door. What if Max is messing with me? He's broke in here before unnoticed. I'll kill him for giving me a nervous breakdown. I lean over to grab my phone to call him but freeze when I don't see it. All my senses rev up to full throttle. I peek over the bed to the floor and close my eyes when I don't see it. It probably fell under my bed, but I *really* don't want to search there.

The TV turns off.

I gasp, holding my breath.

The TV turns on.

The breath I release shakes. Someone is out there and it's not Max.

Max would not play this trick on me.

I frantically glance around the room, looking for anything I can grab to defend myself.

There's nothing. Why don't I have something? A bat. A heavy flashlight. *Something.*

Instead, I jump off the bed and slam my door shut, locking it with shaky fingers.

I should scream. Damn, why did I demand a corner unit? People will still hear below me though. Step by step, I back away from the door.

Click.

I scream when I hear the sound of the door being unlocked. The door swings open and a large figure throws his body on me, his hand covering my mouth.

"Get her legs so she stops kicking me," he demands.

My heart stops.

There is more than one of them.

CHAPTER THIRTY

MAX

"Everything good on your end?"

"Yep. All quiet here," Stone replies. "A neighbor kid brought over a crate earlier. Syd didn't seem too happy."

I chuckle into the phone. "Must be her cat. They have a love-hate relationship." I thought the cat was cool as hell.

"That was her only visitor. She's tried to watch TV a couple times, but other than that, her lights have been off."

"She's exhausted. Hell, so am I."

"Then why the fuck you calling me?" he jokes.

I grumble, running my hand over my jaw. Why am I calling? I trust Stone with my life, so it's not that I'm worried. I just wish it was me there with her and not Stone parked outside her apartment. I was hoping she would call me after she got my text, but if she fell asleep, I wouldn't blame her. We had a long night, and I made sure she'd be feeling me for the days I couldn't be there.

"Did you find him?"

I stare at the large two-story Spanish colonial-style home up the hill, surrounded by desert, cactus and pine trees. "Not sure yet. Kase is getting ready to run surveillance." The house belongs to the head of a drug cartel's daughter which made this trip that much more complicated.

"Good luck and stop worrying about her," he mutters.

I haven't stopped worrying about her in two years. I sure the hell won't stop now. When I hang up, I glance at Kase. "Anything?" I ask as he stares through binoculars. Glancing out the dirty window of our hotel, darkness settles on the impoverished town.

"Nope. I haven't seen anyone come or go." We've been here for three hours, watching.

Plans formulate in my head, but not knowing why he's in there makes it hard to nail one down. The intel we got confirmed he's there. If only I knew *why*. "It's time to take a closer look," Kase says, handing me the binoculars. Slipping out the door, dressed in all black, Kase makes his way up the hill. I try to keep him in my sights through the binoculars, after he parks the car, hidden from the road, but I can't see anything in the darkness. Instead, I focus on the house. It's illuminated by the landscape lights, making it appear to be floating in the surrounding darkness.

"Almost there," Kase confirms into my earpiece a half hour later. I try to find him again with no luck. This is why I hired him. They trained him to be a ghost. "In place. Red Robin's in the air."

I open the drone camera app on my phone. It's designed to search for heat signatures. I count four. "It looks like they're all in one room. I'm gonna get closer and try to see into a window."

"Copy that."

Scenarios run through my mind. Typically they separate imprisoned people. So either he's dead, or he's one of the four. Which begs the question, what the fuck is he doing?

I open another app that shows the camera feed from Kase's earpiece. The screen lights as he approaches a window.

"You seeing this," he whispers.

My jaw clicks. "Yes," I sigh. Four people sitting around a table, playing cards. Rex is one of them. I rub my temple, imagining every way I can bring pain down on him. He's caused our mom so much grief. *And for what?* "I don't know what to fucking think."

The woman stands and wraps her arm around Rex. The other two men at the table continue playing, ignoring them. Rex's body hardens and his hands fist, but he stands up with her with a forced smile. "Something's off," I say, narrowing in on his body language. "You rarely tense when a beautiful woman wraps herself around you."

"Look at his ankle."

My eyes move down his body and the glow of a tiny blinking light around his ankle catches my attention. Well, son of a bitch, he's not here on his own terms. I shouldn't be relieved that he's being held prisoner. And I know I shouldn't laugh, but the bastard finally got himself into something he can't get out of. Seducing a woman to gain access to whatever he's after is his modus operandi. Seems he seduced the wrong woman.

Kase heads back to the hotel so we can figure out our next move. I stare at the phone in my hand and pull up Sydney's number. It's one in the morning, her time. I let out a long sigh, knowing I can't call her right now. How the hell is our relationship going to work if we live on two different coasts and I can't stand being away from her for one fucking night?

Half an hour later, Kase and I sit at the old wooden table, studying the house and the surrounding area. "How are we going to work this?"

I sit back and the unsteady chair creaks under my weight. This isn't the shittiest place I've stayed, but it's damn near close. "If I didn't have something to get back to, I'd let the fucker suffer a little longer." He chuckles and nods. "It's his lucky day. But I want this to be clean. In and out. Let's keep watch tomorrow and hope a window of opportunity opens up."

CHAPTER THIRTY-ONE

SYDNEY

I bite down on the fabric shoved in my mouth that wraps around my head, preventing me from screaming. I swallow back the saliva pooling in my mouth. My hands and feet have ropes around them and are tied to a dining room chair. They immediately blindfolded me so I wasn't able to make out who they are, but I know one of them is a woman. She whimpered when my foot connected to her stomach as I was fighting them off. A lot of good that did.

They've been quiet or not here because the longer I sat in silence, the harder it was to stay awake. When I hear voices, it pulls me out of the light sleep state I'm in. They rip the blindfold off my head and I wince as a few strands of hair go with it.

I meet my captor's eyes in utter surprise.

Shanna and Brett?

I wrack my brain at how these two ended up together. I haven't seen Shanna since the night I passed out on stage and it was obvious she didn't care for me, but this is a whole new level of hate. Why would she do this? Has it been them all along? The texts? The chocolate? And why is Brett involved? He's always been one of the nicest guys that work for Jude. None of this makes sense.

A couple streaks of light shine on the carpet between the gaps of the heavy curtains. Glancing at the clock on the wall, I see it's eight in the morning. If only I could somehow signal to Stone or Hudson that something is wrong. I know they're right outside.

"Should we wait for him to show up?" Brett asks. I nod my head without thinking. I assume they're talking about Max and I smile inwardly knowing how much pain he's going to cause them. Brett lets out a wicked laugh. "Oh, you think he's Superman?" His tone is sharp, so different from his normal laid back voice. "Wait and see what happens when we have his kryptonite." He points at me and picks up a syringe from the coffee table that separates us, filled with a white liquid.

I blink back the tears forming, regret that I wished Max was here stings my heart. One man I loved died, I won't survive if something happens to Max because of me. Brett puts the liquid back on the table and stands up, skirting around the table. Towering over me, he grips my hair, jerking my head back so I'm looking up at him. "Maybe I'll have a little fun with you first." I shake my head, jerking out of his grip.

"Excuse me," Shanna snaps, shooting up off the couch. "What the hell are you talking about? Fun?" She slaps him on the arm and then glares at me for a moment before whipping her glacier stare back at him. "Why would you even say that?"

He holds his hands up and smiles. "I was just kidding, babe. You're the only girl I want to have fun with." He pulls her into a hug but glances over her shoulder, flashing a twisted smile. My stomach rolls in disgust.

She pushes out of his hug and stands between him and I. "Well, get back to work. Make sure the tracker on his car is still working." The irritation in her voice is a relief. She's still pissed and right now, she might be the only thing preventing something bad from happening to me. She spins around. "Don't think I'm on your side," she sneers as if reading my thoughts, getting close to my face. I breathe in a blast of strawberry scent from her gum. "He's my man. You might have stolen my career, but I'll be damned if you'll steal my man."

Stole her career?

Is that what this is about? Revenge for her not getting a record deal? Moxi decides now is a good time to hop in my lap. She stares at Shanna.

"Isn't your cat cute? It's like a little leopard." She reaches down to pet her and before she can touch the orange-spotted cat, Moxi hisses and attacks Shanna's hand. Shanna screams and Moxi sprints out of the room. My eyes widen as I notice blood dripping down her slender white arm. "Go shoot that bastard," she screeches as she darts to the kitchen.

"Would you shut up? Do you want to get caught?"

"Her cat probably gave me rabies," she whines.

I wish. I glance in my bedroom and spot Moxi's eyes glowing at me from under the bed. I try to smile. *Good girl. When I get out of this, you get tuna every day.*

Brett and Shanna come and go, disappearing into my guest bedroom for the next couple hours. "Why hasn't his car moved?" Shanna says to Brett, looking over his shoulder as they walk into the living room again. "You said he couldn't stay away from her."

"I don't know, woman. Get off my back," he snaps. Her fists draw up and she shifts her angry glare to meet the back of his head. "He'll be here," he spins around, meeting her glare, then walks to the kitchen.

They argue in the kitchen. I lean my head, attempting to catch their heated argument, something I could use later against them. *What the hell am I doing?* Focus on getting out of here, Sydney. I twist my hands, hoping to free at least one. The ropes dig into my wrists. Between watching them out of the corner of my eyes and twisting my wrists and legs, I don't notice that I'm moving the chair until one of its legs get stuck on the carpet.

Oh, shit. Shit. Shit.

My cheek slams against the floor from the chair tipping over. I grunt through my gag as the pain radiates from my shoulder to my head. Shit, that freaking hurt. Black Nike's step an inch from my nose and I glance up to a shit-eating grin on Shanna's face.

She squats down. "Going somewhere?" I used to like her voice. She's an incredible singer. Now, I'd rather hear a five-year-old attempt to play the violin. "You're better on the floor anyway like the rat you are. You should have crawled back in the hole you came out of." When she flips her hair, I notice her chewed fingernails and I wonder if planning my demise has been eating at her. Could she be feeling trapped because Brett is making her do this?

I rest my aching head against the rough beige carpet. She paces in front of the couch where Brett is sitting. Tears run down the side of my face. "I'm sorry, babe," Brett murmurs, stopping her and pulling her into his lap. She leans into his body, her eyelids close as his hands massage her arms. I glance up and meet Brett's glare. "I only want you." He whispers into her ear, but his eyes stay pinned on me. She hums as his hands rub her neck. "You need to relax, we'll be here awhile." His hands move down over her shoulders and end up squeezing her breasts. They sit in the only line of sight I have so I squeeze my eyes shut. My being here doesn't deter him, he has no intention of stopping. I think about something else to drown out the sound of her tiny whimpers, but instead of fading away, they intensify in my head.

The sound of a zipper surprises me, so I open my eyes. She's not going to have sex in front of me, is she? Can't she see he's playing her? He bites down on his lip when he has my attention. His hand moves inside her pants and she moans out one time.

I mutter through my gag for them to stop, but it comes out a strangled sound. Maybe it'll pull her out of the trance he has her under. "That's it," he rasps, moving his fingers in and out of her. "You know you want this." He winks at me. His words aren't meant for her. They're for me. "That's it, babe, ride my fingers.

Show her what it's like to be with me. Make her beg for me like you do."

His arrogant words halt her hip movement. Her eyes fly open, and the icy glare sends shivers down my back. Typical narcissist that he is, he doesn't pick up on her demeanor change, rather continues to watch my reactions while he thinks he's getting her off. She tilts her head back to look up at him, catching his attention on me. Her face twists as she yanks his hand out of her pants and she whips around, slapping him across the face and standing.

He retaliates by getting in her face. His fingers squeeze her cheeks in a vice grip, pushing her down on the coffee table. "What the fuck was that for? I'm so tired of your bullshit tantrums," he seethes, his face beet red in the shape of a handprint.

Darkness crosses her face as her hand darts up with the syringe and stabs him in the neck. "I don't beg for anyone, you bastard." Sheer terror sweeps through me as he stumbles back, yanking the needle out of his neck. Panic shoots from his eyes and she meets it with a dark glare.

"That's it, babe," she says, mockingly. "Show her what it feels like to die." Her voice doesn't hold one ounce of remorse as she watches him crawl toward the kitchen with an air of desperation. I can only see his feet when his body stops moving, collapsing to the ground. Tears burn my eyes. This has to be a trick. She couldn't have just killed a man and be okay with it. I flinch as she steps in front of me. "See what you made me do," she mutters, kicking me in the stomach. I writhe with pain as it shoots through my body. I pull a few deep breaths through my nose, working through the pain, hoping another kick isn't coming. Instead, she walks around me, lifts me off the floor and sets me upright.

"He was a means to an end, anyway." She waves her hand in the air, plopping down on the couch and zipping her pants back up. "He was my way to get to you. It's too bad he ended up being an asshole. We had something good going, or so I thought." She shrugs. "He was great in bed though, which makes this suck. How's Max in bed? I bet he's a wild horse."

She smiles, tucking her legs underneath her, an excitement in her voice like we're two best friends having a sleepover and talking about our guys. I'm sure Addison and I have had this exact conversation. Except she hadn't just killed a man.

"Speaking of Max, where is he?" She looks at her phone and frowns. "Why hasn't he moved? His car is still at the hotel." She doesn't know he's out of the country. She groans, pushing up off the couch and pacing. "Nothing is going as planned." She glances at Brett laying on the floor. "I need him to be on his way to start." My eyes widen. *Start what?*

She walks out and goes into the spare bedroom. Panic rises and I glance around the room, wondering what she went to get. When she comes back out, she passes me, humming a song and walks into the kitchen. Whatever she had in her hand was too small to see.

I jerk my head toward the kitchen when someone knocks. It has to be Stone. He's probably wondering why I haven't left today. And if I don't answer, he'll let himself in. Shanna puts her finger to her mouth, gesturing for me to be quiet. She digs through her bag and pulls out a gun. I violently shake my head. No! *Don't do it.*

Another knock. She points the gun at the door. I don't want to make noise, but if he lets himself in, hopefully my strangled scream will at least warn him. When another knock happens, quicker this time, my heart sinks. He won't wait much longer. We both stare at the door with apprehension.

Silence. She glances at me, and I shrug, blowing out a breath of relief through my nose. Shanna walks to the door and looks out the peephole and turns toward me, smiling. "Oh. Looks like it was a delivery guy. I wonder what you ordered? Some lingerie for Max?" She says, unlocking the door. I tilt my head, confused. *I didn't order anything.* She peeks out the door before opening it all the way and grabbing the package on my doorstep.

She opens the package and pulls out a white stuffed bear. "Isn't that cute?" She rolls her eyes and digs through the paper, finding a note. "Ain't Max the sweetest?" She says in a condescending tone. She walks over and holds the card up for me to see. "Too bad you guys won't be okay."

I read the note. *We'll be okay ~ Max.* Relief hits me full force, I swallow hard to bite back the tears, blinking a couple times. Max didn't send that note. He never signs with his whole name, which means it's a decoy.

And now he knows I'm not in here alone.

CHAPTER THIRTY-TWO

MAX

"I think we have our in," Kase says from the other room. I spit my toothpaste out and rinse before walking in there. We've been watching all morning and minus a UPS delivery, there's been zero action. Kase formed an extraction plan if we can't find a way in without force. His plan is the last option, but as the morning wore on, it's become more likely.

He's packing up when I enter the room, holstering his guns and sheathing his knives. "What's up?" I say, confusion in my voice. We both agreed if we carried out his plan, we'd wait until night. It's only two in the afternoon.

"The two guards just left with the woman. And *not* with Rex."

"Let's go," I clip, grabbing my gun and phone off the table. I pull my shirt over my holster and we're out the door in less than one minute. Time is not on our side with so many unknowns. Usually we would watch for schedule patterns, but I'm not giving Rex that much of my time. We're doing this today. Last night, Kase found a dirt road where we can hide the car off the main road. We make the last ten-minute hike up the hill in five.

They've been gone fifteen minutes and I hope we have at least another fifteen. I send up the drone and find he's in one of the back rooms, which is perfect. Blowing a hole out of the wall in front of the house would cause too much attention. The house is far enough on the hill, people below will think a car backfired.

Kase sticks a small amount of C-4 on the brick wall next to a window. Sticking my hand through the bars adjourned to the window, I tap a couple times. The curtains move and Rex comes into view. His eyes widen and he says, "Finally."

I shake my head in disbelief and have half a mind to flip him off and walk away. "Ready when you are," Kase says, standing ten feet back with the detonator in his hand.

"Step back," I say to Rex, motioning for him to move away from the wall. The curtains close and I step aside, motioning to Kase the all-clear.

Within a minute, there's a hole in the wall, smoke permeates the air surrounding us. Rex doesn't wait for the air to clear, he comes barreling out of the hole, coughing. "Big brother, I've never been happier to see you." I stare at him through narrowed eyes. His response, normally snarky when I bail him out, is suspicious. "Dude, that woman is a psycho," he clips, pointing at the house. I chuckle, bending over to work on his ankle monitor. "It's not funny, jackass. She's held me captive for over a month."

I get ready to cut off the transmitter but glance up at him. "I need you to pull your shit together. Once I cut this, it'll ping her, I'm sure. So, we have to move as soon as this is off." With limited resources and time, replicating the wireless frequency so it wouldn't alert anyone when removed isn't possible.

He takes a deep inhale, pops his neck and nods. "Ready."

Kase is already down at the car on lookout. I press down on the bolt cutters, snapping the bracelet in half. We don't waste any time making it down the hill. Rex stays right on my heels until we see Kase.

"No one's come yet," he says, jumping in the car.

I pull in a breath; the adrenaline pumping through me. Now

we wait. Rex sits forward from the backseat. "We need to get the fuck out of here. Why are we sitting here?"

Kase looks at him and back to me. "I thought you said he was good at his job?"

I stare at him through the rearview mirror, shaking my head. If he wasn't so emotional at the moment, he'd know what we are doing. "If your *captor*..." I use the term loosely since I'm sure he was there for disingenuous reasons in the first place "... passes us on the way down, they'll have the small town searching for a silver Ford Taurus in a matter of minutes. If we at least wait until they pass, we can be down the mountain by the time they figure out you're gone. As soon as word gets out, we'll already be on our way out of town." To be on the safe side, I have a contact meeting me at a local garage to switch cars then we have an hour drive to the border.

He throws his body back against the seat, raking his hands through his hair. I kind of feel bad for the guy. "How mad is Mom?"

"I haven't told her you are alive yet." His eyes widen in surprise. "We just found out last night where you were. We were too busy figuring out how to get your ass out of there without fatalities."

"I would have been okay if you came in shooting up the place," he mutters to himself.

"We had that plan, too," Kase pipes up.

I shake my head as he smiles and shrugs, the possibility not even phasing him. Turning in my seat so I can see Rex's eyes, I ask, "What does she have?"

His jaw tightens, he knows what I'm asking. I'm waiting for him to admit he fucked up and I'm not getting blood on my hands for his mess. His focus darts out the window, to the empty road. "There's a diamond I've been searching for. It's the Moussaieff Red Diamond. It's only five carats, but because of its color, it's worth seven million. It was stolen in 2002."

"Shit," Kase whispers.

"We did a job in Mexico a couple months ago. During our planning stage, I heard a rumor that Dante Abalos gave it to his daughter as a birthday present last year."

"It was a fucking rumor. The first time you heard the name Dante Abalos, that should have been enough to make you forget you ever heard anything." Dante is the leader of a cartel in Mexico. When I found out his daughter owned the house on the hill, I figured it was no longer a rescue mission. It was a recovery.

"I had to know. It should've been an easy job. Someone set me up. Sofia knew I was coming."

"Why didn't you tell your team? Or fucking *anyone*?"

He drops his head and sighs. "I'm a selfish bastard, I guess. None of them know about my obsession with the diamond."

"You're also an idiot. And a lucky bastard. You better be glad Sofia liked you enough to keep you around for this long." He scoffs as I turn back when Kase informs us that their car just passed. It takes a car fifteen seconds before it hits the first turn once it passes us. We pull out at twenty seconds.

We're able to pull into the garage with no interference after driving through back roads for a couple miles. Jorge is already waiting, closing the door behind us. I hop out of the car and remove a large manilla envelope from my bag. When Jorge approaches, we shake hands and I hold out the envelope. "Thank you, Jorge. I owe you one."

He glances in the bag and smiles. "I'd say we're even."

We're not even close. He's taking a huge risk helping us and that money means nothing if he's caught. He hands me keys to another car and our stop is quick. Rex stays quiet the entire time until we're back on the road headed toward the border.

"Thank you," he says from the backseat.

I glance in the mirror and nod. "You should call Mom." Kase hands him his phone. I'm not ready to celebrate yet. I'm still angry that I had to leave Sydney to go save his ass. My mind wanders to what she's doing, or what we *could* be doing. My fingers itch to touch her. Just a few more hours and she'll be screaming out my name. Imagining those ice-blue eyes, staring up at me while she sits on the bed naked and wet...

"Mom wants to talk to you," Rex says, interrupting my vision. I grunt and grab the phone from his outstretched hand.

"Hey, Ma."

"Well, I'm glad to talk to you too, son," she says, offended at the tone of my voice.

Despite my frustration with Rex, I crack a smile. "Sorry, I've got a lot of things on my mind."

"I'm sure you do, hon. I don't want to keep you since Rex said you guys are getting on a plane soon, but thank you, Max. I know you and your brother don't see eye to eye on a lot of things, but you don't know how much it means to me that you care enough to help him."

"I only do it for you," I grumble.

She laughs into the phone. "I'm okay with that. Now, both of you get back home as soon as possible." Despite wanting to tell her I'll bring Sydney with me next time, I keep my mouth shut. She'll make a huge deal out of it, plan a party with the whole town. Instead, I tell her I will and hang up.

The closer we get to the US, the easier I feel. Except the line at the border is ridiculous. I slow the car to a stop. "Shit." There are at least a hundred vehicles in front of us. "Have I told you lately how much I hate you," I groan to Rex's reflection.

He shrugs with a smirk. "Mom says you love me."

"So, Rex, you ever use your skills for good?" Kase asks, looking back at him. I bark out a laugh at the absurdity. Rex does nothing out of the kindness of his heart.

"Much to my brother's dismay, I have."

I spin my head around in shock. "Fucking when?" I'm intrigued to hear what bullshit comes out of his mouth.

His jaw clicks and his eyes turn hard as he shakes his head.

"You know what, never mind. You have this ill-conceived notion that I'm only a fuck-up. But you haven't so much as said one word to me in five years, so you don't have a fucking clue what I've been doing."

A horn honks from behind me as I stare dumbfounded at him. Turning around, I inch a whole five feet forward before I whip back around. "Don't guilt me for not calling you. The phone works both ways, little brother. And obviously my ill-conceived notion isn't so fucking ill-conceived since you ended up being held prisoner because you were trying to steal something and I had to bail you're ass out."

He turns away from my glare, his face beet red, the vein in his neck about to pop. "Fuck you, *big brother*. I think I was better off being Sofia's sex slave than being mocked by you." He throws open the car door, gets out and slams it shut, stalking toward the booth.

"Goddamnit!" I roll the window down. "Get back in the fucking car, Rex." He flips me off as he keeps walking. "I'm gonna kill him." The wheel takes the brunt of my frustration as I pound it. I can feel Kase's eyes on me. "What?" I clip, turning toward him.

"I've never seen you this emotional. Do you need to get out of the car and go for a run?" he jokes, referring to the time I made him do it. I glance over the sea of cars, inching forward a little more, pulling in my emotions. I glare at Rex walking in between the cars. "He can't get across," Kase says, waving his passport in his hand. "Give him a few moments to himself. He hasn't had time to process his freedom yet." Releasing a heavy sigh, I nod. He's right.

By the time we pull up to border patrol, Rex is sitting in the shade, leaned up against the grey shack. Kase rolls his window down and tells him to get in.

"He with you?" the Border Patrol agent asks, watching him get in the car.

"Yes." I hand him all of our passports. He holds up mine,

comparing my picture to me, then leans in and does the same thing to Kase.

"Mr. Shaw, Mr. Nixon, nice to meet you." He smiles, handing me back the passports. "Welcome back to America."

It's not uncommon for federal officials to recognize me. Although, thanks to that damn article, new friends are popping up everywhere. I glance at his badge. "You too, Agent Rodriquez." He waves me through and being on American soil puts me in a better mood.

"Call Stone and tell him we'll be there in two hours."

Kase picks up his phone and relays the message. "Hmm," he says.

The way he says it grabs my attention. "What?"

"Stone says she hasn't left her apartment all day." I twist my wrist to look at the time on my watch. Four fifteen. I mean, I knew she was tired, but I'm surprised she hasn't at least left to get groceries. Nothing in her fridge would be good. I pick up my phone and call her. When she doesn't pick up, concern builds in my stomach. "Did you check her apartment before she got there?" Different scenario's flash in my mind but the one that stands out, freaks me the fuck out.

Kase puts him on speakerphone. "Hudson cleared the apartment right before we got there. There wasn't enough time for someone to slip in. Hudson also took the night shift and we're right outside her door. No one went in, Max."

"Are her curtains still closed," Kase asks.

"Yes."

She's just taking a day off from the world. Who could blame her? I drum my thumb on the steering wheel, thinking of the best way to approach this. The minuscule possibility that someone is in there with her, they'll recognize my guys. "Can you see her door from where you're parked?"

"Yes."

"So, if she answered, you'd be able to see her face?"

"Definitely."

"Let me make some calls. Call you back."

I call a buddy of mine who works for another security team in Los Angeles. We come up with a plan. His technical guy is small compared to the rest of the team, so he won't look like a threat. He'll pretend to be a delivery guy. These days random people deliver packages from Amazon all the time, so he won't look out of the ordinary. We just need her to open her door. We call Stone back with the details. Now, we wait. Except this time, with Sydney, I'm the most impatient fucker there is.

"Who's Sydney?" Rex asked from the backseat. I want to tell him to shut the hell up. It's his fault if something happens to her. I would have been there with her, had it not been for him. I pull into the airport, heading for the hanger where we park my plane.

"She's a girl," I bark. In the corner of my eye, I see Kase look back and shake his head. That's his warning that he's about to die.

As we're walking up the stairs to board the plane, my phone rings. My heart slams against my ribs in anticipation. "Talk."

"We have a problem." I'm halted by the tone in his voice. On the last stair, I grip on to the rail and grit my teeth for control. Kase and Rex stand in the doorway awaiting the news.

"When someone finally opened the door, it wasn't Sydney."

I throw my phone across the tarmac. "Fuck!"

CHAPTER THIRTY-THREE

MAX

One word.

Hey was all it took for me to lose my shit on Rex. I stare down at my swollen hand, opening and closing my fist to make sure I didn't break it. It didn't matter at the time he sounded genuinely concerned. Or that he wanted to help. All that mattered was that my girl was in trouble and he's the reason. Now, I'm stuck on this plane going out of my mind.

Kase yanked me off, sending me to the back of the plane. Instead, I came into the bedroom. I always thought I'd be the type to remain calm when someone I loved was in trouble. The voice of reason with Aiden and Kase, *that was me*. I'm the one who told them to pull their shit together. But now I get it. The anger inside me burns and I can't control my actions.

The plane descends from the quick forty-five minute flight from San Diego. Well... usually it's quick. Today, it feels like we've flown across the country.

Kase already has a chopper waiting for us since it'd take us over an hour to get to her place in traffic. Fucking LA traffic. I thought New York City was bad. The chopper will get us as close to Sydney's apartment as possible, and then Hudson is picking us up. I might regret not calling the police or FBI, but I can't risk them fucking it up. If that woman is still there, Sydney's alive. *Statistically*. As soon as the plane hits the ground, I storm out of the room. Passing Rex, holding a bag of ice on his face, I stop and ask, "Is it broken?"

He shakes his head. "Nah."

"That's too bad." I crack a smile, sort of feeling bad, but not really. "You plan on helping?"

He stands up. "If you'll let me."

"Your breaking and entering skills might come in handy." A whisper of a smile sneaks up on his face, but he pulls it back. I stick out my hand and we shake. "Sorry," I mutter. He nods, knowing no verbal acceptance is necessary.

All three of us run to the chopper and we're three blocks from Sydney's apartment complex in ten minutes. Stone pulled the blueprint of the complex and sent it to us while we were in the air.

"I still don't know how the hell they got in there," I say, studying the file, mustering up all the self-control that I know is inside me. Having a little time to think has helped me stabilize my thoughts. "There's a window by her door and a window in her bedroom. Neither are broke."

"I heard a story once," Rex starts and I glance up from the file. "A guy was breaking into apartments by starting at one end and cutting through the drywall to get into the next apartment. I think his record was ten apartments."

"That's fucking commitment," Hudson states in surprise. "It's difficult and loud to cut a hole in a wall, with studs and all."

"But doable. Especially if you know someone isn't home. They don't have to rush," I say, already pulling up Stone's number to send him a text. It makes sense considering Hudson checked the apartment. They probably had something covering the hole that didn't seem out of place.

Me: Find out the lessee to the units behind and to the side of Syd

Stone: On it

We park around her building until we figure out a plan. I instruct Stone to stay put and keep watch after he gets the info we need. He tried to snap a picture, but his phone wasn't quick enough. All we got was that she was a tall brunette.

I open the blueprints again, pointing to the unit behind Sydney's. "Okay, this unit is empty so we'll go through that one and see if that's how they got in. Kase, I want you to fly Red Robin when Rex and I get in. Rex, can you open the sliding glass door quietly?" He gives me an incredulous glare. That's what I was counting on. "Tell Hudson what you need, we might already have it." The two guys get out of the SUV and open up the hatch in the back. "Kase, fly in front of Sydney's unit first and count bodies."

"Got it. You sure you can count on your brother? I mean, I could easily open it up too," he whispers.

I slap him on the back and nod. "I know. But Hudson won't touch Red Robin, afraid to crash it and Stone has to stay where he is. I need you to be our eyes."

The guys come around and Hudson hands us our earpieces. "Hudson get as close to Syd's door as you can, just in case they come out that way." He nods, checks his gun and runs off.

My phone rings and my finger is over the answer button expecting it to be Stone. I pause when I notice it's not him.

"Fuck," I mutter.

Rex glances at it and smirks. "Tell 'em I said hi."

I answer. "Aiden."

"If I wasn't a couple thousand miles away, I'd kick your ass right now," he growls.

"Now's not the time, brother." I lift my chin to Kase, directing him to get in place.

"I need you to tell me you're in the right state of mind to be going in there."

"Remind me to fire Stone." I pace in front of the vehicle, staring up at the scattered clouds. "I'm in control. Can't say I was an hour ago, but I am now."

He sighs. "Don't be mad at Stone. He's worried about you and so am I. If you don't report back in an hour, I'm sending in a unit. *Starting now.*" I'm not surprised to hear the beep of the timer in the background.

"I'll get her, or I'll die trying."

"That's what I'm afraid of. Stay safe, Max."

We hang up, and I tug on Rex that it's time. "We have an hour before the Feds come," I say into the mic.

"There are three bodies. One is laying on the floor not moving, two are sitting across from each other." Icy fear works its way up my extremities, slicing my heart. If they hurt Sydney, no one will leave there alive. Thankfully, they still have a heat stamp, so the person lying on the floor is still warm. And alive, for now. I blow out a ragged breath, calming my racing pulse. I point to Rex and he climbs the first floor rail outside the patio and continues to the second floor. As soon as he clears it, I follow. Pure adrenaline pushes me up.

We wait on both sides of the door for the all clear from Kase. Once given, Rex does as he promised and we're in the apartment within a couple minutes. The dark stale apartment is empty, except a few things on top of the kitchen counter. I flash my light on them. Alongside the food is a tiny empty vial. I pick it up and smell it, but it's odorless. There's a drop of white milky substance at the bottom. A nauseated dread burns my throat, suspicion on the drug and the effects means whoever is on the floor, won't be alive for much longer.

Kase updates us that the people are in the living room. I motion to Rex that we're moving. Sure enough, there's a four by four hole in the wall. Nothing should surprise me, but this does. We stand on each side and listen. The only voice I pick up is a woman's, and it's faint so she's not in the bedroom. I hold up three fingers and count down.

Crawling through the space, I lead with my gun drawn. When a muffled scream comes from the other room, I don't wait for Rex.

"You bitch! You'll drink this if it's the last thing I do!" the woman seethes.

Running into the room, I see the woman straddling Sydney, holding a cup of something over her face. Sydney's struggles help me slip into the room undetected and I tackle the woman, slamming her to the ground.

We both scream as the liquid splashes on my arm and on her. Adrenaline masks the pain as I pin her down and handcuff her. Her piercing screams hurt my ears. When I turn her over, her face is bubbling from the burns. I jerk my head in Sydney's direction, afraid the woman poured some acid on her. Rex is busy unknotting her gag.

"Max," she immediately screams. As soon as Rex has her all untied, she shoots out of the chair and I hold up my hand to stop her. "Max, you got that stuff on your arm."

"Cover your mouth and nose. Both of you get out," I demand, pulling my shirt over my nose, not knowing the exact acid used. I do a quick scan of her body. Thank god she seems fine.

"Not without you," Sydney argues.

"Woman," I grate out. "Now is not the time to argue." I motion for Rex to get them out. Sirens sound in the background. Sydney stares at me and Rex pulls her to the front door.

"I will throw you over my shoulder," he bites out as she fights him. She turns her icy glare to Rex, looking him up and down. "You're a tiny thing, don't think I can't."

She huffs, but ends up running outside with him. Within a matter of minutes, men in hazmat suits storm the room. I brief them on what happened and one of them leads me to the kitchen. We have to step over Brett to get there. I don't even know if he's still breathing. I don't care. It irritates the fuck out of me that we weren't able to catch him sooner. The woman looks familiar, too. I search my memory for where I've seen her. I sigh when it clicks. The night Sydney passed out on stage, she sang before her.

A small patch of skin on my left arm is flaming red. I'm instructed to keep it under the faucet for a good ten minutes. Leaning over the sink, I'm able to take my first breath of relief.

She's safe.

CHAPTER THIRTY-FOUR

SYDNEY

"You've been quiet since we left the hotel," Max says, twisting his body in his seat. I wince when I see the bandage on his arm. "Talk to me."

My gaze meets concerned eyes. I suck in a deep breath and blow it out my mouth. Even though it's been a week since everything happened, I'm tired of dealing with it. The media, the court dates, the phone calls about book deals or interviews. Everything. In a way, I wish Brett had died. That's one less thing I'd have to worry about. Thankfully, he and Shanna are behind bars. Max's fingers weave through mine. "I'm still trying to come down from everything that happened and you getting hurt. It's been non-stop since you found me. Thank you for this." I glance around the softly illuminated plane. I don't know where we're going. Getting *away* is all that matters.

"I told you a million times, I'm fine. My tats hurt more than this," he says, lifting his arm. "And all you have to do is ask and I'll take you anywhere." A small smile curves my lips up as I lean over and place a gentle kiss on his cheek. The way he looks at me like I'm the only person who matters means more than he'll ever know. His tough exterior is a stark contrast to the soft interior he shares with me. He brushes his hand through my hair, pulling me into his kiss to deepen it. "I wish there was a bedroom on this plane so I could hold you," he says against my lips.

Me too.

"Why didn't we take your plane?" Still a private jet, it's larger than his and not as many bells and whistles.

"The guys took it back home. But where we're going, my plane isn't meant to fly that distance."

My eyes widen and I sit up straighter. "Where are we going?" I glance out the window into pitch black, not able to tell if we're over land or water.

He hums and flashes a sexy half grin. "What's it worth to you?"

"Oh, we're gonna play that game, huh?" Slowly, I scrape my finger down his chest, my eyes never leaving his. I bite my lip as I reach the top of his pants. He stops my hand before I can get any further and lets out a groan. He takes his frustration out on my hand, biting it. "Ow!" I yank it back and hit him on the chest. "Don't bite me." His heady laugh fills the plane. It's what I need right now. Laughter.

"That's not what you'll be saying later," he warns, getting up out of his seat. He stands in front of me and leans down, placing a hand on each armrest. His face inches from mine. "Because I promise I'm going to bite, lick and suck every inch of your body." He hasn't touched me since we've been back. His excuse was I needed time to heal, but he has stayed by my side the entire week.

My nerve endings stir and tingle thinking about his lips all over me. The plane tremors a little and I'm almost positive it just had an orgasm too. The flush in my cheeks heat. I open my mouth to respond, but I've got nothing.

He leans down farther, nuzzling my ear. "That's what I thought," he whispers.

The captain comes over the intercom when the plane shakes again telling us to buckle up, we're going through a small storm. My body is going through its own storm right now. Fierce and magnetic, the storm's ready to unleash the impending surge of desire.

Max sits back down and reclines his chair. "Sleep. We've got a while."

I stare at him with twisted lips. "You're really not going to tell me where we're going?"

He crosses his arms and closes his eyes as he shakes his head. I sigh, pulling out a magazine. *And he says I'm stubborn.* After what he just said to me, my body isn't ready for sleep.

THE ORCHID SMELLS SO SWEET, I can taste a hint of spicy vanilla on my tastebuds as a lei is placed around my neck.

"Aloha," the older lady says, smiling. "Welcome to Maui." Her brown eyes gleam, filled with beauty and wisdom. She gazes into my eyes for a beat, like she's searching for something.

"Aloha," I reply when she leans in and wraps her frail hands around me, giving me a soft hug.

"*Nana I Ke Kumu.*" I pull back, tilting my head. Did she just say something? Her whisper was so faint, I wonder if it was just the wind. Her smile widens, and she gently nods her head.

"Ready?" Max says, coming to my side. I glance over, still preoccupied trying to figure out what she said. "Sydney?" I snap out of it and look back to the woman to ask her, but she's gone.

I must be more tired than I thought. "Did you see the lady I was talking to?"

Please tell me I'm not imagining people.

"Yeah. She walked that way." He points and I follow his direction. Still not finding her, I shrug it off. At least I didn't imagine a person. "Are you all right?"

"Are you kidding? We're in Hawaii. I'm just tired." The flight here was long, and I didn't sleep a lot on the plane. It's hard to sleep when your insides are tied in knots from fear, anxiety and desire.

He weaves his fingers through mine and leans down, pressing a soft kiss on my lips. "Let's get going then. Our ride should be ready now."

The drive winds through lush jungle on one side and breathtaking cliffs on the other side. Max still won't tell me where we're going, but it's obvious how he drives the windy roads with ease, he's familiar with them. It's not until we come to a road that winds through the thick jungle and is no wider than one car that I start to white knuckle my *oh shit* handle in front of me.

"Um, Max... please tell me this doesn't last long."

"It doesn't." He looks over and flashes a sexy crooked grin.

"Stop looking at me. Keep your eyes on the road," I say, keeping my eyes glued forward. I don't have to see him to know he's getting a kick out of this.

We turn off on another dirt road, the jeep bouncing on the rough path going uphill. *This just keeps getting better and better.* It's not until we clear the trees at the top of the hill that I loosen my grip.

"Wow," I whisper. The truck rolls down the hill, the ocean right in front of us. The lush green drops off into turquoise blue, hiding the cliff somewhere in front of us. My eyes follow the dirt road we're on and lands on the only house around.

I gasp. "Is that where we're going?" I point to a house, sprawled out alongside the cliff. The isolated house is larger than any house I've seen in this small town by far. It sticks out like a person wearing pink in New York City.

"It is." He downshifts as we hit the last part of our descent, rolling into the driveway. The house is one story, spread out wide but narrow. Windows are everywhere, allowing me to see right through it. Max grabs our bags and I wait at the front door, peeking inside, eager to see the place.

"Max, this place is amazing. How did you find it? It's a *little* off the beaten path," I say, glancing back up the hill, not looking forward to making that trek again.

He laughs as he opens the door. The sea breeze hits us as soon as we walk in and I do a double take. The entire back side of the house is wide open to the outdoors because of the sliding glass doors pushed to the side. Max watches me, staying quiet, as I look around. The modern feel of wood and metal create clean lines throughout the airy home. I'm drawn to the picturesque backyard. Palm trees line the yard and the infinity pool off the large patio looks like it drops off into the ocean. Seagulls sing above us, circling the air.

Arms wrap around my waist, the heat from Max's breath tickles my neck. "Do you like?"

"*Nope.* I can't believe you brought me to this dump." I giggle, turning in his arms. "Seriously, how do you expect me to relax here?"

He picks me up with such ease and my legs wrap around him, my hands link behind his neck. "Who said anything about relaxing?" He wags his brows. Walking with me back inside, he carries me to the bedroom. "I brought you here so I'd have you all to myself. No concerts, no fans, no barriers. Just me and you. *And* lots of sex."

"I like the sound of that."

He lays me on the bed and I let out a wistful sigh. This bed is heaven. I need to leave a great review for this place when we get home. My body relaxes, the jet lag settling in. "How about a nap first?"

"Okay," he gives in. "Only because you'll need your energy later." My laugh tangles with a yawn. He kisses me a couple times and rolls to his side, snuggling me against his strong body. His warmth and the enchanted sounds of the island lull me to a peaceful sleep.

CHAPTER THIRTY-FIVE

SYDNEY

I wake to the sound of voices. Shaking the fog out of my head, I sit up and take in my surroundings. I was almost positive I had dreamt this place. It seemed too beautiful to be real. But it is. The bedroom's wall of windows that looks out to the ocean is wide open. I pull in a deep relaxing breath, letting it out slow.

Voices in the other room remind me what woke me up to begin with. I drag myself out of bed, making a quick stop at the mirror to make sure I don't look like a walking mess. Fixing my messy bun into a cleaner messy bun, I shrug to myself. "I'm not here to impress company, this'll have to do," I whisper to myself.

Max is in the kitchen with his shirt off and board shorts hanging low on his hips, cutting up fruit. I lean against the bedroom door frame, gawking at the gorgeous man. Steel-blue eyes catch mine staring. "Come here," he demands. I push off the frame with my hip and saunter over to him.

"I'm here." My voice comes out more needy than I expected.

My body's reaction to Max is undeniable. It succumbs to his commands without thought or restraint. The notion that I could just hand over all of myself to one man used to scare the ever living hell out of me. Now, it awakens places I never knew were inside of me. This is what I need from a man. This is what has always been missing.

He leans down, scraping his fingers up my thighs, grazing the bottom of my ass under my shorts. "This spot..." He runs his index fingers along the curve again. "Is one of my favorites. You have a gorgeous ass."

He lifts me up on the counter and brings a piece of fruit to my lips, outlining them with its juice. I lick my lips and the sweet bite of guava fills my mouth. "Mmm," I murmur. He does it again, but brings his lips to mine before I can lick the juice off. The taste of him mixed with the sweetness is intoxicating, it's easy to let him pull me under. I squeeze us together with my legs, his hardness hitting my center. He groans into my mouth, his hand grips my swollen breast.

"Fuck. Why didn't I wait?" He mutters to himself, pulling back. I tilt my head in confusion. *Wait for what?* Do I look like I want to wait? He looks behind me, so I twist my body around.

"Oh." I forgot about the voices from earlier. Two women are on the patio, standing by massage tables, setting up. I suppress the disappointment that we have to wait *again*, knowing he set this up. Don't get me wrong, I'm all for a massage, but the building ache in my lower belly is becoming heavy from need. At least, I know I'm not the only one struggling. "Well... I guess you'll for sure get a happy ending," I say, turning back to him. His laugh echos in the open space.

"More like a happy beginning."

"You keep promising things, but I've yet to see you deliver," I say, lifting my chin and twisting my lips in playful defiance, knowing the thin ice I'm walking on. His fingers dig into my hips and the ice cracks as he jerks me into him.

"Sydney, are you wanting to put on a show?" he rasps. "Because I can have you screaming my name in less than sixty seconds and I don't give a flying fuck that we have an audience." I swallow, turned on by his words but also mortified that

I'm thinking of saying *yes*. His brows lift, waiting for me to answer.

This is what happens when you play with fire.

"No," I say with an awkward laugh.

His lip twitches. "You and that mouth will be the death of me." He picks up a mango, bringing it to my mouth. "Now, eat or I'll find something else for you to do with that mouth."

My mouth waters. Not for the mango, but for him. I lean forward to take the mango and run my hand along his hardened bulge at the same time. He shudders in surprise. "I like option number two," I purr.

A low rumble from the back of his throat spurs me on. I tighten my grip. "I wasn't playing," he warns.

"Neither was I."

Strong arms scoop me up and he takes quick strides to the bedroom. He mumbles to the ladies we'll be right back in a language I've never heard him speak. I'll ask about that later.

He tosses me on the bed, pulls down his swim trunks and stares at me like he's about to devour me. "Option two, huh?" He walks toward me, pumping his shaft a couple times and I inch closer to him on all fours.

I hum, pulling him into my mouth. It doesn't take long before deep throated growls are coming from the back of his throat. It's always the few seconds after where he's trying to gain control of his senses, but can't, that I feel like I won an Oscar for my performance. It's empowering.

My eyes roll back into my head when the massage therapist runs her arm up my back. Between the exotic smells and the soft music playing along with the ocean sounds, I'm in pure bliss. Naked, except a piece of cloth placed over the crack of my butt, hands and arms drag along the entire length of my body. Max told me the lomi lomi massage is a Polynesian technique used to get rid of negative energy.

I can't think of a better way to release the shit storm Shanna brought into my life. An elbow digs into the knots in my shoulders as her other hand works my hip. My brain fights to focus on the two areas, but gives up. With more strokes, my body relaxes, reaching a euphoric state. We need to have them come back before we leave. I lift my head, watching the woman dig into Max's muscular back. His back tenses when she hits a knot. A pang of guilt hits me that the tension might be because of me. He needs this as much as I do. Laying my head back down, I push out all the guilt knowing that's the last thing Max would want me to be thinking about.

An hour later, my body is heavy from relaxation. "Please roll over," my masseuse whispers in my ear. Having no care about being naked, I roll on my back. She places the same strip of fabric over my pelvic area and one across my breast, only wide enough to cover my nipples. Hearing Max get situated, I glance over. Holy shit... I shouldn't have. Desire stirs to life seeing Max's naked body. Steel eyes meet mine, desire swirling in them as he winks and then skims down my body. My lady puts a blindfold on me before I get to see him make it back up my body. Yes. Make me blind to him so I can relax.

It doesn't work.

While on my stomach, her touch was relaxing. On my back, every touch seems sensual, like it's pulling the sexual energy from my core because in my mind, Max is watching me. Watching us. I try to think about being on stage, singing. But every thought makes a U-turn and heads right back to Max. What was relaxing minutes ago has turned agonizing. This is so wrong. On so many levels. I focus on her movements, counting down from ten, hoping that will put me back into the zone.

Five, four, three... oh shit! I jump when another set of hands joins in. "Sorry," she whispers but continues with her hand movements. Four hands on different parts of my body, and I know Max is watching now.

"Max," I mutter, my voice needy laced with panic. He chuckles and says something to the women causing them to stop.

I lift my hand to remove my blindfold but Max stops my arm. "Keep it on," he rasps.

All the suppressed desire hits me full force, heating my body. Large warm hands cover my feet, kneading the arch with his thumbs. The pressure of his hands works up my legs. I spread them wider in anticipation as he moves to my inner thighs. His oiled fingers glide over the area and my body shivers when he feathers over my sensitive clit. Much to my disappointment, they keep moving *around* the area I'm silently begging for him to touch. Then he moves up to my torso. I let out a heavy breath and he chuckles, but says nothing.

The palm trees whisper above from the ocean breeze, the air rich with the mixture of the salt and exotic oils. All my senses, except sight, are heightened. Hands envelop my breasts and his breaths deepen with each squeeze. If I was to reach for him, I bet he'd be rock hard. His hands are on the move again, this time, they're headed down. Sliding across my skin to my feet.

This is torture.

When he stops for a few moments, I lift my hand to peek under my mask. "Don't," he whispers, grabbing my hand and placing it back down by my side. I lie perfectly still, waiting. What feels like minutes later, I begin to wonder if he's still outside with me.

"Max?"

Warm lips press against mine and he murmurs, "Shhh. I'm testing my control." I bite my lip to suppress my laugh. "I'm at your mercy, you know that, right?" His lips trail down the sensitive nook of my neck and I tilt my head giving him better access. "Standing here, staring at perfection, while you wait for me, I'm barely hanging on." His raw words glide down my heated skin with his lips. I arch my back when he swirls his tongue around my nipple and whimper. The desire before, now burning a hole in my lower belly, blacks out my other senses and I can't focus on anything else.

The heat from his breath on my clit is enough to make me moan. "Max, please," I beg. I gasp when I'm slid to the end of the table. His hands wrap around my thighs and his mouth clasps to my clit. *Seconds.* It takes mere seconds for me to scream his name as I ride my orgasm out. My fists grip his hair as he continues his assault, sucking and fucking me with his tongue until I'm screaming out a second time with strangled moans.

Before I can come down from my orgasmic high, he pushes me back giving him room to get on the table. He pulls me up so I'm straddling him.

Bright light shines in my eyes and I squeeze them shut. "Sorry," he says, throwing the blindfold off to the side. Giving me a second to adjust, his hands massage my back. My lips curve to a smile when I meet his eyes.

"Hi," I whisper.

"Hey, beautiful."

I rotate my hips, writhing against his cock as it presses against my clit. He lifts me, just enough to slide me back down on him. I moan, my breath catching at the fullness. Our eyes lock as our oiled bodies move in a slow, sensual dance.

"Do you hear that?" he murmurs in my ear as he slides inside of me, fully sheathed. *Only thing I hear is the beat of my heart drumming in my ears.* As he rests his forehead on mine, his eyes close and he wraps his arms around me tighter. The restraint he's been harboring is on the verge of unraveling. "It's your body telling me you were made for me."

Only for you.

"Max." I wait for him to open his eyes. "I love you."

Emotions swirl in his features as his lip curves up to a half sexy grin. "Tink, I loved you yesterday. I love you today and I'll love you tomorrow."

CHAPTER THIRTY-SIX

MAX

"I feel you watching me," Sydney says with one eye barely open. She stretches and rolls to her side, facing me. Ice blue orbs meet mine. "Why are you up so early? It's not even light outside."

"I couldn't help it. You were snoring."

She gasps, pushing me on the shoulder. "I do not snore."

"Don't worry, babe, I won't tell anyone," I joke. She doesn't snore, but I didn't lie about not being able to stop staring at her. I still can't believe she's mine, it feels too similar to my dreams. Except in my dreams, she never told me she loved me. I want to ask her when we can tell everyone, but after what happened a few days ago, she needs time to come down from that horror. So far, I'm doing a damn good job helping her forget.

"Are we staying in bed all day." She yawns, curling up into my chest.

I hum, wrapping my arms around her. That sounds like a fantastic plan. But we can't. "Nope. We're hang gliding this morning." She shoots up, her perky breasts on wonderful display, right in front of my face. Plans can change, right?

"Really?" She squeals in delight. "Hey there hot stuff. My eyes are up here."

"You can't fault me. You practically stuck one right in my mouth." I grab the right one, her nipple pebbling. She slaps my hand, scooting away from me.

"That's not quite how it went." She laughs, pushing off the bed to stand. "When are we going?"

I roll on my back and adjust my hard dick in my underwear. Another problem waking up next to her, my morning wood edges on the side of painful. We had sex so many times yesterday; I thought for sure we fucked the desire out of it. At least for a few hours. But then she had to pop her boobs in my face. That's like offering a dog a steak dinner. And now I'm famished.

She walks to the bathroom, her black lace cheeky panties the only thing on. I groan. "You're killing me, Tink."

Peeking out of the bathroom, her toothbrush hanging from her mouth. She pulls it out. "What am I doing," she slurs, toothpaste almost coming out. She snaps her mouth closed and holds up a finger.

Yeah, seeing white stuff fill her mouth, so much she can't talk isn't helping my dick become soft. At all. I throw the covers off me in frustration and march past her in the bathroom. She stares at me in the mirror with a lifted brow. I step into the shower and turn it on full blast. Ice cold water hits me, causing me to pull in a quick breath.

"You okay?" she asks, glancing into the walk-in shower. "Brrr. That water is cold." She steps back.

"Exactly," I quip. If I didn't want to see the sunrise from a hang glider, I'd be back in bed, warm and satisfied.

The memory of when I threw Sydney in the pool comes jarring back. The water was ice cold then too. She thinks it was because she was messing with me. And that part is why she joined me, but watching her swing her ass, dancing and singing all night was sexy as hell. She had kissed me earlier that day in a bout of adrenaline after skydiving. It took one taste for me to acquire an addiction but I knew Damon had eyes for her so I was trying to quench the flames building inside of me.

It didn't go as planned. She ended up in my bed, subsequently ruining my life for the next year. Hindsight, I should have fought for her. But fuck, it was one night. Who finds their soulmate after being with them one night?

This son-of-a-bitch, that's who.

And here she is now, making me the happiest man on earth. Life is exhausting sometimes, but she's worth every agonizing breath I took because of her.

WATCHING Sydney experience hang gliding was better than the view itself. Her excitement level should be one of the Wonder's of the World. It made me excited and jumping out of planes or hang gliding doesn't get me excited anymore. It's more of a release. But seeing it through Sydney's eyes makes me want to experience everything over again, with her by my side.

"That was incredible!" She launches into my arms after we give the guys our gear, her body wraps around me and she slams her mouth down on mine. I open, taking full control of the kiss I so desperately wanted to give her a couple hours ago before we left. I will take everything she has to give me, selfishly and greedy, without any question. I've never been so consumed by one person. It's fucking unhealthy, but I can't stop. She's my cocaine, an unstoppable craving that isn't satisfied until I devour her.

I wrap her silky strands, heated from the sun, through my fingers and tug so she pulls back. Her lips curl up. "Were you thinking what I was just thinking?" she whispers.

I hope so.

"Marry me?" I murmur.

Her pupils dilate with her widened eyes, but her smile stays. *I guess that isn't what she was thinking.* Her eyes move back and forth between mine looking for validity. She doesn't have to look far. She knows I would never ask if I didn't mean it. And I fucking meant it. Every word. Every letter. Every syllable.

"Yes."

It's my turn to search her eyes. "Do you mean it," I ask, hesitantly.

She nods her head. "Yes, Max. I'll marry you."

I nuzzle my nose into her neck. A tidal wave of relief rushes through me. A laugh escapes my lips as the insanity of the moment catches up to me. I just asked Sydney to marry me. No ring. No knee. Just the words. Why the hell did she say yes? She deserves better than that.

"I'm sorry I didn't plan this better but I feel like I've wasted enough time."

"It was perfect."

"No. You're perfect. In every way. I love you, Tink."

"So, what were you thinking about?" I ask her as we lounge outside. She asked for an afternoon to do nothing except lay by the pool. After the energy of the morning died off, we were both spent.

She rolls her head, glancing over at me, her sunglasses taking up half her face. "When?"

"This morning after we kissed. You asked me if I was thinking the same thing you were."

"Oh," she chuckles, sitting up. She grabs her water and takes a quick drink. Condensation from the bottle falls onto her chest and my gaze follows the drip of water until it disappears into her cleavage. Damn, that's hot. "Our first kiss. Do you remember, after we went skydiving?"

"Did you just ask me if I remembered our first kiss?"

She sheepishly looks down. "I didn't know if—"

I swing my leg over, hopping off the chair and sweep her up in my arms, jumping in the pool. She screams right before she hits the water. She coughs when she breaks the surface.

"You asshole! Didn't you learn the last time you tried to drown me?"

I shouldn't laugh at her pouty lips, but she's cute as hell when she's mad. Swimming over to her, I pull her into my arms and walk her to the ledge. Her back rests against the side of the pool and she wraps her legs around my waist. "I remember, Tink. I tried for so long to forget, except it was etched in my head like a plague on display reminding me about my number one fuck up."

Water cascades down her sun-kissed face, her eyes sparkle like a diamond with the light hits them perfect. "Not too many times you can say your number one fuck up turned into the best thing you ever did."

My smile grows and I wag my brows as my thoughts turn dirty. "You are definitely the best thing I ever did."

She laughs, shaking her head. "Well, if you plan on being *did* some more, that's a good answer."

"Oh, I have plans." I nibble on her ear and she arches her neck, giving me better access. "And you know me, I execute every plan I make."

Chill bumps cover her body. "I hope one of those plans involves a pool," she breathes out. "In Hawaii."

I trail my finger along her bikini bottom, slipping it under. She moans when I swipe it against her core, burying it deep inside.

"It's at the top of my list."

CHAPTER THIRTY-SEVEN

SYDNEY

"I have to go into town to take care of some business," Max whispers into my ear. He runs his nose along my naked spine, making me squirm. I can barely muster enough energy to shoo him off with the slight lift of my hand.

"Stop." I snicker with no emphasis. "I'll be here when you get back." The heat from the afternoon sun mixed with the humid ocean breeze sweeps over my body, relaxing me further into my reverie. I want to breathe this moment forever. I want to feel it grow inside me, cherish every second it consumes my body.

My phone dings, waking me. I roll over and groan. My nipples pebbled from the soft breeze dusting over them. The hum of sensuality vibrating through my body from being naked is empowering. I'm sure Max won't mind if I forgo clothes the rest of the vacation. I listen for him, wondering if he made it back. Rather, I hear my phone ding again. I push myself up, untangling my legs in the cool sheets, and reach to the bedside table where my phone is sitting.

Hulk: Be ready for dinner by 7.

I smile to myself. Everything about Max is perfect. Despite our quick engagement, I can say with absolute ascertainment, I love him with everything that I am. When Damon asked me to marry him in front of everyone, I felt on the spot, caught up in the fantasy that Addison and I were marrying best friends and we'd have babies together that would grow up to be best friends too. I was with him because I needed him to fulfill a fantasy, not because I loved him. And I've come to terms with that mistake. I've realized Max isn't my second choice. He was my clear choice in a hazy world. I let beliefs stop me from tapping into my real desires.

Even though the fantasy hasn't changed, I'm saying yes because I love Max with everything inside of me. He owns my heart. He consumes my thoughts. He sings to my soul. I hold the phone to my heart, getting lost to his tune that lives inside me. Lyrics flash in my head and I pull my phone back, opening the Notes app to write the words down before I forget them. Glancing at the clock, I fly out of bed.

Shit. Shit. Shit. 6:10!

I pull out the only dress I brought with me. It's a simple red, strapless, fitted dress that goes just past my knees. Thankful I took a shower before passing out, my beach wavy hair ends up looking perfect. Mascara and red lipstick finish my sexy look with no need to add any more makeup. *If only I could have a year-round tan.*

A knock at the door surprises me. Man, he's taking this seriously. When I answer the door, I take a couple steps back at the sight of a stranger.

"Ms. Owen, I'm sorry. Mr. Shaw sent me to get you. I'm Carl," he blurts, holding out a dozen roses I missed at first sight. I narrow my eyes at the large Polynesian man dressed in a white linen shirt and black slacks. A tribal tattoo wraps around one of his elbows. He has a lei around his neck and flip-flops on. Looking past him, I see a black jeep.

I take the flowers, not taking my eyes off of him. "Do you mind if I text Max first?"

"No, ma'am." He continues to smile, not offended by my hesitancy. I nod and close the door, locking it. Then look at the entire length of the house, wide open. That lock wouldn't hold anyone back from getting to me.

Noticing a note on the flowers, I pull it off and open the small white card.

PLAN #2 IS IN MOTION. *Carl's a good guy.*
Can't wait to see your face. ~ M

FEAR STILL GUIDING MY SENSES, I place the roses in water and grab my phone. On it is a text already from Max.

Hulk: Carl works for me. I promise he won't hurt you.

Works for him? Taking a deep inhale, I blow it out, releasing the tension in my shoulders and grab my purse. I peek out the front window and Carl is leaning against the jeep, hands in his pockets, waiting. Max wouldn't send just any guy after what happened last week. He's having a hard enough time not taking the blame for leaving me.

"So, you work for Max?" I say, holding onto the handle so I don't bounce and hit the roof. I sit up front, afraid I'll get sick being in the back.

"Yes, ma'am. Hold on," he says, hitting a small dip in the road. *Hold on? I haven't let go.* I grit my teeth so I don't squeal.

"What do you do for Max?" And why does Max have employees in Hawaii?

He glances over and his white teeth flash bright against his tanned skin. "I watch over his house. Among other things."

"His house?" I look back at the hill in surprise, pointing back to it. "That's Max's house?" His eyes widen as he keeps his gaze straight forward.

"You didn't know?" His words come out slow. He mumbles something, not in English.

A weight settles on my chest wondering why Max didn't tell

me. "He didn't say it wasn't his. I guess I just assumed it wasn't."
We make the rest of the trip in silence. I feel bad for Carl. He's
beating himself up for telling me something Max might not have
wanted me to know. I chalk it up to Max assuming I knew it
was his.

When we pull into the restaurant, Max strolls toward the jeep.
"Mmm," I whisper, staring at the gorgeous confident man wearing
white linen shorts and an ice blue button-up shirt. He flashes a
wicked smile, making my toes curl. Carl laughs, interrupting my
gawking. My cheeks flush. "Sorry," I blush, looking away
from him.

"Stay here," he softly commands, getting out. He walks up to
Max and they speak. Max chuckles, slapping him on the back,
shaking his head. I already know how that conversation went. Max
walks over to my door, opens it and takes my hand.

"Hey, beautiful. Red is definitely your color." His gaze trails
over my body and he bites his lip. I'll never grow tired of him
looking at me like he wants to devour me. "Let's go before I
change my plans." The unmistakable alpha side of him shows as
he ushers me in the front door like he owns the place. *Hell, maybe
he does.*

We're led to a table with two round cushioned wicker chairs on
the beach. Wicker lanterns hang above us creating a romantic
ambiance, but it's the purple and pink sunset that catches my eye.
Between us and the beach are tikis lined in a semi-circle.

"There will be a show in a bit," Max says, linking his fingers
with mine on the table. There's always a sense of ease when I'm
with Max, even though he's the most intense person I've ever been
around.

As I bring the wine to my mouth, a tiny voice says, "Are you
Sky Owen?" Placing the glass down, I turn and smile at the young
tween standing by our table, terror in her eyes as she squeezes a
small journal against her chest.

Max removes his hand from mine, sitting back in his seat and I crinkle my nose from the loss of touch before turning back to the girl. "I am," I say. Her eyes light up. "What's your name?"

"Sadie. I'm sorry to bother you. My mom said it wasn't you, but I knew it was. I was just hoping you would sign my journal for me." She holds it out, and it shakes from her nerves.

"Oh my gosh, I'd love to." I take the journal. No pen. I glance up, looking for a waiter. Instead, Max holds one out. I blow a quick kiss to him as I take it. "Ok, Sadie, what song is your favorite?" I ask as I sign it and hand it back to her.

Her words fall from her mouth faster than I can keep up, telling me about how her friends all dance to one song, but sing another song. How a boy texted her another song, and that one is probably her favorite. I just smile and nod, listening to her excitement.

"I'm sorry," the mom intervenes, coming up behind her. "Sweetie, we should let them eat." Sadie takes a breath.

"Okay," she sighs.

"Sadie, it was great meeting you."

"I can't wait to tell everyone," she squeals. "Can I get a picture of you?"

I glance at Max wondering what he's thinking. He winks at me, flashing a reassuring smile. "Of course, I love pictures." Sadie pulls a phone out of her pocket handing it to her mom and stands next to me. Her energy vibrates through her body.

She wraps her arms around me for a quick hug. "Thank you so much!" She runs off showing everyone in her family the picture.

Silence hangs between Max and I. Breaking it, I say, "Don't tell me you're afraid to touch me in public."

He leans on the table, lowering his voice. "This is uncharted territory so I'll need you to guide me, here. The one thing I didn't plan for tonight was fans. We talked about telling our friends, but…" His words trail off, not wanting to bring up why we didn't go through with our plan. Getting kidnapped kind of puts a halt on things.

"Obviously, we'll still tell our friends. I mean, unless you plan on keeping our marriage a secret?" I bite my lip to hide my smile.

"That smart mouth is going to get you in trouble," he rasps. I lean forward, an inch from his chiseled face.

"I like trouble," I murmur, closing the distance and kiss him. *Is this guidance enough?* Pulling back, satisfied with my leadership skills rarely used with Max, I say, "You're the king of this territory so don't go soft on me now."

He laughs to himself. "The fact that you think anything about me is soft is shameful. I'm obviously giving you the wrong impression. Respecting your request to wait to tell our friends, yes... soft, never." The heat between us expands from his unwavering gaze, a testament to his dominance and I have to turn away for a breath. I focus on the waves rolling up on the beach. "But I'll let that one go since you said I was king." I'm met with a cocky smirk when I turn back.

I smile, nodding. "Like there was any question."

"There's only one question."

I tilt my head and take a guess, "Soft or hard?"

"That is *usually* not a question." The confidence in his voice makes me shift in my seat, the tone shooting straight to my core. He smiles knowingly, as he waves the waiter over and tells him we'll be back. Standing, he reaches for my hand and guides me down to the beach. I take off my wedges as soon as we hit the cool sand. There is nothing more romantic than walking hand in hand with the man you love down the beach at sunset. Max stops us when we reach a more private area of the beach and pulls me into him.

"Dance with me?" he asks.

There is never a day I'll say no to that. I nod and he reaches into his pocket and plays a song. Old Dominion floats out of his phone singing "*One Man Band*." The sun is a kiss away from disappearing into the horizon. Our bodies sway to the music. Max sings to me the part about getting tattoos and trashing hotels. I giggle remembering the poor table. His raspy voice is thick with emotion, but he carries the tune and it's sexy as hell.

"God, I love you," he whispers into my ear when the next song begins. The honesty in his words is unbounded and raw. I glide my hands up his jaw and stare into his eyes. "I've never said those words to another woman." His admission surprises me. I mean, he's thirty. "I was just waiting for the right woman to say them," he says, reading my thoughts.

"Sorry I made you wait so long." Even though my past pushed me to where I'm at today, I wish I would have been more truthful with myself regarding my needs.

He wraps an errant hair behind my ear and I watch his Adam's apple move as he swallows. He clears his throat and I wonder what's making him nervous.

"Max, what's—"

He covers my lips with his thumb, halting my words.

"I've always craved a rush, but you're the only rush that's ever satisfied me completely. I was stupid before... but I can't say things happened the way they did for a reason." He looks down and shakes his head before finding my eyes again. I nod in agreement but stay quiet. "We both lost someone, and I'd never say anything to lessen your loss because I know you loved him. You have grown and spread your wings so wide on your own, I'm in awe of your bravery. But I can promise you, I will move mountains to keep you mine forever. That river between us has dried up and you're the only person who can quench my thirst. I need you, every day." I hiccup through my tears as he drops to his knee and pulls a ring out of his shorts. "This is how I should have asked you," he murmurs, holding the ring between his finger and thumb. It catches the light and glistens. My heart is overwhelmingly captivated by his words, it's hard to talk. "Sydney Owens, *a.k.a Sky*, will you officially be my wife?"

I kneel, the sand cushioning my knees. "It was official hours ago. I haven't changed my mind," I sob, holding out my hand. He slips the platinum round cut diamond ring on my finger. I sniffle and take in a deep inhale, blowing it out, trying to calm my racing heart. "Max, you're the wind that keeps me flying and I've never flown so high and it's all because of you. You have always been there for me, through the worst and now the best. You mean everything to me and I can't imagine a life without you. But you have to promise to continue to sing to me."

He chuckles with the shake of his head. "Only for you."

Tonight, every shadow of guilt or apprehension that ever filled my heart, has been destroyed by Max's love for me. He does more than complete me, he makes me better.

CHAPTER THIRTY-EIGHT

SYDNEY

I bite my lip, holding the phone in my hand, staring at the ceiling, the sting of reality invading my dream. After last night, I don't want to wake up. I'd be fine living here forever with Max.

"What did Graham want?" Max asks, rolling to his side. He pulls my nipple into his mouth, sucking hard. I moan, my eyes rolling back, succumbing to his insatiable hunger.

"Did you ask a question?" I murmur.

He growls and yanks the sheet over me. "I can't help it. Your naked body is too hard to resist."

"Nobody asked you to stop." I roll on top of him, straddling his hips, holding the sheet up to my chest.

"Tell me what Graham said…" He yanks the sheet from my hand, pulling it out from between us, running his hands up my bare thighs. "… And I'll keep going."

"Graham wanted to know if I was up to doing a country fest type concert in two weeks. Lots of artists, goes on all day and night type thing," I blurt out quickly, making him chuckle. Despite his promise, he lifts me off of him and covers me again as he scoots over, leaving a good foot between us. His hand props up his head and his expression turns serious.

"Are you ready for that?"

"I was ready for *something*," I say snarkily, giving him the evil eye.

A slow cocky smile crawls across his lips, not helping ease the ache between my legs, and he reaches for my hand, holding it between us. "There'll be plenty of time for that later. Let's talk about this. I want to know where you're at too."

"Fine," I sigh in defeat. Nerves drown out the desire as my mind replays the fear. Was what happened enough to ruin my career? Does Max want me to stop since we're getting married? A downward spiral evolves as my thoughts race about our future. Being here, caught up in everything Max, I haven't considered what happens when we *leave*.

He squeezes my hand and dips his head until we lock gazes. "Sydney, you don't have to do it if you're not ready."

"Is that what you want?"

Confusion registers on his face. "What do you mean, is that what *I* want? This isn't my decision."

I roll out of bed, needing a little more than a foot of space between us. A pool of dread knots my stomach as I wrap the silk robe around me, pulling the belt tight. Max raises his brows.

"I know it's not your decision." I swallow as the knot moves to my throat. "But what if my decision is to keep singing?" He sits up, leans against the headboard with a confused expression. The stark contrast of the white sheet against his tan body only makes his sculpted body stand out more.

"Are you worried what I'll think if you keep singing?" I nod slowly. "Tink, I want you to be happy doing what you love. There have been no assumptions made that if we're together, you would drop your dreams. You've earned your place in that world and I'd never take it away."

My eyes cast down as embarrassment stirs in my belly. *Especially after that answer.* "Sorry," I whisper, sitting on the edge of the bed. Wishing I could have half of Max's confidence.

"Don't be sorry, babe. There's a lot of unanswered questions about what's next. But I'm on your side wherever that is." I peek up and softly smile. "Now, I can't promise that I won't be an over-protective husband."

"You? Overprotective? Noooo."

He pounces from his spot, pushing me back and ends up strad-dling me. "Okay, smartass," he says, tickling me. I writhe under him, squealing for him to stop. He leans forward on his hands, steel-blue eyes lock onto mine. "You underestimate how deep my love for you is."

He's wrong, I feel it, deep inside my bones.

"It scares me to fall this hard for someone, I feel so out of control, it's mind bending, yet I'd fight the world alone to keep it. *To keep you.*"

The rawness from his words melt into my heart. I cup his jaw and nod, tears pool in my eyes. "I'm yours, Max. Forever." He lowers onto his elbows and runs his thumb across my cheek, catching the tear that broke free.

"Forever isn't long enough," he whispers, leaning down and dusting featherlike kisses down my neck. He reaches between us, pulling the knotted silk belt loose.

For the next hour, our hearts and souls strip bare. With no words, Max shows me how deep his love is for me.

"I WOULD PAY a million dollars for that picture."

I glance over my shoulder, wondering who Max is talking to. He's staring at me from the bed, his hands behind his head and the white sheet covering only one of his legs and outlining his hard cock. I roll my body so my back is against the doorframe instead of my hip. "What picture?"

"I lied. I don't want that picture anymore. I want that one." He points at me. "The silhouette of your naked body in the doorway, the sun shining behind you, blue skies as the backdrop. It's flawless. Don't get me wrong, the one with your tight ass was glorious, knowing that anyone could fly by and see your beautiful tits. But this one..." he groans, licking his lips while he adjusts himself "... is breathtaking."

I glance at his phone on the nightstand and smile. "You only get one, so you better make it perfect."

His smile reaches his eyes as he grabs his phone. I glance out to the ocean, and standing here naked, out in the open, waiting for my picture to be taken, is probably the most provocative thing I've ever done. Granted, no one can see me unless they fly by in a helicopter. But it's a possibility. I've heard a few fly by. I loll my head in Max's direction when he keeps telling me to hold on, don't move.

"Max." I smile. "Take the picture."

"There. Don't move." He takes the picture and winks. "It wasn't perfect until I had your eyes on me." He stares at it and hums. "Damn, Tink. You couldn't have given me a better present."

I giggle and crawl up on the bed, sneaking a glance at the photo. It surprises me to see how sensual I seem. "Wow." My sneaky glance turns into a flat-out stare.

"You are so beautiful," he softly sings in my ear, goosebumps pebbled my bare skin. The tune *"You Are So Beautiful"* by Joe Crocker snaps me out of my gawking and I pull up on my elbows.

His voice, rich and deep, is sexy as hell. "We should sing a duet."

Humor crinkles in the corner of his eyes. "Nope. Don't get used to it, Tink. That's your job, not mine."

"You know where to find me if you change your mind."

He laughs. "Tell me what you were thinking earlier." It takes a couple seconds to register his shift in conversation. "When you were staring out to the ocean. I called your name a couple times, but you didn't hear me."

"Ohhh." I slowly nod, the thoughts coming back. "I decided I want to do the concert. If I stop, she wins. It's what she wanted all along — for me to fail. That's why she tried to sabotage my performances."

"I guess we're going to Dallas."

I cock my head to the side, wondering how he knows it's in Dallas. "You've already looked it up, haven't you?"

He finds me humorous. "Babe, I already have a security plan in place. And Stone is putting your new security team together."

"Please tell me you weren't texting while I was riding you," I tease, wondering when he found time to do all that. The nap I took wasn't that long. And when I woke, Max was passed out.

He hops off the bed, slapping my ass on the way up. "I'm great at multitasking, but my head up here" —he taps his forehead— "is useless when your hot pussy is milking my dick."

My cheeks flush from his dirty words. He pulls up his shorts and comes back to sit down next to me. "So, beautiful, when do you want to get married?"

"As soon as possible." The words fly out of my mouth, surprising even me.

His smile is disarming, and I'm glad he saves them for me. "I can arrange a wedding before we leave."

It's crazy that I'm tempted to say yes. Could I get married without Addison here? I'm sure she'd get over it. My shoulders slump into the bed. What am I thinking? She'd kill me.

"Getting married to you, here, would be amazing. But our friends should be here. I don't need a huge wedding," I slip in so he doesn't think I plan to go bridezilla on him.

His lips twist as he thinks and then his smile returns, reaching his eyes. "I have a plan." His plan intrigues me. So far, his plans have been perfect. "But first, I want to take you to my house."

CHAPTER THIRTY-NINE

MAX

W hen your woman has been staring at her engagement ring for at least twenty minutes and then she looks over at you and says, "I've been thinking," you brace for the worst. Conflict swirls in her eyes and my chest tightens, readying for war. She's not getting away from me that easy.

"Okay," I drawl, reading into every move she makes. She swirls the ring around her finger, the very thing causing her distress. I don't get it. We had an amazing week in Hawaii.

She licks her lips and says, "I don't want to tell Addie and Aiden, yet."

Fuck. This again?

"Not because I don't want them to know." Her hand covers mine and she squeezes. "This is our first time at your house and I want... I need more time to learn about you without distractions from our friends. We can tell them after the concert." I release a heavy sigh filled with relief, looking out the window. The foreign feeling of insecurity is a bitch. The town car pulls off the main highway, headed toward my house. "Am I being too selfish asking this?" She turns in her seat toward me, worry etched into her features.

"No." I shake my head. "I just thought you were going to say…" I stop myself, not wanting to throw my doubts out in the open. Cupping her neck, I brush my thumb across her pouty lip. "Never mind. Selfish be damned, I'm happy to have you all to myself for a little longer."

Pulling her to me, her lips melt into mine and I get lost in the taste of her. She's a drug, the euphoric vibe when I'm with her is more intense than any adrenaline rush I've experienced. It's a constant craving and I hope, for the sake of my sanity, I'm able to control it someday. She breaks away from the kiss when the car stops and the craving spikes again.

Damn, I'm in trouble.

"Wow," she says, looking out the window. "I forgot how big this place is."

Dirty thoughts come to mind, but I keep those to myself. I want this to be our home base so I need her to like it here. "And I want to show you every square inch of it." I laugh to myself. This conversation is much different in my head.

The driver opens the door and I reach for Sydney's hand, pulling her out behind me. "Addie will be so jealous," she snickers. I glance down and her smile matches the gleam in her eye as she stares at the house.

"Of what?"

"I'm about to learn what's in the mysterious house of Max Shaw." I bust out with a laugh, swinging her up into my arms, carrying her toward the front door. She wraps her arms around my neck and holds on. "Well… unless she already knows." Her voice turns down.

I stop walking right before I hit the first step. "Tink, you are the only woman I've ever brought into this house that will see *every-thing*. I don't want there to be any secrets between us other than the ones I can't tell you for your safety." She pulls her head back a bit and raises her brows. "I'm in the security business and that means there are things I can't share. But this house isn't one of them." My dad's secrets in this house passed onto me when he died. Only my team and Aiden know about them. And now she will.

"I'M NOT AFRAID. YOU ARE." Syd's voice trembles behind me. My laugh echoes all the way down the dim-lit stone spiral staircase leading to the underground tunnel. We just finished touring the half of the house where I run my operations. The weapon room, the command center with all the monitors, the boardroom, each of the guys have a bedroom so if we have a late night, they can crash here. But last of all is the underground rooms. We slipped through a secret door, masked as a wine cellar, right off the kitchen.

I stop and turn on a step; her eyes almost level with mine as she stands on the next step higher. "There's nothing down here that's scary, babe."

"That's what the guy says in every horror movie out there." She runs her hands through her hair. "I'm thinking I would be okay to *skip* this house secret."

The last thing I want is for this place to scare her. "Listen, just think of it as the magical castle from Beauty and the Beast instead of an Amityville Horror house." She stares at me through round eyes, making me chuckle.

"If a clock talks, that would be just as scary." She closes the space between us as her voice carries, echoing down the chamber. "I know this is your house and I should have nothing to worry about, but holy shit, Max, I am almost certain there are ghosts down here. What did your dad use this for?" Her body shivers.

"You were already aware he was a philanthropist, right?" Even though he wasn't a great father, he was a great man. She nods her head. "He helped hide battered women and their families until the organization could give them new identities and a new life, away from their abuser. This is where they would stay temporarily."

"Wow." Her expression lightens. "That's amazing, Max." Her

lips twist in thought. "Is that why you help fund the women's shelter?"

In Hawaii, I told her about all my other endeavors, including the women's shelter. I nod. "He left all his money to me and since helping women was important to him, I wanted to keep that spirit alive. Obviously, I didn't want to continue hiding people in my house," I smile inwardly at the thought because it's happened a few times as we've had to hide dignitaries when working a government contract. But it's not regularly. "So, that was the next best thing."

"You two are a lot alike. The innate need to help people runs deep in your blood."

"I used to fight it. Last thing I wanted was to be like him. Until he died, and I learned everything about the man. My view of him transformed into more of a role model, a man I strived to be."

"He'd be proud of you. You're so much more than him, though. You don't push aside your feelings for fear of what you'll look like in the business world. Your compassion for Lulu is proof of that. And she's not even yours."

"You couldn't be more wrong," I say, rubbing my thumb on her back. "I'm just like him. I never wanted to get married, especially didn't want kids. In my head, having a family wasn't worth the risk in my business. They're a liability."

Sydney tilts her head back, twisting her lips, as she mulls over my words in her mind. "Hmm. Not sure how this makes me feel."

"That was all before you. Now, the reward is worth the risk. And there is still a risk. But what I've learned in the last few months is there are risks everywhere. Even in your job."

She nods. "That there is."

"After meeting you, I started wondering if my dad had just never met the right woman. My mom was a faceless woman, who got pregnant. The foreign feelings I had after kissing you once, was a mind fuck. One kiss was all it took. Your taste was like pure dopamine and the chemical reaction fucked with my head."

"And you fought it."

"I did." I close my eyes, remembering how angry it made me to watch her with someone else. Let alone one of my best friends. I blow out a harsh breath, not wanting to go down that memory lane again. "If my dad had met someone that triggered this much of a reaction as you did to me, he would have chosen love too."

"I'm happy you chose love." She plants her lips on mine. When she pulls back, I groan, demanding more. "Okay, I'm ready to see the basement."

"Of course you are," I say sarcastically, adjusting my snug pants. She bites her lip like she's sorry, but that sweet look is nothing more than a front. She loves that she controls me, even though I try my hardest to prove otherwise. Rather than try to prove it now, I think about where we're going.

And the perfect spot where I'll strip her down and show her how much her control affects me.

I unlock the door at the end of the tunnel and her eyes roam around the gathering room. "This furniture doesn't look like eighties stuff."

"It's not. When I moved in, I updated everything, even down here. Just in case I ever needed it." I pull out a chair at the end of the long conference table, watching her peek into each room. Every room is the same with two double beds and a small table with two chairs. Similar to a hotel room. The restrooms and kitchen area are out here.

"Are you done looking?" I ask when she takes the whole tour.

"Yep. It's so cool. Definitely, not the dungeon I was thinking. Maybe, you should've updated the scary stairway."

I chuckle, shaking my head. I love that hallway. The mystery of it has always intrigued me, but I'm not about to argue that right now. I have other things on my mind. "*Maybe*, you should bring your sweet ass over here." I pat my legs and wag my brows.

Desire flickers to life in her eyes as she walks over. "Yes, sir," she purrs, swinging her leg over mine, straddling me. My fingers dig into her thighs as my thumbs graze her clit through her leggings. Her body shudders and her eyes roll back as she melts against me.

"Take your shirt off," I command. She toys with the hem of her shirt for a couple beats and I lift a brow. I won't mind putting my handprint on her ass. She scrunches her cute button nose but lifts her shirt over her head. A black lace bra covers her beautiful tits. She throws her shirt on the ground and then goes to pull mine off. Sitting forward for easier access, I raise my hands so she can take it off. Her fingers tickle my torso as she unbuttons my jeans. She laughs when I suck in my stomach.

"Is Max Shaw ticklish?"

I grab her hand, inching to my stomach. "You won't find out right now," I say, bringing her hand to my hard cock. She grips it through my jeans, pressing her palm up the length of it until her fingers brush against the head at the top of my underwear. Impatience strikes, so I stand, putting her on her feet while I pull my pants and underwear down. She follows suit, taking off the rest of her clothes. She looks at me and I love that she waits for my direction. It fucking makes me crazy with desire.

Sitting back down on the cushioned chair, I stare up at her perfect petite body, holding my hand out. She slips her candy apple red fingernails into it and I guide her back on top of me. "Country girl, I want you to ride my dick like you have eight seconds to hold on."

"Is that all it'll take?" she purrs.

"Fuck, I hope not."

When she slides down my cock, swallowing it with her wet pussy, I lean back and groan, the burning need for her enveloping me to the point of obsession. She rides me, slamming down and moaning with pleasure each time. I don't dare move knowing the second I do, I'll come. Hard.

I might have lasted more than eight seconds, but not more than eight minutes. The sight of her getting off on my dick, there was no way I could hold out.

"Damn, if I would've known you were a rodeo star…" She pushes off my chest, sitting up. Her flushed face brightens with a smile.

"I have a hand full of tricks, you just need to find out what they are." Jesus Christ. My dick just got hard again.

"That sounds like a challenge I plan to win by the time we leave my house."

"Do you want kids?" she asks hesitantly, peeking up at me. Her silky white skin pebbled as I skim my fingers over her bare back. I just found another trick of hers. *She's very flexible.* I'm kicking myself wondering why the fuck I haven't given her free rein before.

I freeze my movement and eye her with a lifted brow. "Why, are you pregnant?"

She slaps my chest and pushes up to a seated position. "No, Max," she says, her frustration with my question loud and clear. She nods to herself, the conversation she's having in her head, doesn't include me. "I mean, we're getting married, this is stuff I should know already. But, I gather you don't," she says, her voice rich with disappointment.

What? How did she come to that conclusion? I sit up, raking my hand through my hair, wondering how we went from amazing sex to this. "Tink." She ignores me, running her palm against the sheets. Stopping her movement with my hand, I squeeze it and wait for her to look up. "It was a joke. Obviously, my comedic efforts didn't go as planned." Her lips break a smile. "I want kids. I want however many you want."

Her eyes narrow. "What if I want five?"

"Then we'll have five. But, nothing comes in odd amounts.

Four-pack, six-pack, eight-pack, there are never seven-packs. We'll either need to have four or six." She chuckles. I pull her hand, guiding her back to me, relieved we've moved past the unnecessary emotions.

"I've always wanted four kids," she says, holding up and wiggling four fingers. I nod, smiling at the thought of our kids running around this place. The killer games of hide and seek. The hiding possibilities endless. "I'm sorry about my comment, I assumed you didn't want kids. You had mentioned before you didn't and it caught me off guard wondering if that was still how you felt."

"The person I was before you doesn't matter anymore. You changed me." The words don't do justice to my feelings. I could never express to her the impact she's had on my life. Showing her how much I love her for the rest of our lives will have to suffice. I pull her swollen lips to mine, hoping I'll be enough for her forever. That this will be enough.

"I love you, Max," she murmurs against my lips as if reading into my insecurities.

"How about a Dallas wedding?" I say, an idea being driven from those same insecurities. She pulls back, tilting her head. "We can fly everyone out for the concert and then get married."

Her eyes widen. "You make it sound like that's an easy task. Max, that's less than one week away."

I lift a brow. One thing I know about Sydney, she likes to fly by the seat of her pants. "Are you saying you can't plan it?"

"I didn't say that," she boasts, her spine straightening. "I was just *saying* we would need to get busy planning. Like, right now."

"So, is that a yes? Will you be my wife by next week?" She nods, her smile bright against the dim room. Relief, that she'll be mine soon, builds in my chest.

Her lips meet mine for a quick kiss before she hops off me. "Time is a wasting, my future hubby." I lie back and watch her slip on her clothes while she sings, *"Goin' to the chapel and we're gonna get married..."* by The Dixie Cups.

My future has never looked so fucking hot.

CHAPTER FORTY

MAX

"How am I supposed to watch the sunset when you're on top of me?" Sydney lets out an adorable huff and tries to move off me. I shake my head. "Where the hell do you think you're going?"

She slaps me on the chest. "Make up your damn mind." The wood of the dock, hard under the blanket I'm on, creaks as I shift to a sitting position. Sydney wraps her legs around me and leans back on her arms. An angelic glow shines behind her from the setting sun.

It was her idea to come down to the docks at the lake my property borders and watch the sunset. I had a better idea when I rolled her on top of me. First she needs to be naked. We'll watch the sunset as we make love.

"How about we get nak—" My phone vibrates in my pocket, stopping me and Sydney's smile widens. "Ignore it."

"I'm not sure I can ignore something vibrating against my core."

When it goes off immediately after, I sigh. She scoots back enough for me to reach into my pocket. There is no better cock blocker than your mom calling. When Sydney sees who's calling, she tells me to answer.

"Let's tell her."

My heart hammers against my chest hearing her say she wants to tell someone. And my mom, of all people. "Hey Ma," I say, putting her on speaker. "You're on speaker and Sydney is here."

"Oh. Who's Sydney?"

Sydney pinches her lips together. "Hi, Ms. Shaw. It's Sky, but you can call me Sydney."

"Like Sky Owens?" she squeals.

"Ma," I say, shaking my head.

"Sorry, I'm just so excited to meet you. Even if it is on the phone." She tries to contain her excitement, but it's useless.

"It's nice to meet you too, Ms. Shaw."

"Oh, please call me Susie."

"We have some news," I interrupt, hoping to move this conversation along. "Sydney and I are getting married." When it sounds like the phone drops and then silence, Sydney and I stare at each other. "Ma, where did you go?"

"I'm here. I think the phone line crossed with someone else's. You know when that happens? Like when me and Julie were talking once and then for a few seconds, a man's voice comes on the line. It's the weirdest thing. But it only lasts for a couple seconds. Funny thing, you were just getting ready to tell me something, and the line switched with someone telling their mom they were getting married." She lets out a humorless laugh. Sydney grimaces and buries her face into my shoulder. This is not how I imagined my mom reacting.

"Ma—"

"Max, can you please take me off speaker?"

Fuck.

Sydney pushes up with tears in her eyes, and it shocks my heart. "Ma, I'll call you back." I hang up the phone without waiting for her response.

"Hey, look at me." Her eyes flash to mine and I wipe away her tears with my thumbs. "She's surprised, that's it. She will love you."

"What if she doesn't," she cries. "I mean, my own mom didn't. What if yours hates me too?" Her insecurities are wreaking havoc in her eyes.

I blow out a ragged breath knowing deep in my heart, my mom will love her. They are so alike and she's hounded me for years to get married. I shake my head. "Tink, she won't. Let me call her back and talk to her. You'll see." She nods and tries to push off me, but I hold her thighs down. "You are not going anywhere." I'm determined to fix this. The two women I love more than anything will be on the same side whether or not they like it.

Sydney chews on her lip as I hit my mom's number. I keep it off speaker, just in case my mom's a wild cannon again.

"Is she pregnant?" I drop my head at her first words. See, wild cannon just exploded.

"No. She's not. Why are you being so rude?"

"Son," her voice levels. It's the same voice she would use when I fucked up. "What am I supposed to think? You've known her for what, two months? Is she after your money?"

My eyes widen, surprised by how mean she's being. I rub my jaw as Sydney stares at me. "First, we've known each other for over two years. Second, that was uncalled for. You don't even know her." My voice hardens as I become defensive. Sydney's head drops.

Silence hangs between me and my mom until she sighs. "I'm sorry, Max. You're right. You caught me off guard. I don't want you to get hurt. You should bring her here so we can meet."

If she thought I caught her off guard before, wait till she hears the rest. "Actually... we're getting married next weekend. In Dallas. I planned on sending the plane to pick you and Brad up. Rex will be there too."

She gasps. "Why the rush?"

"Because I want her by my side permanently as soon as possible," I grind out, not liking that I have to justify my actions. Even if it's to my mom. I pull in a deep inhale, grabbing Sydney's hand and bring it to my lips. "Because I've loved her for over two years and I finally was able to make her mine."

She sniffs in the phone. "Max, I've never heard you talk like that before." I roll my eyes as my mom's voice morphs into sweetness. "I still would like to meet her before you get married."

"Ma, we're at the ranch and only here for four more days."

"Okay. Send the plane in three days and we'll come there and visit for a day before we all go to Dallas."

I mouth to Sydney, "She wants to come here to meet you." She nods in agreement. It's probably the best plan. I'd hate to ruin our wedding weekend fighting with my mom.

"You win," I say into the phone. "We'll see you in three days."

CHAPTER FORTY-ONE

S weat makes my shirt stick to my back as we take a quick break from our soundcheck. Nerves mixed with excitement about tonight has my body heat at an insane level. Also, the insane summer humidity I'm not used to anymore doesn't help. Max is sitting on a speaker, watching everyone. He's more relaxed now that I'm not in danger.

Or maybe because I'm about to be his wife.

My teeth tug on my lip, the thought sending butterflies to my belly. *Max Shaw's wife.* The whirlwind of the past few weeks, the island, the proposal, the time we spent together, seems like a dream. Max asked me once we got back if I regretted saying yes now that I've had time to think and I'm back in reality. *Definitely not.* And now, all our friends are on their way here for a surprise wedding. To top it off, Max's mom does love me. The couple days we've spent together have been wonderful. I can't help the flutter in my belly watching Max with his mom. It's a sexy attribute to see him cherish his mom.

Staring at the empty stadium in my hometown, I wonder how many people coming tonight know the real me. Memories of sitting out in the lawn seats watching my favorite band pop in my head. It's surreal to think about. There's one person who won't be here, though. *Mommy dearest.* That woman would never admit that her daughter, the one she never wanted, was successful. She probably tells people that I lip sync.

"You all right," Max says, coming up behind me. I shake her out of my head. I was never good enough for her, and it wasn't without trying.

I sigh and spin in place, looking up. "Yeah. Just being here, takes me back."

"Do you want to see her?"

I shake my head, biting my inner cheek, not surprised he can read me. "She's not worth my time. She's had twenty-six years to make time for me, that road is a dead end."

He nods, shoving his hands in his pockets. "Damn, it's hard not to pull you into my arms right now." I scan the surrounding area, light technicians and stage prop guys are busy doing their job. Two guys from the band are fine tuning their instruments on stage.

I wrinkle my nose and step into Max's space, lifting on my toes. I place a quick kiss on his lips, tugging on his bottom lip as I pull back. "That'll have to due until later."

He narrows his eyes with a wicked grin on his lips. "I don't think that'll last until later." As he takes a step forward, I take a step back.

"Max," I warn. "There are reporters everywhere. One kiss is easy to hide." I seem to have awoken the beast. When he takes another step forward, my eyes flicker around, looking for something to distract him. Tug chuckles to the side of us, watching everything.

"I thought you were keeping it on the down-low until tomorrow."

"We are," I clip, not taking my eyes off Max, afraid he's about to lunge. From the corner of my eyes, I see Tug get up from his drum set and an idea pops into my head. "Hey Tug, Max used to play drums."

"Sick. You wanna heat her up?"

Max pops a brow up, slowly nodding his head while his eyes rake over my entire body. I clear my throat, shifting my body from foot to foot as his devilish expression does exactly what Tug suggests. Except he's not supposed to heat me up. "The drums, Max." I point to the sticks Tug's holding out.

"This is fun watching you squirm," Tug jokes. Max jerks his head to Tug, his expression hardens and I still. What the hell? Tug's smile drops, his eyes widen. "No, bro... not like that... I mean... not sexual at all," he stutters, trying to find his voice. "I mean, Sky's like a big sister to me." Max gets a hold of his feelings and his shoulders relax. "Here, have fun." Tug jerks out his sticks again, passing them to Max before striding off stage.

I pinch my lips together and wait for Max to say something. Rather than addressing what just happened, he stalks around the drum set and sits, twiddling the sticks in his hands.

"So..." I drawl, not giving him a chance to redirect. He stares at me and I blow out a breath. "I think you just scared the piss out of Tug."

"Good."

I sigh, looking up to the rafters. Max rarely lets his emotions get the best of him. "Tug is a good guy. He didn't mean anything *by it.*"

Max beats a stick against a drum and I jump in surprise. *Why is he being an ass right now?* I cross my arms and glare at him.

"I'm sorry," he finally says. "It's because we're engaged and no one knows that has me on edge."

"Do you want me to put my ring on? I will. The only reason I'm not wearing it is because we both agreed we wanted our friends to hear it from us before they heard it through a media outlet. But you're not my dirty little secret, Max. I love you and I want to tell the world I'm yours."

His head drops and he shakes it. Lifting up, regret is written all over his face. "No. Let's keep to the plan. I just hate not being able to touch you."

"Tonight, you can make up for it and touch me however you want," I tease, helping lighten the mood.

His lips lift to a smile as he beats on the drum, his eyes never leaving mine. When I recognize the song he's playing, I throw my head back, laughing. Jay strings his guitar, joining in. Not wanting to miss out playing with Max, I grab my mic and turn it on. My foot beats to the music and I jump in singing *I Can't Get No Satisfaction* from the Rolling Stones.

Claps surround us when we finish. I stare at Max, his shirt soaked, sticking to his six-pack and there's nothing I'd rather do than straddle him and let him play me right now. He looks wickedly hot.

Swaying my hips, I shimmy around the drums, approaching Max from behind. I whisper in his ear, "Meet me in my dressing—"

"Look who I found begging to get in," Graham announces loudly, walking onto the stage. I stand tall and glance at who he's talking about, taking a couple steps away from Max.

"Sydney!" Addison runs across the stage and I run to meet her halfway. Our arms wrap around each other. "I mean Sky," she quips as she pulls back, smiling.

"I didn't know y'all were coming up here." I glance around Addison and the group of our friends make their way over to us. Aiden, Jaxon, Ryan, Macie, Harper, and Katie join Max, slapping backs and hugging each other. The only one missing is Ryker. It's football season, so I'm not surprised.

"I couldn't wait to see you," she says. She glances at Max. "Did you quit your day job?" He grins, wiping the sweat from his forehead off on a towel.

"Nope. Just crossing something off my bucket list."

I was ready to cross something off my bucket list too. *Screwing a rock star in a dressing room.*

"You guys sounded awesome," Katie says, looking back and forth between us.

Jay walks over, thankfully, and I introduce him to everyone. He pats Max on the back and says, "We know who to call if Tug is sick."

"This is so cool." Harper and Macie walk to the front of the stage and twirl around. "Is Preston around," Harper asks excitedly, scanning the area.

"No. He hasn't gotten here yet." When she pouts, I add, "Don't worry, I'll introduce y'all later." Her face brightens up. "I'll meet you guys at the hotel in a bit. I have to finish up here."

Max and I have some unfinished business.

"All right, girls, you heard her," Aiden says, signaling them to walk. "You coming, brother?" he asks, patting Max on the shoulder. Max's eyes find mine and I try my hardest not to show any emotion.

"I'm going to stick around and make sure everything is set for tonight." Aiden taps his finger on his lips, studying Max. Then his eyes turn to me. Shit. He'll see right through this.

"Max, everything is fine here. We just have to finish going over our set. I'll see y'all tonight," I squeak out, waving my hand around.

Ignoring the heated expression on Max's face, I say goodbye and head backstage to my dressing room.

Alone.

Definitely not getting any satisfaction.

"IF you just stopped being so stubborn. You and Max look good together." Addison says, flipping through a magazine that has a picture of Max and me on the cover from the music awards night.

"Did you bring that with you?" I laugh, watching her shrug a shoulder. It's last month's magazine, so she didn't pick it up at a store recently. We're old news now. I feel bad that I haven't told her about us, but Max and I swore to each other we would tell them together.

"Well, she's right," Katie adds, looking up from painting her toenails.

Addison, Katie, Harper, and Macie arrived a couple hours ago and we're all relaxing in the hotel before the show starts. The last time we were all together was at Damon's funeral. I push those thoughts out of my mind. The faded guilt will always be a memory away, but I can't continue to live my life suppressing my feelings based on my past.

"He's leaving next week, ladies." It's the truth. They just don't know I'm going with him. We've decided when I'm not on the road, we'll live at his place. It'll be a great reprieve from the spotlight. As much as I love it, this tour has opened my eyes about being in the public. It's invigorating and scary at the same time. To be famous, it seems you have to surrender all your privacy and I can't live that way. This way, I get the best of both worlds.

"And?" Addison continues.

"*And*, I live in Los Angeles." Still not a lie. Although, I slip into the bedroom to avoid further questioning, hoping they don't follow.

Nobody follows, rather Addison yells from the living room. "Why hasn't he left?"

I knew she would ask since I'm not in trouble anymore. I blow out a breath and peek my head back in the living room. "It's Max. He needs to make sure everything is safe before leaving. He's already vetted every security guard." She nods slowly, weighing my answer in her head.

"I guess," she says, unsatisfied with my answer. Shit, this is harder than I thought.

"Would you stop? I need to get my stuff together. No more talk about Max." I've never been a good liar, especially around Addison.

Harper jumps off the couch. "Yes! We need to get ready because

Preston Scout is about to meet his future wife and I need to look ah-mazing tonight." My mouth drops open, mortified of what Harper plans on saying to Preston. I guess it won't be any worse than he normally hears.

"Harper, don't make me regret introducing you."

"Regret? You watch, he'll be thanking you tomorrow."

We burst out laughing. At least she got the conversation away from Max.

"HEY DALLAS, HOW'S EVERYONE TONIGHT?" The humid air fills with screams and it echoes across the seats all the way out to the lawn seats. Cool blue covers the stage from the lights burning above. Lights from phones twinkle all over the stadium. I have one more song left of my set.

I glance at the right of the stage where my friends are standing. Addison jumps up and down along with the crowd. Max flashes me a smile. I'm ready to scream at the top of my lungs that he's mine. Instead, I turn my attention back to the crowd, a flurry of buzz flowing through my veins for what I'm about to do.

"I have one more song for y'all tonight. It's a cover for a song that seems appropriate right now. Y'all know about rumors?" I tell myself not to turn toward Max. This wasn't in our plan and I'm not sure how he'll feel about it, I mean, he can't be too mad. *I'm about to be his wife.* "Well, sometimes, there's a little truth in them."

As soon as the crowd figures out what song I'm about to sing, the place erupts. I can't help the quick glance in Max's direction and I wink when our eyes meet. He shakes his head, smirking, obviously not surprised.

The melodic words flow out of my mouth as I sing *"Rumor"* by Lee Brice.

Flashing lights pop off, ending my set and the stage manager hands me a bottle of water. I down the whole thing before exiting.

The set breakdown happens instantaneously with the new set for the next artist.

The girls bum rush me, congratulating me on a great show. I'm waiting for the questions regarding my song choice when Max walks up and pulls me into his chest. "What do you say we make it true?" he asks, repeating a line from the song, before slamming his mouth against mine. Gasps surround us as the surprise sinks in, followed by hoots and hollers. I laugh against Max's lips.

"It's about damn time," Aiden quips.

Max digs his head into my neck, whispering, "God, I love you. Even your mischievous little mouth."

"Ready to face this crowd?" I ask, tilting my head toward our friends.

"Fuck, yeah, I'm ready."

CHAPTER FORTY-TWO

SYDNEY

"You're a horrible best friend." Addison picks up her martini and glares at me over the rim of the glass. Putting it back down, she continues. "I don't know if I should be furious or excited."

"I pick the latter." I softly smile. They still don't know why they're really here or that we're engaged. We're all at dinner and about to announce it. If Addison's mad now, she's about to be livid.

"Of course, I'm happy for you guys." She leans over and gives me a hug.

"Well, there's more we have to tell y'all," I say, trying not to choke on my words. A pang of guilt that I've been engaged to two of these guys' friends kicks my nerves into gear.

"We're getting married tomorrow," Max burst out. *My mouth drops.* Way to break the ice. The entire table breaks out in so many questions, comments and gasps that I can't decipher any of it.

"I take it back," Addison says, pinching my side. Ow! I jerk my head to her and she's crossed her arms tight across her chest.

I wince, shrugging a shoulder. "At least we're not married."

"Ooohhh!" She playfully growls. She's not upset, slightly hurt, but I can see she's ready to celebrate. "I would have told every dirty secret you had. *To the tabloids.*"

I pinch her back, laughing. "No, you wouldn't."

Chaos ensues after that. Question after question about how we got here. The one question no-one asks, the one I was most afraid of, is *why so soon?* I tell everyone how he asked me both times. We both talk about times we were together on the tour.

Addie grabs my other hand. "Lulu will be ecstatic that her favorite aunt and uncle are getting married." She freezes and I cock an eyebrow up in question. "She'll hate that she's missing it."

My smile widens. "She's not. I already talked to Amy, and she's bringing the kids up." Amy was like a mom to me. There's no way I wouldn't invite her.

"She knew you were getting married when we dropped the kids off?" She huffs. I bite my lip and nod. Amy and Suzy were the only two who knew, and they were sworn to secrecy.

"How's the living arrangements going to work?" Aiden pipes up over the crowd, his arm around Addison's shoulders.

"When Sydney is on tour, I'll be with her—"

"And when I'm not, or not recording," I cut in, "we'll live at Max's house." Max is having a recording studio built into his house as we speak. We'll also search for a house in the LA area next week.

Addie squeals beside me and Aiden rolls his eyes at his wife. "Are you going to start a team in LA?" Jaxon asks.

He bobs his head a couple times. "Sort of. The team I hire will be solely for Sydney's security, though. When I'm with Sydney while she's touring, I don't want to focus on anything else except her." The girls coo around the table. They might think that's romantic, but Max is pure business with my security.

"Shaw Security will manage perfectly without me. Kase will take lead when I'm gone."

Aiden's back straightens, and he leans an arm against the table. "What? What about Stone?"

Max chuckles, shaking his head at Aiden's displeasure. "Stone didn't want it. Kase has experience leading teams before and the guys all agreed he should do it."

"He's only been with you for a year," Aiden argues.

"What is with you?" Addison snaps. "Kase seems like a great guy."

"He's not bad to look at either," Harper purrs and Addison's smile grows, pissing Aiden off more. I glance between Aiden and Max. Max has a shit-eating grin on his face, loving this. Yet, it wasn't too long ago when Max tasked Kase with something else rather than standing post outside my hotel room when I asked about him. We spent the day with Kase and his girlfriend, Ellie, last week so at least Max is over the jealousy.

"If *someone* else was working for me, I wouldn't have to fill that job."

"Fuck that. You screwed that up, hiring him. That would mean he'd be around my wife all the time." He gives his head a hard shake.

"He's asking his girlfriend to marry him next week," I say, laughing at his ridiculousness.

"I don't care. I don't need my wife ogling some SEAL whenever we're around him."

"I don't ogle," Addison spurts out, hitting him in the arm. "What the hell is wrong with you?"

While they argue, I lean over to Max and whisper, "I bet you they disappear in ten minutes."

"I give it two." Sure enough, a couple minutes later, Addison excuses herself to go the bathroom and Aiden follows a minute later. Their need to prove to each other they are each enough hasn't changed, if anything it's gotten worse. "How about we sneak out too?" He whispers back, sticking his hand in between my thighs.

I slap it away. "Nope. You're cut off until tomorrow night."

He jerks up. "What? Why?"

"Because, it's the night before the wedding. It's like bad luck… or something."

"That sounds like some bullshit women made up."

I shrug, smiling because I just made it up. "Probably. But you can wait." He eyes me for a beat before leaning over and kissing me. I already know what he's trying to do. When he kisses me like I'm his lifeline, it turns me on faster than a light switch. Not this time. *My vajayjay is on lockdown.*

Pulling back to end the kiss, Max looks at me in anticipation and I shake my head. His shoulders drop and he sighs. "If there ever was truth to the adage that opposites attract, you two would be the poster couple." Jaxon laughs.

I slip my petite hand into his large strong palm and squeeze. "We each take over where one leaves off."

We're perfect for each other.

After Addie and Aiden join back up with us, complete with wild hair and rosy cheeks, they both declare we split up and start our bachelor and bachelorette party. Max and I already talked about this and decided we didn't need to go out one last time as single. But it seems our friends won't let us make that decision.

It's crazy to think about how much my life has changed in just over a year and a half. I was always the one ready for a party. I was *that* girl, dancing on the bar, having men do shots off my belly. When I didn't get hired at Coyote Ugly, I was livid. I would have been the perfect person. Except, I failed the bartending part of the test. Still. *I bet they regret it now.* I get to sing on stage for a living, making a shit ton more money and don't have to sling one drink.

"Oh! And paybacks are a bitch," Addison declares, standing. Harper and Katie join her, cheering as I think back to Addison's bachelorette party. When I made her get on stage and practically hump a guy. This should be fun. Max growls at Addison.

Aiden laughs. "How's it feel, brother?" He pulls Addie into his side. "Just skip the prison part, okay?"

"I can't promise anything." His smile drops and he glares at her. "Kidding. I'm kidding. I promise, no fights tonight."

Addie ended up in jail at the end of her bachelorette party. It was an interesting night.

"Knox is going with you guys," Max states, looking up from his phone. The stern expression on his face means, *don't argue*. I wasn't going to. I'm in the spotlight now and after what happened with Shanna, I'm okay having a bodyguard follow me around.

Half an hour later, we're pulling up to Gilley's in a limo when I hear my phone ding. Digging it out of my purse, I bust out a laugh. Max just might be worse than Aiden. He's only quiet about it. Harper leans over to see.

Hulk: listen to *Eyes On You* by Chase Rice

"I haven't heard that song," she says. I roll the privacy glass down and ask the driver to play it on the speaker. We listen and the sweet undertone of the song is drowned out by the innuendo that Max is always watching me. *So, behave.*

"What is with these cavemen we have?" Addison snickers.

Feeling spiteful, I reply.

Me: *So What* by Pink

"Ohhhhh. You're brave," Harper says over her shoulder, scooting over to get out of the car. "I can't imagine Max being a fan of that song."

Katie, touching up her lipstick by looking at her reflection in the tinted windows, stops and looks back at us. "I know Max, and I can guarantee you the boys'll join us before the hour is up." Not that that was my plan, but I wouldn't be upset.

I forgot that Katie grew up with Max and I instantly forget about the text. "Katie! Guess who I met? Rex." A rep from the club meets us at the limo and escorts us past the line outside. People yell my name and a wave of phones come out. I wave and smile.

"Who's Rex," Addie asks, ignoring all the fanfare.

Katie's red lips curve up. "Wow. I haven't heard that name in years."

"Who's Rex," Addie and Harper both say again.

"Max's brother." We both answer together.

"Wait. What? Max has a brother?" Harper says, her voice filling with interest. "Where does this brother live? And is he single?"

"Don't get your hopes up, Harp," Katie says, wrapping her arm through hers. "Rex is the unattainable. From both the law and the women." I glance at Katie as we're led to the VIP section and sat at a u-shaped booth that faces the oversized dance floor. If she wasn't already married, I'd ask if there was a story behind that comment.

"What the hell does that mean?" Addison asks.

"He's the real life Danny Ocean."

I laugh at Katie's reference. It was my exact thought when I found out what he did. "Really? Max's brother is a thief?" Addison's gaze jumps from me to Katie. We both nod our heads.

"And y'all get to meet him tomorrow."

I feel the vibration of my phone and hope it's Max telling me he's here.

Hulk: And here I was trying to be sweet

"Ha! As if," I say out loud. Addie glances a quick peek. My fingers move quick with a text back.

Me: liar liar pants on fire

The bubble pops up immediately. My screen is still lit up when I get back a response.

Hulk: Something will be on fire. And it's not my pants. More like your ass if you're thinking like that song

I pull the phone to my chest, hiding it. Addie smirks. "What did it say?" I shake my head. She doesn't need to read this. "I don't think I've ever seen a guy make you blush."

Stuffing the phone back in my purse, I decide it's best to stop our texting now. Or my new rule about no sex will be broken quickly. Because dominant Max is my favorite.

CHAPTER FORTY-THREE

SYDNEY

"Do you take this woman to be your forever? Because doesn't that encompass everything?" Graham states, glancing at Max. I roll my eyes. Leave it to Graham to change the traditional vows.

Why did I ask him to marry us? Right. Because I love him like a brother.

When Max looks at me, those steel-blue eyes that stole my heart, captured my soul and made me feel again softens as he says, "Yes. I will love you, cherish you, remain true to you as long as I live."

"Sk—" Graham stops and shakes his head and I smile, giving him a reassuring nod. This is the first time he's used my name since I crashed into his home so I'm not surprised. "*Sydney,* do you take this man to be your forever?"

We decided not to do our own vows. Max would rather show me how he feels than tell me in front of everyone. He said he doesn't need to prove it to them. Instead, we each picked out a song to dedicate to each other at the reception.

"Yes. I will love you, cherish you and remain true to you as long as we both shall live."

As we exchange rings, tears blur my vision and I swallow the emotions getting the best of me. Max cups my neck, his thumb wiping a tear away. Leaning his forehead against mine, he whispers, "I love you, Tink. You'll never know how much my heart beats for just you." The tears run down my cheek. "Thank you." I lift my head, our lips are a whisper away as we close in.

"Stop!"

We freeze, our lips barely touching. "You can't take this away from me. Okay, Max, you may now kiss your bride," he proudly announces. Max smirks right before he fuses his lips to mine. The world ceases to exist for a couple moments. It's just us. Two lost souls twisting together. Our new song begins, and it encompasses our past, present and future. *Do you feel it?* I want to ask him. I want to know if it's as loud and clear to him as it is to me.

Claps and whistles seep into our bubble until it's so loud we don't have a choice but to let it envelop us. "I love you, too," I say, breaking away. The attendees jump to their feet in the little white church house, cheering as Max and I turn, hand in hand.

"Ladies and gentlemen, I proudly present to you, Mr. and Mrs. Shaw."

"ARE WE DONE YET?" Max walks up behind me and whispers into my ear. I tilt my head, leaning back into him as he nibbles my lobe. Spinning in his arms, I smile up at the gorgeous man. He's lost his tie somewhere, the top couple buttons open. He rolled his sleeves up, displaying his tattoo and the veins in his forearms. I cup his chiseled jaw, his five o'clock shadow tickles my palms. "Please?"

"The reception started fifteen minutes ago and you look like you've had a rough night already."

"You know how much I hate these penguin suits."

"But you look sexy as hell," I purr.

"That's *not* making me want to stay longer." His voice is deep and pleading, he grabs my hands and brings them to his chest.

"This holding out bullshit hasn't made tonight easy. Seeing you in that dress, it's fucking killing me."

"Holding out?" I laugh. "Max, it's been one night." The flash of a camera lights up Max's face. This will always be known as the picture where he's begging for sex. I almost feel sorry for him.

"See. Killing me," he snickers, pulling me to his chest. We sway to the song playing. "But I'll wait. It just gives me time to devise my plan of action."

"You sound like you're saving someone." I giggle into his chest.

"I am. Me."

And he says I'm dramatic.

Our night continues as we float around the room, twinkling lights above our head, moving from table to table to greet everyone. In between tables, Max throws out a word. A hint at what he's planning. So far, I've heard handcuffs, wedding cake icing, blindfold, ice, balcony, anal. *Anal?* I tense at the last hint, staring up at his lazy smile, slightly panicked. Max is not a small man. *Anywhere.*

He lifts a shoulder in a non-committal shrug, guiding me to the next table like what he just said was as casual as *let's eat.* "Just thinking out loud," he whispers into my ear.

I adjust the tight-fitted lace dress against my heated body, wondering why I picked such a form-fitting dress. The only part that flares out is the bottom. I wanted simple, but as soon as I put on the vintage fit and flare lace dress, I fell in love. This morning, Graham set up a dress fitting for all us girls with seamstresses ready to make any adjustments. Most of them didn't need any since Graham had been sneaky and got all the girls' sizes beforehand. He had a few dresses I had already picked out, flown in from Los Angeles.

Max's hand rests on my ass as we talk to a few of the band members and their dates. We don't stay long as we want to talk to everyone who came out on such a last-minute notice.

"Helicopters." Harper beams, pointing up to the ceiling. "It's crazy, there are helicopters outside, trying to get a shot of you two. This is so cool." I giggle at her excitement. I'm used to it now, nothing surprises me.

"It's all because I'm marrying *hashtag AMA's most wanted*." I air quote the name I know he hates.

"I'm going to hashtag your ass if you call me that again." He yanks me against his hard chest, his eyes bore into me. I lift a brow in defiance.

"What exactly would you hashtag on my ass?" I snicker.

"I'm sure you don't want me to hear that answer," Harper says, sneaking away.

Max's eyes cast up, contemplating. "Hmm. Something like... Max's property. If found, return stat."

"That is so caveman of you."

He shrugs. "Aaannnd? I'll get the same tattoo with your name," he says, wagging his brows.

I smile up at him knowing he would.

"I'm stealing your woman," Addie states, pulling me out of his arms. "We haven't danced together in forever."

"See, that's why you need that tattoo." Max points at Addison.

I laugh at his seriousness. "Addie won't be looking at my ass anytime soon," I joke, over my shoulder as I'm being pulled on the dance floor.

We start two-stepping around the floor like we did in the old days. "What tattoo are you getting on your ass?" Addie asks, smiling.

I shake my head. "There won't be any ass tattoo." I laugh. Addison would kill me if I branded myself that I was someone else's property.

"Can you believe how much our lives have changed since we graduated college? It's insane to think about."

I think back to the day we were laying on the lawn at the University of Texas the last day of college. It feels like that was a different life. We were both young and trying to find our place in the world. It definitely didn't go the way either of us had imagined.

"It is. I wouldn't be where I am today without you."

"Shut up. You went to California—we won't talk about why—and kicked ass out there. *On your own.* You are a strong, independent woman, Syd. Own it." She stares at me, waiting for me to accept her words.

"But, had you not—"

She spins me around to stop me from talking. When she stops me and we continue moving around the dance floor, she repeats, "Own. It."

"Fine," I sigh. "I'm a strong, independent woman."

"That sounded as believable as you liking vanilla ice cream."

Memories flash in my head and I burst out laughing. "You'd be surprised how that's changed too."

Before she can ask about it, Graham comes over the speaker, requesting Max and I join him on the dance floor. Max is at my side in a matter of seconds, claiming what's his. He playfully stares Addie down. "Mine."

"I swear you and Aiden must have been the stingiest children ever," she snickers, making him chuckle.

"Max and Sydney decided instead of writing their own vows, they would dedicate one song to each other tonight. First is Max's song."

Max wraps one arm around my waist and links our hands with his other. "You're the most gorgeous woman," he whispers, giving me a chaste kiss while we wait for the music to start. Whistles and catcalls surround us. Max rolls his eyes at our obnoxious friends.

The song *"Speechless"* by Dan + Shay floats out of the speakers. Word for word, I listen so I don't miss a beat as we sway to the music. Max sings a few parts to me. Goosebumps pebbled my skin from the heat of his words and the passion in his voice. By the time the song ends, tears are streaming down my face. He cups my face, swiping the tears away with his thumb. "You told me you liked my singing," he teases.

I slap him. "Stop. That was amazing. You're amazing." I lift on my toes and bring my lips to his. My nerves kick in when Graham talks again. My song choice is from my heart and *my voice*. This song is about Max.

"The next song is from none other than Sky Owens-Shaw. You guys might know her." Laughs surround us as Max tilts his head in confusion. I bite my lip, hoping he likes it. "Without further ado, here is Twisted Wings."

Twisted Wings

You hid in the shadows
watching over me
I tried to make you understand
You should've set me free

But you held on tight
Your grip tighter than your ego
Your determined mind
You're the unsung hero

Every heartbeat,
Every breath,
Every flight,
Belongs to you.
The power in those steel-blue eyes
Made these twisted wings come true

I'm not running anymore
Take all of me
All of the love in my heart
You hold the key

I'm the breath you need to live
But you're the wind I need to fly
I'm weightless when I'm with you
I never want to lose this high

Every heartbeat,
Every breath,
Every flight,
Belongs to you.
The power in those steel-blue eyes
Made these twisted wings come true.

My wings are stretched out wide
I'm flying on my own
If it wasn't for you by my side
My twisted wings would've never flown

Every heartbeat,
Every breath,
Every flight,
Belongs to you.
The power in those steel-blue eyes
Made these twisted wings come true.

It's weird hearing myself. Especially when I'm singing about the man staring down at me with a mixture of emotions swirling in his eyes. I wait with bated breath for him to say something. Both his hands cup my face. The room silenced and dark around us, making the moment even more intense.

"I don't even know what to say, Tink." He nods a couple times, swallowing. "Wow. I can't believe you wrote me a song."

I clear the nerves stuck in my throat. "Did you like it?" My voice barely a whisper.

"Did I like it? Babe, I loved it. Thank you."

As soon as his lips hit mine, the room erupts in cheers and I melt into him. He pours all those emotions into his kiss.

"Thank you," I say, pulling back. "Thank you for choosing me."

He winks at me with the sexy smile that made me fall for him years ago.

"Anytime, Tink."

THE END

EPILOGUE

MAX

One year later

"Push, babe, push."

"What the fuck do you think I'm doing!" Sydney screams. My head pulls back wondering where my sweet Tink went. Her super-human power grip digs into my hand as her face turns beet red like it's about to pop any second.

"C'mon breathe with me." I soften my voice, trying to help her calm down. Mimicking the breathing techniques we learned in Lamaze class, I pull in a few quick breaths and release a longer one. Syd's crazy eyes pin me in place. "You fucking breathe again, I'll suffocate you with a pillow." My gaze jumps over to Addison, sitting on the other side of her, wondering if she's just as confused as I am. She barely shakes her head, telling me to be quiet in her subtle way.

When did I become the enemy?

Syd lays back, her chest moves up and down rapidly while she takes a break. "You got this, Syd. I see her head," Addison says, wiping a cold cloth over her forehead. Sydney lifts her head, tears pooling in her eager eyes.

"You can?" Her voice is sweet as sugar as she looks at the

mirror placed strategically at the end of the bed. I glance over and can see the head crowning. My baby girl is about to come into the world.

"Okay, Sydney, I need you to push one more time," the doctor instructs.

She pulls her body up, gripping behind her thighs, and starts to push. "She's almost here, babe," I say, wiping the hairs stuck to her face behind her ear.

"Next time you try to stick your dick in my pussy, I will rip it off and shove it down your throat." If her head could spin all the way around, I'm certain, it'd be doing it right now.

It's just an empty threat, but my whole body shudders at the thought. I glance at the doctor wanting to tell her that Sydney is a sweet woman and she would never cuss like this in front of her kids. The doctor's tight lipped, hiding her smile while she works. *What am I doing wrong?*

The cries of a baby fill the room, already demanding our attention. The nurse takes her and wraps her in a blanket, placing her in Sydney's arms. I blink back tears staring at the tiny human. Ember Reese Shaw. Her large round eyes are wide open as she quiets and listens to Sydney talk to her.

"Look what we created," she murmurs, glancing over at me. She sighs, wiping a lone tear off my cheek. "I don't think I've ever seen you cry."

"What is happening to us? You turn into the devil and I've turned into a pussy." She softly chuckles as I lean over and kiss her forehead. "She's perfect, babe."

"Okay, momma, we'll go clean her up while you finish here." The nurse bends over to take Ember out of Sydney's arms and I shoot up, my chair sliding across the floor.

"Where are you taking her?"

"It's okay, Dad, we're just taking her to the nursery to get her weighed and cleaned up," she responds in a placating tone.

My spine straightens. "You switch my baby, there's not a corner you'll be able to hide in." Sydney yanks on my shirt, hushing me.

The nurse chuckles, lowering Ember into a little rolling bed. "It's okay. I've heard it all," she says, looking up with a bright smile. "But I can say, his is the most convincing. I promise you won't be leaving here with a different baby."

I narrow my eyes at the woman, pulling my phone out. "The pink package is rolling out," I relay to Stone, not taking my eyes off the bundle of pink. "And run a background check on Nurse Finley." Her head lifts and she rolls her eyes.

"Max, stop," Sydney says, slapping my thigh. "The last person you want to piss off is the woman handling our child."

Shit. She's right. "Scratch that. Buy Nurse Finley any car she wants."

Sydney covers her face with her hand and the nurse rolls the bed out of the room, laughing. Well, at least she's not leaving mad.

Addison walks from across the room and leans over to give Sydney a hug. "She's precious. And already has Max wrapped around—" She winces, doubling over on the bed.

"Addison," Sydney and I both say together. I round the bed to her side.

"Oh, no." She snorts, holding her protruding belly, looking down. I follow her gaze to the puddle on the floor. Sydney gasps and follows it with a squeal of delight.

"Looks like we're not done having babies today," I say over my shoulder, rushing out to get Aiden.

Five years later

"Remember when you were excited to play hide n' seek with her?" Sydney exhausts, pulling the curtain away from the window, looking for our half-pint. We've been looking for her for an hour. "Ember Reese, you win. You can come out now." Her voice travels through the huge house as we walk out of the sixth bedroom we've cleared. The undertone of irritation is covered by sweetness in her voice. Although she should know by now, our daughter is not a quitter. "We have to find her before everyone gets here."

"I know the quickest way to get her out of her hiding spot," I say, stopping her in the hallway and pushing her body against the wall. She glances at me surprised. Pressing into her, I pull her leg up to wrap around me. "I think she can smell when daddy is getting fresh with mommy." She laughs and nods knowing I'm right. Bending over to bring my lips to her natural full red ones, I revel in the taste of the woman that still owns me.

"Mommy! Daddy! You're supposed to be wooking for me."

I chuckle against Sydney's lips as Ember forces herself in-between the two of us. Sydney drops her leg and we both look down at large ice-blue eyes and a head of wild blonde curls.

"What do you think we were doing?" I say, throwing her up in the air. Her giggles fill the hallway. Her giggles morph to squeals when she hears the doorbell.

"Everyone is here!" She dashes down the stairs before Sydney can even tell her to be careful.

Sydney and I walk down the stairs hand in hand. "Can you believe she's five?" she says, looking over at me.

I sigh, shaking my head. "Can we have another one?" Her eyes widen and she hits me on the arm. "What? You're the one who wanted five."

"Yeah, I hadn't had quick stop Emmy yet." I chuckle at our nickname for her. She's been running since she was ten months old and hasn't stopped since. I never thought a pint size human could tire me out. She has proven me wrong. Repeatedly.

We watch Aiden and his crew file in. Ember runs to Brooklyn and the two fall to the ground in a hug and a fit of giggles.

"Do you ever wonder what they're laughing at?"

Sydney just smiles. "Best friends will always have their own language. You might as well stop trying to understand." She drops my hand and runs to Addison, giving her a hug. I wait for the uncontrollable giggles, but they never come. I can't help but stare at Addison's belly. Fucking number five. Aiden wasn't kidding when he said he wanted ten.

I just want one more.

Sydney's career skyrocketed, and she's at a point where she's calling her own shots. We've talked about her taking the next year off to try for baby number two.

"Feel like having some target practice," Aiden chuckles, standing beside me on the last stair. We both listen to the choppers outside, flying overhead as they try to get pictures of Sky.

"I would if I could." Truthfully, they don't bug me as much as the guys who get up in our face when we're out. Those fuckers deserve what they get. The few cameras I've had to buy was worth the look of fear in their eyes. We've come to a mutual understanding for the most part. I'll get a rogue paparazzi now and then. He learns where he stands in this relationship real quick. Far, far back.

We watch as our friends pile in the house. It's hard to believe the changes in all our lives over the past eight years. The kids outnumbering the parents. That's always a bad idea.

Addison waddles up to us, staring up at Aiden. "Hey, do you think you can help me wrangle Mason before he pulls out his penis and does wall art?" I burst out laughing. Their two-year-old son is a hellion, but this is a new talent I hadn't heard of. "He's very proud of his art," she says sarcastically.

Aiden walks away shaking his head. Lulu strides up to me, taking his place, and wraps her arms around me. "Hey Uncle Max."

"Hey, Lulu."

She rolls her eyes and huffs. "Can you please stop calling me that? I'm not a child kid anymore."

I bite my lip to stop from laughing. "Sorry, I forgot, you're a tween." I extend the last word for emphasis. Witty little girls are funny, witty big girls are a pain in the ass. But she's still my favorite.

"Can you talk to mom?" I glance down, tilting my head wondering what she's wanting me to talk Addison into. "Aunt Syd said I could sing with her on stage at the concert next month if mom says it's okay. I bet you can guess what she said." She sighs.

"You know I can't change your mom's mind. Why won't she let you?"

"She says *it'll go to my head being this young and I'll lose sight of my priorities.*" She attempts to mimic Addison's voice.

I bob my head. "It's statistically true."

"That is a bunch of crap. I already know how good I am, how much more could it go to my head from being on stage?"

I chuckle at her lack of humbleness. "Obviously not a lot. Maybe that's the problem."

She stomps away angrily. "I thought you wanted what was best for me," she snaps over her shoulder before slipping outside. Shit. I don't look forward to these years.

"Wow. You made someone angry," Sydney says coming from the kitchen. She blows her hair out of her eyes and then wraps it up in a bun. "Man, those five-year-olds are crazy for slime."

My eyes widen. "Between pee on walls and slime, we'll be cleaning for days."

"Pee? Who peed on the wall?"

"Nobody. Yet. Well, I hope. And Lulu, was already angry. It wasn't me," I say, holding my hands up. "She really wants to sing with you next month."

"I know, I feel bad. I shouldn't have said anything to her before talking to Addie."

Pulling her into my chest, I say, "Can we keep Ember five forever?"

"I wish."

Jett comes running out of the kitchen with Ember on his tail.

"Jett, wait. You're supposed to give me a birfday kiss." They disappear out the front door.

My mouth drops open. *What the fuck just happened?* My gaze jumps from Sydney to the door and back to Sydney. She laughs like what just happened was amusing. It wasn't.

"That's so cute." She beams.

"Cute? Fuck that. Aiden!" I scream, storming out of the room. "Aiden!"

"He's outside with Mason," Addison says, holding a blob of bright pink slime in her hands.

I spin in place and take long strides outside. "Dude, you need to keep your son away from my innocent little girl," I snap when I see him sitting on the tree swing. Aiden bursts out laughing, his gaze behind me. I whip around and watch Ember tackle Jett, giving him kisses all over his face.

"Brother, you are in trouble."

TWISTED WINGS PLAYLIST

Listen to the entire playlist on Spotify
"Twisted Wings" (Original song out of the book) by Tina Saxon
and Jaime Deraz
"Lost Boy" by Ruth B.
"99 Red Balloons" by Nena
"So What" by Pink
"Eyes on You" by Chase Rice
"One Man Band" by Old Dominion
"All to Myself" by Dan + Shay
"You Are So Beautiful" by Joe Cocker
"Mercy" by Shawn Mendes
"Get the Party Started" by Pink
"Shut Up" by The Black Eyed Peas
"Rumor" by Lee Brice
"Chapel of Love" by The Dixie Cups
"Everything's Gonna Be Alright" by David Lee Murphy, Kenny
Chesney
"Speechless" by Dan + Shay

NOTE FROM THE AUTHOR

Did you love Max and Tink together as much as I did? I know it took me forever to write their story, but this story was so different from the others and I wanted it to be perfect for you. Sydney deserved her happy ending. Hey, at least no one died in this book ;).

Who am I working on next, you ask? Ryker. And this story is DYING to be told. The current title (which can change) is *Wild Distortion*. I can't wait for you to read this epic romantic suspense. Granted, if you know me at all, you know you'll be waiting a few months. Hopefully not a year! But, if you've held on with me through this book, THANK YOU!! Readers are amazing people. When I receive an email, or read a post about how much you enjoyed my books, it makes my freaking week! Just know, I have so much love for y'all.

If you haven't heard, the song Twisted Wings from the book was put to music and sang by Jaime Deraz. She did an amazing job!! You can find it on iTunes and Spotify!

Tiffany, Lori, Traci – I don't mean to repeat myself, but you three are the solid base to my unsteady author life. Your support for me is unwavering and I LOVE YOU THREE to death!

Melissa Ellen, my best-author friend, thank you for pushing me to finish. It's the push I needed! I look forward to all our book adventures. Here's to many more!!

To my husband, who is always there to offer one liners (whether or not I ask for them), I love you! Thank you for letting me follow this crazy dream of mine and being there for me 100% of the time.

My amazing book team, I couldn't have done this without you! Hang, my friend, you are so talented and patient.

Y'all want to know how picky I am with covers? Hang sent me the cover, and I liked it, but when I tilted my laptop screen a little backward, the lighting of the picture changed and was exactly what I wanted. So, I took a picture of it and sent it to her. She, of course, tried to mimic it with her laptop but couldn't get it. It was a funny conversation. Anyway, she got it right, and it turned out perfect!!!

Ellie (and company), thank you for making my words look like I know what I'm doing. You and your team are always top on my list.

Until next time friends!

Xoxo

Tina

BOOKS BY TINA SAXON

TWIST OF FATE Trilogy

Aiden and Addison

Fate Hates

Fate Heals

Fate Loves

Twisted Wings

Max and Sydney

Blinding Echo

Kase and Ellie

Wild Distortion (Coming 2020)

Ryker and Aspen

Join my reader group to get to know me and get early access to what I'm working on!

Saxon's Sirens on Facebook

FOLLOW ME!

Facebook

Instagram

Website

Pinterest

www.ingramcontent.com/pod-product-compliance
Lightning Source LLC
Chambersburg PA
CBHW060951120726
47910CB00002B/591